Dime

Also by E. R. Frank

America

Friction

Life Is Funny

Wrecked

Dime
E. R. FRANK

Atheneum

NEW YORK LONDON TORONTO SYDNEY NEW DELHI

*For Amy and Bill, my exceptional parents, who have
always given me an abundance of love and books*

An imprint of Simon & Schuster Children's Publishing Division • 1230 Avenue of the
Americas, New York, New York 10020 • This book is a work of fiction. Any references
to historical events, real people, or real places are used fictitiously. Other names,
characters, places, and events are products of the author's imagination, and any
resemblance to actual events or places or persons, living or dead, is entirely coincidental.
• Text copyright © 2015 by E. R. Frank • Cover illustration copyright © 2015 by Neil
Swaab • All rights reserved, including the right of reproduction in whole or in part in
any form. • Atheneum logo is a trademark of Simon & Schuster, Inc. • For information
about special discounts for bulk purchases, please contact Simon & Schuster Special
Sales at 1-866-506-1949 or business@simonandschuster.com. • The Simon & Schuster
Speakers Bureau can bring authors to your live event. For more information or to
book an event, contact the Simon & Schuster Speakers Bureau at 1-866-248-3049
or visit our website at www.simonspeakers.com. • Also available in an Atheneum
hardcover edition • Interior design by Mike Rosamilia; cover design and hand-
lettering by Russell Gordon • The text for this book was set in Hoefler. • Manufactured
in the United States of America • First Atheneum paperback edition May 2016 •
10 9 8 7 6 5 4 3 2 1 • The Library of Congress has cataloged the hardcover
edition as follows: Frank, E. R. • Dime / E. R. Frank. — First edition. • pages cm •
Summary: Fourteen-year-old Dime, a foster child in Newark, New Jersey, finds love
and family as a prostitute, but when reality sets in, will Dime have the strength
to leave? • ISBN 978-1-4814-3160-6 (hardcover) • ISBN 978-1-4814-3161-3 (pbk) •
ISBN 978-1-4814-3162-0 (eBook) • [1. Prostitution—Fiction. 2. Families—Fiction. 3.
African Americans—Fiction.] I. Title. • PZ7.F84913Di 2015 • [Fic]—dc23 • 2014023579

Acknowledgments

The author gratefully acknowledges and warmly thanks:

Frank Albanese, Kathy Farrow, Laurie Lico Albanese, Stephen Lucas, Jessica Roland, Alexandra Rosenblum, Amy Rosenblum, Claire Cohen, Jim Rosenblum, William Rosenblum, and Stacy Liss, for taking the time to read the first miserable drafts and telling me they were good.

Rachel Cohn, Maria Fredericks, Carolyn Mackler, Wendy Mass, and Patricia McCormick, for giving so generously and graciously of their time, wisdom, encouragement, and connections.

Justin Chanda, for magically coaxing out the missing parts and doing so with wit, wisdom, and charm.

Sharon Freedman, for buying me that ticket in 2011 and also for the cookie.

Richard Jackson, for every bit of our history and

friendship, and especially for his Winter and Spring 2014 e-mails, calls, and instruction to relax.

Heather Schroder, for her welcoming certainty, patience, and professionalism.

Jennifer Hubert Swan, for that long phone consultation about books, both real and imagined, and for her support over all these years.

The Polaris New Jersey staff and clients of 2011–2013, for allowing me in, especially a certain two (you know who you are) whose resilience, humor, and decency are beyond words. I hope I got things a little bit right.

I ain't cynical. . . . Tellin' the truth's not cynical, is it?
— Dill, *To Kill a Mockingbird*

THE PROBLEM IS the note.

It has to be perfect or else my entire plan will be ruined. It has to be so perfect that its reader will have no choice but to do the right thing, see it all the way through.

I've been in a lot of dilemmas in my life, but never one as complicated as this. I've thought up more versions of the note than I can count.

There is so much that needs to be said.

Chapter One

WHEN I FIRST understood what I was going to do, I expected to write the note as Lollipop. But in the six weeks since then, I've had to face facts. Lollipop has lived in front of one screen or another her whole life, possesses the vocabulary of a four-year-old, can't read, and thinks a cheeseburger and a new pair of glitter panties are things to get excited about. Using her is just a poor idea.

Back in August, Daddy assigned Lollipop to me, saying, *You school her.* I must have been doing a good job hiding my insides from him, or he wouldn't have. L.A. was still the only one of us who was allowed to touch the money. If she found out, it would be the second time she'd learn about Daddy asking me to hold coins. Which would only make things worse than they already were.

Lollipop didn't know the difference between a twenty and a one. "What's that?" She held out her hands, nails trimmed neatly and painted little-girl pink. She was polite, even if she was stupid. "May I touch it, please?"

"Nobody touches the money but Daddy."

"Listen to you," Brandy said from the couch where she was dabbing Polysporin on the cut over her eye that was taking so long to heal. "Cat gave back your tongue?"

"You're touching the money now," Lollipop said. She leaned her head in close to get the best look she could. Then she sniffed. At the one first. Then the twenty. "It stinks."

"Stop," I told her. "Money is dirty. You don't know where it's been. Don't put your nose on it."

Brandy grunted. "That there the funniest thing I heard all week." She didn't sound amused.

I pointed. "That's a two." I pointed again. "That's a zero. That's twenty."

"I know that says twenty." Lollipop pretended to be offended. She was obviously lying. "What's that one?"

"A one next to a zero is ten. You didn't even learn any of this from TV?"

"They have numbers on *Sesame Street* all the time," Lollipop said. "And *Little Einsteins. Mickey Mouse Clubhouse.* They have it on a bunch of stuff. So I know them, but I never paid attention to what's more. Only I know a hundred is a lot and a thou-sand is even more than that. A thousand keeps me pretty in pink."

"Do you know letters?" I asked.

Lollipop nodded. "Yeah," she said. "TV and Uncle Ray taught me those."

Brandy grunted again. "I bet he did."

"Do you know how to read?"

"Some signs." Lollipop scrunched up her face, thinking. *"Exit."*

I waited.

"Ladies. Um. *Ice."*

I waited some more.

"Maybe that's all the signs I know. But I can read two books."

That didn't seem likely. "Which ones?"

"'In the great green room, there was a telephone and a red balloon . . .'"

Some kind of a hiss or a gasp or the sound of a punctured lung came out of Brandy.

"'. . . and a picture of the cow jumping over the moon.'"

Brandy flew off the couch as much as anybody still limping can and smacked Lollipop so hard that Lollipop fell, a perfect handprint seeping onto her cheek. She didn't cry out a sound.

Not a whimper, not a squeak. She just got still, like a statue knocked over. You have to respect an eleven-year-old who gets smacked like that for no good reason and keeps quiet. That Uncle Ray trained her well.

"Brandy!" I stepped between the two of them. Brandy wasn't weak, but this. This was a whole side of her I never knew existed.

Her face was twisted up again the way it had been the other day with Daddy, only now it was beat up from him, fat lip and bruised eyes.

"What was that?" Brandy asked Lollipop. Her cut seeped blood right through the shiny Polysporin. "What was that?"

Lollipop answered as plain as she could manage. She didn't move any part of herself but her mouth. "*Goodnight Moon.*"

"Get off the floor."

"Brandy." Those flames that were lit in my belly the day we took Lollipop rose up, flaring. Was Brandy going to turn vicious now, on top of everything with Daddy? But Lollipop was standing, calm as anything.

"Don't you ever say those words again." Brandy smacked Lollipop's other cheek. Lollipop went down. This time tears oozed like rain dribbling down a wall.

"Daddy's going to kill you," I told Brandy. Even saying

Daddy made me want to slide through the floor and die, but there was nowhere to slide to and no way to die, so somehow I just kept on.

Brandy slipped around the corner to the alcove where my sleeping bag was. I heard her zipping into it. *L.A.'s going to kill you!* I wanted to shout, but the cat took back my tongue again. Anyway, probably Daddy was getting home before L.A., who was doing an outcall. So Daddy would get to Brandy first.

I hauled Lollipop up and propped her on the couch. I made sure the bills we had been studying were in my back pocket. Then I wrapped ice in a paper towel and held it to both sides of her face. She had white features and good, light-brown hair. Her skin was the color of wet sand. Mostly she seemed white, but with that color, it was confusing. She was prettier than the rest of us. Baby-faced.

"What's the other book you know?" I asked her. "Whisper." I didn't want Brandy hearing anything else that might make her charge back out here. But it had been a long time since anybody could talk to me about any kind of book.

"'Be still,'" Lollipop whispered. "It's monsters. There's more, but I can't remember it right now."

Somebody who smelled like barbecue potato chips used to cuddle me on her lap and read to me. I didn't remember the reader; just that salty, smoky scent and something scratchy on my left shoulder every time a page was turned. I remembered the books, though: *Goodnight Moon* and *The Snowy Day*.

"'A wild ruckus,'" Lollipop tried.

"Rumpus." I used to love *Where the Wild Things Are*.

Chapter Two

SIX WEEKS AGO I just assumed I would do the note as Lollipop, but in a fast few days, I changed my mind. Now I keep going back to the idea of Brandy. I could make up the parts I don't know, even though I know more than she ever meant to tell me. *A long time before Daddy, I was a little girl living with my grandmother. Every night she gave me a bath, and every morning before school she did my hair with me standing on the couch so she wouldn't have to bend and hurt her back.* . . . Brandy told me a lot. I liked hearing her stories: *I'm white but my people are black. My mother had blond hair and blue eyes and sent me to my father's mother before she died when I was a baby. My best wifey is Dime. She's street but she speaks well because she's educated. Don't even try to figure that out.*

Except if I were really trying to tell it the way Brandy

would, it would be: *A long time before Daddy, I was living with my grandmother. She do my bath every night. She do up my hair every morning. I'm white by my mother, but my grandmother and everybody else I'm from, black. Now I got a bunch of wifeys. One called Dime. She black but talk TV white. Don't even try.*

I wouldn't have thought she would be one to give up and lay her head in the lap of the life, but sometimes people are surprising. She likes knowing how things are, how they're going to be, who's going to take care of what. Brandy doesn't enjoy the work the way L.A. sometimes does, but the truth is that she just can't picture herself without Daddy. Even with everything that's happened.

Me and my Daddy, Brandy might say. *Maybe I'm not his only. But he take care of me so good. Nobody else ever done nothing for me since my grandma. My Daddy save my life every day. He got me clean, he give me food, he give me a couch to sleep, a place to stay and clothes. He the only one who ever love me.*

I could use Brandy. Easily. But we've been through a lot together, especially in this past month and a half, and I don't want things to end badly. If I wrote it in her voice and she found out, she wouldn't like it at all. She would think I stole her. Or worse, that I was making fun of her.

So that leaves L.A. Only I can't get inside her head. She's too old, for one thing. Twenty-two is a whole other world from sixteen like Brandy. Or fourteen like me. Eleven like Lollipop. And even though I'm hard now, I'm not evil. I don't understand evil, which is why I don't understand L.A.

If she had come home first that day I was trying to teach Lollipop about coins, she might have nearly starved Brandy half to death for bruising Lollipop's face. She might have held back Lollipop's food too, *for bothering Brandy* she would say, slapping Lollipop's head. Daddy would never know about it, and even if he did know, L.A. was the Bottom Bitch and could keep us from eating or smack us if she wanted to.

When Daddy walked in, Brandy was pressing more ice on Lollipop's one cheek and brushing concealer on the other, trying to make the two sides match again.

He took a good long look. "What happened?" At first nobody answered, since it was hard to know who he was asking. "Dime?"

But before I could open my mouth, Brandy did. "I swatted her." I saw her hand shaking holding that brush, but otherwise, she was cool as a cucumber. "She mouthed me, so I swatted her. She ain't going to do me like that again."

Daddy smacked Lollipop on the top of her head. Lollipop went statue. Then Daddy smacked Brandy on the top of her head. Two times. For the second time, he used his fist. Brandy kept her mouth shut, but she fell down hard and had to keep the pain tears back. The cut above her eye began seeping blood again. Even so, she stood right back up.

Daddy took Lollipop's chin and eyed the handprints. "Better cover that shit up." He moved her head left and then right so he could examine both cheeks. "Before you get back to work." He grabbed the beer and the cash I was holding out for him and disappeared into his room. I waited for the lava inside my stomach to cool down, but a second later he poked his head out again. "Lollipop, you learn money yet?"

She looked at me, panicked.

"She started off well," I answered.

"She better learn fast." He tilted his head at me. "Get us some dinner." Brandy cooked better than I did. But it was my turn.

"Am I cooking for L.A.?"

"Nah," he answered. "She out the night."

That's what I thought. She wouldn't come back until noon the next day, which was good. It was Brandy's turn with Daddy after work, so Brandy would be happy. And I wouldn't have to pretend with him and be terrified he would read my mind. *I have nobody. I have nothing.* I could burrow into the sleeping bag instead and try to sleep all day, instead of being awake, hurting with the burn in my belly and everything else.

So time is passing and I'm not closer to figuring out the note than I was six weeks ago. I can't write it as any of them. Not Lollipop, not Brandy, not L.A. But I also can't write it as myself, because my own voice can't possibly accomplish what has to get accomplished. What I mean is that I'm not young and stupid and baby pretty and compelling like Lollipop, in that way that might make some people somewhere take notice and be upset enough to do something. And I'm not chill and sometimes funny like Brandy in a way that might make some people somewhere pay attention and listen enough to do something. And I'm not cruel and half-insane like L.A. in a way that might disturb some people somewhere just enough to stand up and do something. I'm just serious and boring. In a way nobody ever notices. Or listens to. Or cares much about.

Still, despite everything, despite my plan, I'm not actually suicidal. I don't want to die yet, because there are things I have been hoping to do. Like fly in a plane and also a hot-air balloon. I would give anything to be in the audience of *Wendy Williams*. Or any live talk show. There's that man, John Edward, who can talk to people in your life who have passed. I would love to be in his audience, but I have heard they are sold out for years in advance. I'm not even mentioning *Oprah*, because that ship has sailed, but I would give just about anything to meet Oprah.

Also I want to swim in an ocean and meet an elephant. In the wild in India or Africa. But if I never get overseas, maybe at a zoo somewhere, or at one of those preservations. I have loved elephants ever since I was small, way before I knew there was a book called *The Color Purple* with Shug living inside it, loving elephants. When I first got to that part near the end, I could hardly believe it. Especially since Shug is the sort of person I wish I could be, even though Celie is the one I'm more like.

But before I opened the pages of their story and after years of liking elephants all on my own, I saw something astonishing on TV where I was working. I got to see the whole thing because I was tied up and by myself. This female, more than fifty years old, had lived every kind of way all over the world. In the wild, then a zoo, then a circus, then a traveling road show, and all that. She had been loved a little but mostly neglected and abused and sold about a million times. Then finally some rescue people found her and took her to a preservation just for elephants. On her first night there, she was in a cage meant to help her transition to her new life and to the other worn-out elephants living it up in their retirement. Well, this other female was walking back from the fields or the forest or whatever it was and spotted the caged one from far away. And I swear those two elephants recognized each other. The caged female started making all kinds of noise and trying to pry the metal bars apart, and the other one started running and trumpeting, and the two of them nearly tore that cage to pieces trying to get to each other. And when the people finally had the sense to open up the gate, those elephants draped their trunks all over each other and stood so close, you thought they were going to sink right down to the ground in a big-eared pile. But they stayed upright, entwined, touching each other all over with the tips of their trunks, patting and feeling and checking, and looking and massaging, as if they never wanted to let go. That was something incredible. You just knew those two had been close once a long time ago. You just knew they had given up hope of ever seeing each other again. You just knew they had never been so happy to see anybody ever in their entire lives.

The first time I read about Celie reuniting with her sister, Nettie, in *The Color Purple*, about the two of them falling into an overjoyed heap right there on the porch, I thought of those elephants. And to be honest, I cried.

I also want to be pregnant and give birth to my own baby, but that's never going to happen, even if I don't kill myself. But if it did, I would name a boy August and a girl June. And if I had my own child, I would take care of it better than any mother ever did in the history of motherkind.

What I tell myself is that I know I'm doing the right thing. And that I am brave. It requires courage to betray the people closest to you and then take your own life before they kill you themselves.

Chapter Three

FOR SOME REASON I was just remembering a teacher I had when I was in kindergarten. Ms. McClenny was light brown with freckles all over her face and arms. She smelled like Murphy Oil Soap, which was what Janelle used to wash the floors each month. I loved the smell of Murphy. Three other girls and a boy got pulled out two times a week with me to visit Ms. McClenny's room in the school basement. She sat us in a circle of red chairs that fit our behinds perfectly and handed us each a hardcover copy of whatever she had picked out: *Corduroy* the very first day, and later on, *James and the Giant Peach* or *The Mouse and the Motorcycle* or *Dinosaurs Before Dark*. When we finished our turn reading aloud, Ms. McClenny let us choose a lemon drop from her bowl. *To refresh your voice.*

When that boy, Shawn, started crying at the end of every pull-out period and begging to stay and read some more and the rest of us didn't cry but begged, too, Ms. McClenny convinced somebody important to increase our pull-out class to three times a week. After that, every Friday we moved from the circle of chairs to the green and blue and orange square patched rug where we could sit or lie down or *stand on your heads if the spirit moves you.* On Fridays we listened while she read aloud. By the end of the school year, Ms. McClenny had read to us every page of *Peter Pan.*

In first grade we were back to twice a week. Sometimes we didn't stay in the basement room but instead walked up the stairs to the school library. Ms. McClenny showed us the different sections and how to browse. *You can pull any book off the shelf and look at it for as long as you like.* She explained there were libraries everywhere and that we should ask our parents to take us to the ones near where we lived. *When you're a teenager,* she had said, *you can get your own library card.*

I had her for pull-out during second and third grade too. I remember sitting on my hands in that red chair, listening so hard to *Number the Stars* that my fingers fell asleep.

And now that reminds me of another book I read last year about a girl who lived when millions of Jewish people and others were murdered by Nazis. Somehow I skipped a lot of it, but one thing that caught my attention was that Death is the narrator. Remembering that makes me think Sex could narrate my note. After all, just like Death, Sex happens to everybody.

It is tiring to be me, is how Sex could begin. *I am incredibly busy all the time without ever a rest. Sometimes I am busy in a way that feels extremely good. That is when two young people are in love, and I come around and help them out. That is some good stuff. It's okay with older people in love, but older people are just not as attractive.* Janelle stole HBO off the neighbor's cable, and HBO didn't care if certain characters were unattractive or fat or practically grandparents—everybody had sex on HBO. *So I prefer young people, because their bodies are still beautiful. Don't get me wrong: It's cool when it's two people not in love, but it's not as good as it can be. I am never my best self so much as when two young people in love invite me around.*

Sex would just be warming up. *But sometimes is not most of the time. Most of the time, I am busy with making money for somebody. This is my job, and honestly, it is just not any fun at all. Yes, it's true that there's some good feeling when I'm chilling with whatever man hit me up for company. But often even then, I have to deal with his bad mood or his ignorance or his general nastiness. Even if the dude is pleasant to pass the time with, the girl is a whole other story. You see,* Sex would explain, *when it's for moneymaking, the girl rarely enjoys herself. And most of the time, she does not want me around at all. It's hard work, because of how the girl acts like she likes me, when she would rather eat a cockroach-stuffed rat than party with me.*

And while I'm complaining . . . Sex would be on a roll now. *I never ask Violence to be in my company. I deeply dislike it when he comes by, but family is family. I wouldn't have chosen Violence for a cousin, but what can I do? I don't invite him. He just shows up.*

Sex would have a lot to say. *Another hard part of my job is that I am forced to do things I really shouldn't have to. For instance, I have to work with children.* Sex would sigh as he wrote this part. *I am not fit for work with a human body that is too small to do what I need it to do or a human brain that is too young to understand me.* Sex would write with his teeth gritted. *But somehow, the powers that be tell me I have to add children to my job description. I do not appreciate the extra stress.* After Sex introduces himself like that, he would get to the point of the note.

Anyway, he would continue writing, *this is not about me so much as it is about a situation.* Maybe he would begin a new paragraph here. *There are a lot of people involved, including one child. Three children, depending on whether you think of a fourteen- and sixteen-year-old as children. If you consider how old each of them was when her story began, then we are thinking about four children. Since three of them had not reached the age of ten when I was forced to meet them, and the other was not quite fourteen.*

L.A. used to tell Brandy everything, and Brandy never promised to keep quiet. So I know more of L.A.'s story than I want to and plenty of Brandy's. And Lollipop's is coming out a little more every day.

There are four females living in a stable in Newark, New Jersey. They have a Daddy and a clean place to sleep and food and clothes. You could say they are being taken care of real nice. Sex would pause here. *Or. You could say the secrets they are keeping are like a poison eating their souls from the inside out.*

I will tell you about it.

Chapter Four

I MET L.A. last winter. I'd had a fight with Janelle, and she kicked me out into the freezing cold. *After all I done for you when you was small and now you going to do me like that? You going to do this baby like that?* Walking up and down Chancellor, I imagined I could still smell her gin and Coke and hear her indignance. She hadn't given me a minute to grab a book. I couldn't go to school without my coat or knapsack—Trevor and Dawn would ask questions I didn't want to answer—so now I would fail both tests and baby Sienna might not get her medicine, either. She was tiny and cute as a million buttons.

"You okay?" some girl said to me. I'd seen her pass across the street before. I remembered noticing that I liked her high boots. They were tall and brown with a tassel on each zipper. "I asked if you okay?" I think I'd seen those boots go by a few times since lunchtime. Since not eating any lunch.

I nodded. A bus cruised past, lumbering and loud.

"You been out here crying all day." She had straight hair with a golden stripe down the side and golden Spanish-colored skin mixed up with black features.

"I'm fine. Thank you."

"Hmm." She raised her eyebrows. "You uppity." That seemed like an old-fashioned word. "Here." She took off her coat. A white down vest edged in white fur. She held it out to me. "Put it on."

In nothing but an old hoodie and worn-thin jeans, I was so cold it felt like I wasn't wearing any clothes at all. Not even underwear. But I had my pride. "I have to catch the bus." Mist came out of my mouth, white and thick, like the fur on the coat. I was shivering, and my teeth were chattering.

"You not catching no bus, girl," she said. "You watching them buses go by." She shook her vest at me impatiently. "You even have any money?"

Embarrassed, I kept my eyes on her tassels but held up my dime so that she could see it.

She sighed. "Just take the damn coat."

So I took it. It wasn't the warmest ever, but it helped. The fur was soft beneath my fingertips.

"I'll come back by here with some food later," she told me.

She came back forty-five minutes later with a cheese-burger, fries, and a Coke. I ate it all in about a minute, standing up because there wasn't anywhere to sit down. "Thank you."

"Where you staying tonight?" She had her arms crossed over herself. The mist was coming out of her mouth too.

I shrugged. I could probably go home by now. It had been hours. Most likely Janelle had forgotten about me. Even though this was the first time she had ever shouted me out the door. *I have two tests today.* I rarely talked, much less spoke up, so it wasn't easy. *I already went to Rite Aid for Sienna's nose spray Tuesday.* That errand made me miss a quiz plus homework. *Can you send Jywon?* He never went to school anyway. She had bounced the wailing, feverish Sienna on her shoulder, disgusted. *Jywon nothing but a boy. I am not sending him for no medicine. You see this baby burning up. What is the matter with your brain?* I had been surprised. Jywon wasn't a boy. He was sixteen. *Soon as I start asking you to do for me, you going to give me attitude? Selfish. You the most selfish female I ever kept. Get out and keep out. You overstayed your welcome.*

She had started mixing gin in with her Coke a few months before, after they took Vonna to move back in with her mother. I'd never seen Janelle drink much besides a beer now and then, but the day Vonna left, Janelle sat motionless at the kitchen table for close to four hours and then stood up, walked out the door, and went to buy as many of those blue bottles as she must have had cash for. That was when she started getting mean, saying things and slapping my face for the first time. After Vonna's mother got arrested again and Vonna returned to us four days later, I'd hoped that Janelle would go back to her regular self. But she kept that Booth's gin and bought more when the bottles ran out.

"All right then," this girl said to me now. "I'll take back the coat. I'm L.A. You ever need anything, you come back around here."

I slipped off the coat and handed it to her.

"What's your name?"

I wasn't trying to be rude. I just didn't like to talk. So I didn't answer.

Janelle let me back in and even made a plate for me, but I couldn't get warm. Vonna and then Jywon used up all the hot water, so I couldn't take a hot bath or shower. I shivered in my bed that night and two more. Then we argued again because Janelle wanted me to skip school to watch Sienna at home while she went to tussle with Medicaid about Jywon's eyeglasses. *I'm trying to graduate eighth grade,* I started to explain. She put her hands on her hips and shot her head forward. *I'm trying to take care of all y'all kids! You big enough to help, but you think school more important than fever and a boy about to go blind?* Jywon was only farsighted; he wasn't going blind. I didn't even think she was going to Medicaid; I think she wanted to sit at the kitchen table, looking out the window and drinking her gin and Coke. But she yelled and whacked my head with her fist, and Sienna was screaming again, and I couldn't take it. It was too late to go to school. So I went back to the street and walked all the way up and all the way back, over and over to keep warm.

L.A. showed up with another cheeseburger after a few hours. She had on the same white down vest with the fur. She asked some questions but then forgot about me, maybe because I didn't say much. She chewed french fries and walked along, talking and talking. ". . . fighting with my aunt all the time. Kicked out every minute. Her men always trying to get with me." She shook her head and took another fry.

I sneezed. Then I sneezed again. I had nowhere to wipe my nose. I used my hoodie sleeve. I wanted her to offer me that coat again.

"You sick," L.A. informed me.

I was. I wanted to go home and crawl back to bed, but

Janelle took my sheets for Sienna. She said she would get money from welfare for new sheets, but I had a feeling it would be a while, and then what about a blanket? I was skinny, and I got cold fast.

"You should come by me. My boyfriend cool. We got heat. You not warm enough where you at, is you?"

"I can't leave," I coughed. "They'll put me as a runaway."

"You think anybody care? That lady ain't going to notice you missing until next Christmas."

It was strange. It was nine or ten years since I'd been living with Janelle, but I knew what L.A. said was true. I'd been there the longest, but Janelle liked me the least. Not when I first came, and I was small. But by the time a few years had passed, after Vonna had moved from a crib to a bed and when Ms. McClenny let me bring home *Charlie and the Chocolate Factory* and I asked for us to read it together, Janelle called me a show-off and told me not to bring any books around anymore.

Foster mothers can be complicated. A lot of them don't like you when you get older. Denise and Jenny both told me that, even before Denise went home to her aunt and before Jenny left Janelle's for a group home. It wasn't just Janelle, they told me. It was all of them. *You going to see,* they'd both said, at different times. *Soon as you get a little bigger, you going to see.* They were each only at Janelle's for a few months, but they were older than Jywon, practically grown, and they knew things. They were right: Even before Janelle began drinking, she stopped being nice to me. The drinking just made the not nice turn into nasty.

"You coming or not?" L.A. asked.

I followed her home. It's no use wishing I hadn't. Because I did.

"This her," L.A. said. "Dime girl."

Her boyfriend was tall and dark and looked like a cross between Chris Brown and Kanye. A perfect cross. He smiled down at me. "Hello, Beautiful." Nobody ever called me beautiful in my entire life. I was so surprised it took me a minute. And then I sneezed when I was trying to say hi back.

He had a gold letter *D* on his front tooth. "God bless you," he told me.

For the first time I heard the meaning behind those words. I felt like God had just blessed me. And I wasn't even sure I believed in God. My legs and belly felt shaky in front of his brown eyes, which angled downward a little at the outside edges. He had a scar cutting his right eyebrow in half. It's hard to describe, but he looked like a gangster puppy dog.

"Get this girl some hot food," he told L.A. She turned on

the stove and pulled out a bowl and a spoon. "Sit down, Dime," he told me. "Make yourself at home." He was pointing to the couch. I sat on it. It was black and felt like the way I imagined real leather would feel. Opposite the couch, mounted up on the wall, was a huge TV. Huge. I sneezed again.

He settled into a thick, brick-colored armchair across from me. He put his feet up on the glass coffee table. He was wearing some kind of soft-skinned slippers. They looked so warm. "L.A. been telling me about you."

I wasn't sure what that meant.

"She been saying you in a bad situation where you been staying."

I hadn't told L.A. anything about Janelle calling me selfish so much lately or keeping me out of school for babysitting or errands while she drank and hit me and twice threatened to cut me or me having to slap away Jywon all the time. So I wasn't too sure how she knew it was a bad situation. But then again, I guess a thirteen-year-old girl sitting at a bus stop in the cold with no coat for hours is probably a pretty good tip-off something's not right.

I shrugged.

"When I talk to you," he said softly, "you got to answer me."

I stayed quiet. He slid his slippers off the table, leaned forward, and put his hands on my cheeks. Almost like he was going to kiss me. And also like he was a little bit angry. I was scared of him being angry, but at the same time his hands felt so good and his eyes felt so good, I didn't want him to let me go.

"You understand?" he asked.

I started to nod, but his hands got just a little bit firmer on my cheeks. They were so big. And warm. I wanted them to stay on my face forever. "Yes," I said. "I understand." I didn't want to disappoint him. He was looking at me like he saw me. Like he really wanted to hear my voice. Like I mattered.

"Soup." L.A. brought it to the coffee table and set it down in front of me.

He let go of my face. I wanted to ask him to put his hands back. But instead I picked up the spoon and ate. He watched. Only I didn't feel watched: I felt seen.

"She going to be good," he said to L.A. I didn't know what he meant. "You did good."

L.A. beamed. She had nice teeth just like his. Big and white and straight. She looked like a little girl when she beamed like that. I only ever saw her light up with him.

Chapter Five

THAT ONE DIDN'T know me yet, Sex would write about me in the note. *What I mean is, she knew about me because she read books and watched HBO. And she heard people talk. But she hadn't met me face-to-face. L.A., though. Well.* Sex would pause his writing fingers for a second. *L.A. knew me from a tiny little girl. Practically a baby. I was not happy to meet her that first time or all those times after. No sir. But her father and uncles and my nasty cousin in tight with them forced the issue. It bothers me to this day.*

L.A. didn't share much with me after those first two cold afternoons pacing Chancellor, but it seemed like she had shared her whole life with Brandy. And Brandy could be loquacious.

It made it easier for the one with the gold D on his tooth, though. He took one look at L.A. all those years ago, and he could tell she was going to be cake. "Hey, Beautiful," he said to her. "What you crying for? What? You got to repeat the eighth grade again? Well, how many times you done the eighth grade? Twice? Twice already? Nah. You not stupid. They just ain't teaching you right. Wipe those tears, Beautiful. Here. Use my scarf. That's all right. We'll wash it when we get home. Sure, baby. You come home with me. You can use my phone and call your mama to tell her you ain't lost. You ain't got a mama? All right then. You call your aunt then. Sure, baby. I don't care if you don't go to school. . . ." I didn't understand it back when Brandy used to tell me. I don't think Brandy understood it either. But I've grown up since. *It's not hard to sweet-talk a girl looking to feel special. Not hard at all.*

Chapter Six

HE SAID I should call Janelle. He tapped the speaker on his phone and handed it to me.

"I'm staying with a friend," I told her.

"Where at?" I could hear the gluey Booth's in her voice.

L.A. and her boyfriend both shook their heads.

"Over by the McDonald's on Clinton," I lied. He smiled at me with all those straight teeth and the gold letter *D* glittering. He was the best-looking man I'd ever seen.

"You don't got no clothes."

It was true. "L.A. is the same size as I am," I lied again, glancing at him for the smile. L.A. was taller and more curvy. Janelle would never know.

"Her mother going to get you to school?" The way she spoke, I could almost smell the alcohol.

"Yeah." Even though I didn't need anybody to get me to school, because I liked school.

"All right," Janelle said. "Come on home in a couple days."

I gave the phone back to him, trying to pretend I didn't care that Janelle didn't even ask to speak to any mother. Trying not to worry about whether L.A. would lend me clothes and if so, how foolish I might look in them.

"You know how to cook?" he asked me as he tapped off the phone.

"I can do some."

"You going to help L.A.," he said. "We having company tonight."

We roasted a chicken and made rice and green beans.

"That back burner gets stuck on." L.A. showed me. "You got to keep a eye on it."

I did the rice, keeping my eye on the back burner, turning the dial this way and that, until I got the feel of how it was broken but could still be made to work at the same time.

I met Brandy that night. They said she was L.A.'s cousin. I didn't understand how that could be, since she was white. Which was different all on its own. She skipped me serving the beans. I wasn't going to say anything, but Daddy did.

"You forgot Dime," he told her. She spooned beans onto my plate silently.

Later she took the last of the rice just after Daddy asked if I wanted seconds. I hadn't even answered him yet, but he picked up her plate, tilted it, and used his knife to slide her rice onto mine. I never had a father or an uncle before—Janelle's men moved in and out and she barely let them talk to us kids—so I thought he was doing what fathers and uncles did. Just looking out for me. Taking care of me. I liked that. It felt good.

Chapter Seven

THAT ONE WITH the gold D *played the girl they call L.A. perfect,* Sex would explain. Brandy was a good storyteller. She told me L.A.'s story as if she had been right there, watching the whole thing. Sex would know just how to tell it again. *"Her?" D acted like the other female was nothing. "Satin? That there ain't nobody. She ain't nobody important. Here. Take her sweater. It look better on you. You look like a queen now. What? Nah. She won't care. I bought that sweater. That's mine. Not hers. She leaving soon, anyway. She won't even know it's gone. Turn around now. Whoooo. Beautiful. You look beautiful." That's what these dudes do. They play the girls like nobody's business. "What? I'm not worried about nothing. Nothing. Just the rent. I'm a little behind, but don't you worry. Help? How you going to help? That's real sweet of you, Beautiful. I'll think about it."*

I hadn't understood it at all before. But now it seems so obvious, it's embarrassing.

It's a game of the mind, and that's the problem. These young girls, they don't understand anything except false promises, love lies, new clothes, and a meal. Their fathers and uncles and mama's boyfriends and cousins and brothers and boys around the block made these girls confused. So confused they don't know which way is straight.

Chapter Eight

THE FIRST TIME I stayed there almost two weeks. My fever broke the second night, and even though I still didn't feel too well, I went to school just like always. L.A. and him worked all the time. I thought L.A. worked selling clothes in the day. I thought she worked at a restaurant at night. I thought she switched from being like a friendly big sister to a bitch because she was working so hard. He drove her to work in his gold Honda, but she always took the bus or walked home. So she was tired. That's how ignorant I was. I thought he worked for the phone company. I don't know why I thought that, but I did. That's how even more ignorant I was.

In the beginning I slept on the couch and never noticed when L.A. came in, passed right by me, and went to her room. I slept hard. The blankets and sheets were clean from an old mini-refrigerator box in L.A.'s room. She gave me clean sweat-pants and a T-shirt from another box. They were big, but they worked fine. I washed my panties and socks in the sink.

The third night, after he dropped her off at work, he asked me to wash dishes. He sat down to watch TV but looked at his phone every few seconds too. That's what he did every day for about an hour before he went back out.

"Get me a beer," he called. I put a newly clean fork into the rack and pulled a forty out of the refrigerator. I was nervous in that heart-beating way I had just being near him. He made my head dizzy and my body hot. I'd read enough to know those were signs of being in love, but I was embarrassed in front of myself and didn't want to admit it. He was old. Thirty at least.

He patted the couch next to him. I gave him the beer and sat down. "Want one?" he asked.

I shook my head.

"You got to answer me when I talk to you."

"I'm sorry." I didn't want him mad at me. "I don't drink beer."

"Huh." He took a swallow, looking at me. I didn't want him to look anywhere else.

"You too good for beer?"

I started to shake my head, but remembered to answer. "No. I'm just too young."

"You funny is what you is." He smiled. "I wouldn't let you drink no alcohol anyway. That right there a test. You passed." He put his forty on the glass coffee table and then pulled a bag out from behind the couch. He must have hidden it there when I wasn't looking. It was fancy, with white tissue paper crinkling out from the top. "Take it," he said.

I wasn't used to getting presents. I stayed still.

"Go on." He picked up his beer again. "Look."

It was two sweaters with vertical ruffles down the center of the back and sleeves that widened, like bells, at the wrist. Three soft T-shirts, two pairs of jeans, and fake-leather black boots. High boots. Four pairs of socks and five pairs of panties in five colors and a hot-pink bra. One sweater was red, like a valentine. One was gray. At the bottom of the bag, puffing up like a pillow, was a coat. Black with gray fake fur lining the hood.

"You got to have clothes."

"How did you know my size?" I'd almost never been given new clothes before, and not this many all at once. I couldn't believe it.

"I know your body." He moved closer, laying his arm across my shoulders and kissing my forehead. Nobody ever kissed my forehead. I loved the feel of that kiss. I loved the feel of his arm, too.

"Thank you."

"What's wrong, Beautiful?" He sipped his beer.

"Nothing."

He sat back a little to look at me better. "I know your face now," he told me. "And I know something just then bothering you."

Nobody had ever looked enough at my face or cared enough to see if I was bothered. It had been a long time since anyone had ever noticed any kind of feeling of mine. Maybe Ms. McClenny from way back in pull-out class. *You feeling okay, honey?* She had touched my cheek with her Murphy Oil Soap–smelling hand. The new baby Janelle had been keeping was sent home after only a few weeks, and I hadn't slept for hearing Janelle cry all night. *You feverish?* Then Ms. McClenny pulled my head to her round hip in a sideways hug before tucking me under a blanket on the square patched rug. *Close your eyes and rest until the bell rings.*

"Don't get mad?" I said.

He shook his head. "Nah. Tell me."

"Maybe L.A. wouldn't like it if she saw you had your arm around me."

His teeth were so gleaming and perfect. They looked like candy. The gold *D* shone.

Don't laugh, I wanted to say.

When he smiled, the angled outside corners of his eyes slid down even more. "You priceless," he told me. "Don't you worry about L.A. She know I like you, and she know it ain't none a her concern."

He liked me? I wasn't sure what that meant. But his arm was wrapped around me again, and he was looking at me in that way he had, that way that said I was something.

"Matter of fact"—he put his forty back down again and turned me gently so that we were face-to-face—"I don't even want you to leave. That's how much I like you." He rested his forehead right on the spot where he had kissed me. "You can be one a mine now." His? "You can stay here long as you want with L.A. and Brandy."

"Brandy?"

"She moving in real soon," he explained. "Another one called herself Satin was here awhile, but she just left out." He lifted his forehead off mine but stayed close. I could feel his breath. "So I told Brandy I'm a help her out. And now I met you." He looked right into my eyes. "And you something extra special."

And then he kissed me on my mouth, just a quick brush, just for a second, and I knew I'd never wanted anything more than to be his.

Chapter Nine

"WE GOING TO lose the apartment," her Daddy told L.A.

That's how Sex would keep on with the note. He would write L.A.'s part just how Brandy told me what she knew.

L.A. fell for his bullshit. "I got dogged at work. They didn't pay me. Now I owe rent. Not much, but the landlord. You know how he is. He want his coins. You can help. All you got to do is go meet my friend. You go meet my friend, and you do what he want, and you bring me back the money. What? Nah. Just this once. It ain't nothing. You done all that before. You told me so with all them uncles and them when you was small. Nothing you don't know how to do. You can do it this time on your own choice. You can do it and earn some money instead of it just getting stole from you for free. I bet you're real good at it too. You had all that experience. You can put it to good use now. What? Us? Nah. Not until you bring me some money. Maybe then I'll let you get with me like that. Nah. He ain't going to ask you to do much. Just go chill with him. Don't give him a hard time. Take his coins and bring it to me. Yeah. Then we good for rent. Think about it, Beautiful. Think about how you can make yourself useful. Make me real proud and bring me my money and then I'll get with you like that. Yeah, you think about it."

It made sense to me then. Perfect sense. When you're young, you're stupid.

The men. The money. I like my job so much better when it's just young love instead. That's what Sex would write.

Chapter Ten

WHAT I KNEW was that right as L.A. was showing up, this one they called Satin was on her way out. She was old. I thought she was twenty-eight or maybe even older than that. She was the Bottom Bitch, but something happened. Brandy said Satin got in a car with the one they called Stone and chose him. Brandy said Satin had made two thousand dollars that day and broke to Stone right there in his car. Just handed him all that cash that was supposed to be for our stable. I heard on the street that Satin was out of pocket somehow: looked Stone or Whippet straight in the eye or didn't step off the curb into the street when she was supposed to. Also I heard somebody else randomly recruited her for his and she said yes and never came back home. Whatever it was, L.A. took Satin's place. And Brandy and I got added a long time before Lollipop arrived. I only ever saw Satin once or twice. She was small and skinny with patchy, ashy skin. Her face was bony, like a skeleton's. L.A. said it was her HIV finally showing up. Brandy said it was smack; maybe even tweak. All I could see was that Satin looked so old.

Chapter Eleven

BRANDY MOVED IN on my fourth day. He gave her the couch and sent me to a sleeping bag in the alcove. *Brandy been talking to me longer,* he whispered. *She got seniority, so she got the couch. But don't you worry, Beautiful. We going to fix up that alcove nice for you.* He gave me a new pillow with a royal-blue pillowcase.

Those first days, I still slept hard. Nothing woke me until seven, and then my eyes popped open as if I had an alarm clock in my head. I didn't want to miss school. I didn't want to miss Trevor and Dawn. Even though I barely ever said anything, they didn't just count on me for homework; they talked to me some too. I didn't worry they would bother me, the way I worried about other kids, sometimes jumping each other in the hallways, pulling out knives. Or disrespecting the weak teachers with language as foul as Janelle at her most drunk. I didn't want to miss Mr. Stewart going off about how bumblebees and dolphins share the same physics or about Hilary Clinton or global warming or whatever topic he thought was okay for world history. I didn't want to miss his class, even though I was only getting Ds in it and he didn't seem to know my name.

I hadn't gotten any As or even Bs for three years—not since English in fifth grade at middle school. But still I didn't want to miss that feeling I got from knowing an answer even though I never raised my hand. That feeling people get in books like Peter must have had during his snowy day when he made footprints and then stick tracks in the snow or Mandy when she lay in the grass and gazed at the pansies she grew herself from seeds. Charlie Bucket when he peeled back the wrapper of that second chocolate bar and saw the flash of golden ticket peeking out. I only got that feeling from school or from books.

And from him when he looked at me or smiled at me or put his arm on me or kissed me. He didn't do any of those things very much. I thought he was trying not to get L.A. or Brandy jealous. Because a few times he'd whispered to me, *You know you my favorite, right? L.A. own her place, and it important. And Brandy reliable. But you. You smart, Beautiful. You special. I got plans for you.* He would be whispering so close to my face. *Big plans.*

I spent more and more time thinking about him, wishing he would whisper to me again, touch me.

So I began leaving Trevor and Dawn after the last bell, rushing, hoping he'd already driven L.A. and Brandy to work and come back home. Then he and I would be alone together without the others for about an hour before he left. Maybe we would watch TV. Maybe he would wrap his arm around my shoulder. Sometimes we played games on his phone. Angry Birds. He always laughed when I beat him. Sometimes he would send me into L.A.'s room, or he would go into his because he wanted privacy. I would hear him playing some kind of video game or talking on his phone. Whispering or shouting or just making conversation. When he was whispering or just talking, he would have a way he spoke—a tone—that made me mad. Jealous. It was the same tone he used with me when he told me I was the best. I didn't like hearing that tone for someone invisible on the other end of his phone.

But sometimes he would come out and tell me things. It was always topics and not details. Money or Stress or Business or his Brother Down South and the Russians or if somebody pissed him off at the gym. Until he mentioned that, I didn't even know he went to a gym. I thought his body was just natural.

Sometimes he would wrap his arm around my shoulders, pulling me close and kissing my eyelids, giving me that good feeling. *You the best,* he would say. He would notice my homework spread out on my lap. *You the smartest individual I know. I got big plans for you.* I felt like I was really somebody.

I was carrying a forty and a plate of Doritos and guacamole over to him. I was walking too fast and somehow I tripped, smashing the side of my head into the corner of the glass coffee table.

"Whoa." He was next to me before I even realized what had happened, lifting me gently onto the couch.

My head throbbed.

"Stay there." As he disappeared into the kitchen, I saw a streak of rust on his arm. I touched above my left ear and felt stickiness. I sat up fast. He wasn't going to want my blood on that couch.

"Lie down, now," he said when he came back in.

"But I'm bleeding."

"Lie down, fool," he said gently, and I did.

"Hold these."

I held out my hands to take a box of Band-Aids, a tube of

Polysporin, and a tiny white Advil bottle. He shifted me carefully over onto my side and began wiping and pressing. I winced.

"Ain't nothing," he said. "Heads bleed." He dabbed some more. "Band-Aid's not going to stick with your pretty hair. Hold still. I'm a press hard a minute."

I held still, while he pressed hard. It hurt, but not badly. I didn't make a noise.

"You brave beside being smart, huh, Beautiful?" I felt him smearing on the Polysporin, and then I held still again while he checked his work.

"You good now." He helped me sit up, sliding his warm arms under and around me. I could hardly look at him, what with the beer-soaked carpet and the green mush all over the armchair. Doritos in pale bits where his feet had crushed them, and his gold *D* and angled eyes and scar. With how our bodies were touching and how he was taking care of me.

"I'm sorry," I whispered. He eased the Advil container from my sweaty palms and shook out two pills.

"Open." I obeyed. He tucked the pills inside my mouth. My head pounded. I had to close my eyes because I was too agitated and embarrassed to watch his face so close to mine, to see his warm fingers slip between my lips. I swallowed with nothing but my spit, and then I felt him move to kiss my forehead. Without even deciding, I raised my mouth to catch his. He pulled back and chuckled. I was disappointed and relieved both at the same time.

"Relax, Beautiful." His voice was so soft. My entire body began to shiver. "I'm a clean this mess."

"I'll do it," I said, even though I could hardly think or move with the shivering.

"Nah." He waved me off. "Relax."

I'd never seen him lift a finger to clean anything. That was mine and Brandy's and L.A.'s job. I shivered and tried to calm myself as I watched him work. He knew where the Windex was and how to use a wet washcloth instead of a wet paper towel on the brick-colored cloth chair. He knew to blot the beer puddle on the carpet instead of wipe it. He knew how to use a vacuum cleaner.

"What you gawking at?" he asked me with his butt in the air while he Windexed the underside of the coffee table.

"Nothing."

"Oh yeah," he said, pretending to be mad. "You laughing?" He shook his head and tossed a wadded-up wet paper towel at my feet. "Now she laughing."

L.A. yelled if I was loud and woke her up, because she and Brandy only got home from work and into bed right before my eyes flew open in the morning, and they were tired. So I tried to be as quiet as I could be leaving for school. Brandy never yelled from the couch, but then again, she slept through almost anything.

About half the time when I walked in around three, they would be showering and getting ready. The two of them dressed up in outfits he bought them. Adult, sexy high heels and low-cut, sparkly tops. They were only allowed to wear those to work. At home it was just sweats and T-shirts. L.A.'s fur-lined vest was more stylish than my new black coat, and Brandy's gray wool looked warmer than mine, plus it had square white snaps on it. But my fresh clothes were nicer than their day-time sweats and T-shirts. I was worried they would be mad about that, but they didn't even seem to notice. I thought it was strange, because after living with her for so many days, L.A. seemed like the type who would notice and not like it.

They always gave their tips to Daddy. That's what I started calling him, because everybody else did. And because that's how he acted; making sure we had food and shampoo. Protecting us. *Nobody going to mess with you when they know you mine,* Daddy would say, and I knew that must be true. He was tall and built and dressed well without being too flashy, and people always showed him respect when they came around our place.

Daddy would get annoyed at the others if he thought there wasn't enough money.

"Where the rest?" he asked Brandy.

"That's it," she would say. "It's all there."

"That's not shit."

"Cold," Brandy said. "People ain't going out."

"L.A. got me three times that," Daddy said.

L.A. smiled.

"She been working longer. Got her regulars," Brandy tried.

"You better get you some regulars," Daddy said. "You ought to be making more than L.A. White quota higher. That ain't rocket science. You better step it up."

I did my homework and pretended I wasn't listening. I didn't want to know what it all meant. I still wanted to believe that L.A. was selling clothes during the day and working at a restaurant at night. I wanted to believe she and Brandy shared the same shifts, seating fancy people at candlelit tables or maybe taking drink orders from a group of grown girlfriends or from a family party. Like how it is in restaurants in the movies.

But it was hard to ignore the truth. Those tips weren't tips. They were pay. For what L.A. and Brandy were really doing. I tried not to look at the money changing hands, because Daddy got tense if we seemed like we were too interested in it. He never gave any to L.A. or Brandy. It wasn't their job to manage the coins. It was his.

A few days later was Saturday, and I was reading in my alcove in the morning while everybody else slept. I heard what sounded like some sort of animal: a big dog or small bear, but then I realized it was Brandy, making noises on the couch. I slid out of my sleeping bag. She was mostly asleep.

"Hey." I perched on the edge of the leather and shook her shoulder. There was wetness under her. Sweat. "Brandy," I said. "Wake up."

Then L.A. was next to me, in her white tank top and gray sweats, sucking her teeth. "Thought we was done with this shit," she muttered. She leaned over Brandy, tapping her face light and fast. "Wake up, girl." She kept tapping. Brandy was still making those snuffing sounds. "Shut up."

Brandy opened her eyes. There were tears coming out of them. I didn't know you could cry in your sleep. "Get off." She pushed us away and sat, huddled. Her red T-shirt was soaked.

"Dime, get a towel," L.A. ordered. "Brandy, get up off that couch. Daddy going to be pissed off you messed up this leather."

I thought about when I had been bleeding on it. He wasn't pissed off at all then. What was L.A. talking about? Brandy stood up and crossed her arms over her elbows. She shuffled out of the way and then sank onto the rug, leaning against the armchair.

"You okay?" I asked.

"Get me a damn towel," L.A. hissed.

Brandy wouldn't look at me. She just rocked forward and backward, arms crossed, fingers tucked under armpits. I got a towel from the bathroom. When I came back, L.A. took it and began wiping down the couch. Brandy was still hunched on the floor. Then Daddy banged out of his room. For a minute, he looked as pissed off as Janelle. But he glanced at me and softened.

"I got it, Daddy," L.A. said. "Don't worry about nothing."

"Yeah?" Daddy asked Brandy.

She shrugged. "I'm good." Her voice was almost a whisper. She didn't look good. Daddy threw me a soft look, his *you special* look, and then he went to her.

"I'm good," she mumbled.

He knelt down in front of her, and she stopped rocking. He took her face in his hands. It made an ugly feeling well up in me, even though I felt bad for Brandy. He stroked her hair back out of her face. I wished there was something wrong with me so that he would stroke mine like that. "Ain't nothing but a dream," Daddy told her.

L.A. kept wiping the couch, behind me. I could hear the towel sanding the leather. Daddy scooped Brandy up, standing and holding her like a baby, her legs dangling over his right arm and her head resting on his left. "You want smack for real, I'll go buy you some," Daddy told her quietly. "But think on how hard we worked to get you off that shit."

Brandy nodded a tiny nod. "I know."

"And if I get you some—which I will do, you just say the word—you know I can't have none a that up in my household."

"I know." Even from where I was standing, I could see her body trembling.

His voice was so gentle. "I get it for you, then you got to leave."

"I don't want it."

"You sure?" Daddy asked. She nodded again. "Come here, baby," he said, and I turned away because I couldn't stand my own jealousy. But then Daddy called to me. "Dime." I turned back. He rested his chin on top of Brandy's head and winked. Then he disappeared with her into his room.

I tried not to listen to them, but it was hard. The apartment wasn't that big. L.A. stomped back into her own room as soon as the couch was dried off, and that left me alone to hear them and to imagine what was happening. It wasn't difficult, especially because I was imagining it was me in there instead of Brandy. Wishing.

Chapter Twelve

"COME ON, BEAUTIFUL," Daddy said, as soon as I walked in the door after school. I could tell from the quiet that L.A. and Brandy were already gone.

I looked at him, nervous.

He slipped the knapsack off my back, then gently turned me around toward the door. "About time I took you out."

It's like what I used to say to Vonna. *Come on. I'm taking you out.* And she would jump up—actually jump—and keep jumping all the way to the door. We never went anywhere real, because there was never anywhere to go. But I pretended. I would use my bus pass and take her across Newark, telling her we were about to see a circus. She would play along, and when we got to the cluster of fabric and wig shops all around Academy Street, we'd stop and lean against a construction barrier wall somebody once put up and never took back down. *Watch the elephant parade,* I would say, when four fat old ladies all together shuffled into a store across from us. We could see everything through the plate-glass windows. *Wait, there's a clown.* I would point to a man in another store holding up a platinum wig in one hand and a magenta one with bangs in the other. *He going to put one on?* Vonna would giggle. *Watch,* I would tell her as he picked out a third wig. *Maybe he's going to juggle.*

Out by the curb, Daddy opened the door of his Honda for me and then trotted around to his side. I'd never been inside it and was surprised at how clean it was. The radio didn't work, though, and the floor mats were worn thin. We drove on streets I'd never seen and parked in a lot he was going to have to pay for later, with a ticket that slid out from a machine.

Out on the sidewalk, Daddy slipped his hand down from my shoulder to my bottom and then wiggled up under my new coat until his palm slid into the back pocket of my jeans. His warmth felt good in the freezing cold, and the way his hand told anyone who could see that he was mine felt even better. He steered me through streets with cafés instead of dollar stores, through men and women wearing business suits mixed in with the regular people. He chose a café and sat opposite me inside a booth.

"You want a hot chocolate?"

I nodded.

He ordered two with whipped cream and a plate of french fries for us to share. He dipped a fry into his hot chocolate. "That some good shit," he told me. "You try it."

I tried it. He smiled, eyebrows angling, when I switched back to my ketchup. Then we were quiet awhile. I ate my fries as slowly as possible, wanting to make everything about the way I was feeling last as long as it could, hoping that we would never have to stand up and he would never turn away from me.

"You got any questions?"

I shook my head, nervous again. There were things I wanted to tell him, but they weren't questions. They were just things I wanted him to know. *I love royal blue, and you gave me that royal-blue pillowcase,* I wanted to say. *Once I had a gym teacher who looked a lot like you only not as cute and he was bald. My favorite smells are barbecue potato chips and Murphy Oil Soap and also the smell of A & D ointment, which is what you put on babies' bottoms.*

"You been with me a time." He popped another fry into his mouth. "Thought you might have a question." I didn't want to think about questions. I didn't want to think about what I knew he was asking me.

I used to play checkers a lot with my foster brother, Jywon, and I beat him every time even though I'm younger. I taught Vonna and another boy Janelle kept for a while who we called Truck, but those two couldn't beat me or Jywon. We had a tournament one weekend, and the winner was supposed to get everyone's dessert for a week. I won, but Jywon wouldn't give up his ginger snaps. Truck tried to beat Jywon for cheating me, but he was too small.

That's what I wanted to tell him, but instead a question came out after all. "Last week. That Saturday morning. Brandy was dreaming about heroin?"

"That's what you want to know?" Daddy smiled. "You funny."

I didn't feel funny, but he looked happy with me, so I didn't mind.

"Yup. Girl was skinny as a rail and half-dead when I found her. She ain't had her a dream like that in a good while."

Do you love Brandy a lot? I wanted to ask, but I couldn't. Daddy knew, anyway. It was like he could read my mind.

"I got a big heart." Daddy smiled. "I got room for a lot of loving." He tilted his head and let me see his gold *D* and looked straight into my eyes the way he did. "And you." He stopped smiling. "You real special."

His voice was like a blanket, and I closed my eyes for half a second, imagining I could crawl right into it. And then

I was talking. "Once I won the class spelling bee, and that same year I had stitches in my chin when I was nine when I tripped running up the stoop, and Janelle let me eat Froot Loops all day long for a week after that because I loved Froot Loops and she always spoiled us if we were hurt."

He finished his hot chocolate, licking his top lip for the whipped cream. "Sound like your Janelle done a good job with you when you was coming up." He nodded, and I nodded because Janelle had been good at a lot of things a long time ago, even if she wasn't good at everything and even if that gin made her evil now.

"Did you ever think you saw someone you thought you knew and then when you got up close to say hi, it wasn't the person you thought?"

"Did that yesterday." Daddy seemed surprised. "That happen to you, too?"

I nodded. I'd never talked so much in my life. "Who was it?"

"Who was what?"

"Who was the person you thought you saw?"

"A old associate."

I ate a few more fries.

"Dime."

I stopped eating at the serious tone of his voice. "I can't

do what L.A. and Brandy do," I whispered. I looked down at my place mat. It was white paper with a row of old-fashioned bottles drawn in bright colors.

"You know what they do?"

I nodded without looking up. He didn't get annoyed that I had only nodded and not spoken.

"You sure?"

I nodded again. "But I can't do that." *Except with you.* I shivered the way I seemed to when I was around him and now at the thought of doing *that* with him. I glanced up fast and then back down. "I'm a virgin." I was more than a virgin. I felt my face heat up.

"You ever even been kissed?"

I shook my head, my face even hotter from how he wouldn't let me kiss his mouth the way I wanted to when I hurt my head.

"Dime." He was gazing at me again, like I was the only person in the world. "They do it because they want to. Ain't nobody expecting you to do nothing you don't want."

He looked away and rubbed his face, as if he felt tired or sick.

"Are you mad?" It was hard to ask.

"Nah, I ain't mad," he said. "I couldn't never be mad at you." He dipped a fry in ketchup and ate it, chewing slowly.

"Just stressed." He frowned at something he was thinking about. "Don't worry about nothing."

"I'm sorry," I whispered.

"What for, Beautiful?" He leaned forward, resting his forearms in a triangle pointing toward me.

"Just. I don't know."

He slid his hands over to mine and covered my fingers with his. I loved how strong they felt. Just like his voice, only solid.

"You know I'm a take care a you, right?"

I nodded, trying not to smile about it too much, trying not to burst with how good it felt.

He picked up both of my hands in his and bent his head to kiss them. "All right then."

He must have been more stressed than I even knew, because I heard them arguing in his room before L.A. went out the next afternoon.

"You know how it go," he was saying in a low, mad voice. "You know how it go. It the same every time. What you bothering me for about it now?"

I couldn't hear what she said, exactly, except I could hear how mad she was too.

"You just do what you do, and it going to go down how

I say. Six months, L.A., like I told you. Then we going to—"

She interrupted him, with something about a *little bitch*. Then I heard a thump, and it was quiet. I think maybe he swatted her or pushed her onto a bed or maybe a chair. I looked over at Brandy, who was waving her hands in the air, trying to dry nail polish. She changed it once a week, working over flattened grocery bags so she wouldn't stain the kitchen table.

"She talking about you," Brandy said. "'Little bitch' is you."

I knew L.A. didn't like me much, but hearing that hurt. At least Daddy stopped her. I loved how he protected me. "Get used to it," Brandy told me. "They fight a lot. Not going to be about you all the time neither." She blew on her tips. "It ain't ever personal with L.A. anyway."

". . . back to where your uncles and them can do you for free, without even taking care a you?" I heard Daddy ask, and then something muffled. "So you just . . ." Then Daddy got quiet again. It stayed quiet for a long time.

"L.A. tell you all about her special self yet?" Brandy asked me.

Now I heard something else. At first I thought it was L.A. crying, but then I realized it was her making another sound. Then the music went on in there, loud, and Brandy rolled her eyes. "I hate that song."

I hated knowing what they were doing in there. Hearing them argue bothered me, but it bothered me more picturing what was going on now.

Brandy shook her head. "Now she going to be late, and he going to blame her."

I stared at my books until Brandy spoke up again. "L.A. had a lot of boyfriends before Daddy," she told me. "But once anybody find Daddy"—she spread her purple nails in a fan on top of the table—"hardly nobody choose to leave."

This was the third Sunday, and the third time we all ate dinner together, early, at four. L.A. and Brandy were going out to work after. Tonight Daddy looked distracted. He wasn't glancing at his phone and thumb typing at all. He was just nursing his forty and staring at the center of our round table, not eating.

Brandy looked at me over our spaghetti and meatball plates and then at L.A.

"What?" L.A. said. She wasn't so smart sometimes.

Brandy jerked her head at Daddy.

"What is you looking at?" L.A. asked impatiently.

Brandy sighed so loud it was almost a groan. "Daddy, you okay?" she asked. Now L.A. looked more carefully at Daddy.

He rubbed his face. "Nah."

L.A. sat back and crossed her arms. She glared into the air above the table, not looking at any of us.

Daddy shook his head. "Dime, you got to go back home."

Back to Janelle? Back with Jywon and being kept home from school and the shouting and the smacks and that ugly smell of gin? Not here? Not with Daddy, whispering and warm?

"Close your mouth, girl," L.A. told me, still glaring. Was she mad I was going to have to leave? But I thought she didn't even like me.

Daddy's face was sad. He frowned, crunching up the scar in his eyebrow. "Saw her by your block," he told me. How did he know where Janelle lived? He must have asked around. He must have found out. He must have wanted to know more about me, because I was so quiet I could hardly tell him anything. "She all liquored up," Daddy said. "She ain't doing good."

I didn't want to go home to Janelle all liquored up. The last few times, she threatened me with the big knife we used for chicken and carrots. What if she got my eye? Why was Daddy saying I had to go back to her?

"She need you, Dime. You a smart girl. You mature."

I heard L.A. snort. Daddy ignored her, and so did I.

"You got to go help her out a her mess."

"Don't make me." How could I leave him? He was the only one who ever took real care of me.

"This ain't no place for you," Daddy said. "Ain't right, me keeping you."

L.A. lifted her head and began to eat her spaghetti. She slurped the noodles hard, rude, but Daddy still ignored her.

"Please." He had never kissed me properly. Only that one time, so light and fast. I at least wanted him to kiss me properly. "I don't want to go."

"I'm real sorry, Dime," Daddy said. He squeezed my leg beneath the table and left his hand there. "I ain't making rent. Might have to get me a tenant for that alcove."

I remembered the afternoon he'd taken me out and we'd had hot chocolate. "But before you said—"

"I know what I said," Daddy interrupted. "I'm a try to figure it out." He shook his head. "Meantime, it is what it is."

Brandy drank her Sprite. I could tell she was purposely not looking at me. Would she be glad to see me go, or would she miss me?

"Go pay your Janelle a visit." Daddy was still holding my leg, massaging it a little, trying to make me feel better. "You pay her a visit, stay awhile, and maybe I come up with something by then."

L.A. stood up so fast, she knocked the table, making the

silverware clatter. Daddy slid his hand off my leg. She grabbed Brandy's plate and her own and began to clear the table.

"I wasn't done," Brandy protested.

"You done," L.A. said. "We late anyway."

Daddy ignored them, as if they weren't even there, just looking at me, sad.

After L.A. and Brandy left, Daddy didn't disappear into his room. He sat on his chair, staring at me cleaning up in the kitchen. He wasn't holding his phone or asking for a forty. I kept cleaning and cleaning because I was confused and nervous and trying not to cry, thinking about leaving Daddy.

"Dime," he called after I had wiped the counter three times.

I turned around to him.

"You know I don't want you to go."

"Yeah."

"Come here."

I went to him. He pulled me right onto his lap, my legs dangling sideways off the chair. "You know why I wouldn't let you kiss me that time you cut your head?"

He was holding my face in his hands, the way he had the very first night I'd met him, only this time my body was on his, so close. I felt hot and shivery and scared and crazy. I shook my head, and he didn't get mad at me for not answering with words.

"Because you so special." He dipped his head toward mine. He kissed my lips softly. I couldn't think over the feeling of rushing everywhere inside me at once. "You young, but you act grown." He looked into my eyes. "Can't help myself none. I just love you." He kissed me again, using his tongue for a quick second, and I felt the surprise all over my body, like the electric shock from the bad outlet in Janelle's kitchen, and then he pulled away again and sighed and made a little rumbling sound.

He loved me. I had hoped he loved me. I had thought maybe he loved me, but now he was telling me so. I pressed my body into him, holding my face up, wanting more.

"Nah, Dime," he said, pulling back, pulling himself together again. "You only thirteen."

"Please," I said.

"Wish you could stay," he told me, resting his forehead on mine.

"Let me."

"Uh-uh," he murmured. "Ain't going to work out."

But he picked me up, just the way he had picked up Brandy that time she had her nightmare. He carried me to his room. I was so small compared to him, I felt like a newborn baby. He shut the door with his foot and lay me down in a bed with slippery, smooth sheets.

He stroked my arms with his big palms and kissed my cheeks and my mouth. "One more minute," he whispered. "One more and then you got to go."

"Let me stay." I whispered it so quietly because it was hard to talk with how good my body felt beneath his strong hands and soft lips and because it was hard for me to talk anyway.

He sat up suddenly, frowning and bunching up his eyebrow scar as if he was mad, but I could tell he wasn't mad. "You best go, Beautiful," he told me. "Before we do something that ain't right."

"No," I said. "Please." I reached out for his hand and put it on my cheek. "Please."

"Dime, you killing me," he said, and I loved how much he loved me.

"Please."

And then he was stroking me again and kissing me. "You sure, Beautiful?" he asked.

"Yes."

"You don't want to stay a virgin?"

"No." I was almost crying with wanting so badly for him to hold me close.

He kissed my lips again, and opened my mouth with his for much more than a second. I pulled back, scared. He pulled back too, kissing my forehead instead, stroking my arms and stroking my legs and stroking my whole body over my clothes, and by the time he bent to kiss my mouth with his tongue again, I wanted him to, and he knew just how to kiss and stroke until nothing felt surprising or scary but just good, and he took a long, long time peeling off my jeans and T-shirt and pink bra and panties and a longer time stroking and kissing me even more, quietly, all over everywhere, everywhere, making me feel so good, so so so good that when his body finally eased into mine, it felt like we were flying.

It was impossible to say good-bye. He kept kissing my face.

"You so beautiful," he kept saying, pressing his forehead against mine. "You so beautiful."

Somehow, finally, we separated. He opened the door, gently pushing me out of it, and I had to walk to Janelle's. It was still freezing out. I zipped my new coat and shifted my fancy bag with my new things inside it from one hand to the other. I tried not to cry.

It was a long walk, long enough for me to cry anyway and remember every single moment of what had just happened. Every kiss and stroke. Every sensation from every part of my body. I couldn't believe I wasn't a virgin anymore. I couldn't believe how lucky I was that my first time had been with Daddy, who loved me and knew how to make me feel so good. How could I leave him now? How could I go back to Janelle's? But he had said that she needed me, that I was supposed to be with her, and he needed his alcove back to rent out, or else he wouldn't have a place to live. *I love you,* he had said, after we flew together, and he was cuddling me in those smooth, smooth sheets. *You so special. I do anything for you. But your Janelle need you, and it ain't right me keeping you just because I want you so bad.* Then he rearranged our bodies so that he was spooning me, pressing his warm nose into the back of my neck and holding me close.

A man I'd never seen opened the door. "Jywon out," he said.

"Who is it?" I heard Janelle shout, and then she was next to the man, who stepped aside.

"You back now?"

I nodded.

She grabbed my bag, but she was holding a gin and Coke, and some of that spilled over my things. "Damn it." Then she took a drink. "Well, get in here." She opened the door wider, and I walked past her and the man.

"This her," Janelle told the man.

He looked at me and nodded. "She just like you said."

"This Earl," Janelle told me. "Earl as in James Earl Jones. He stay with us now."

She never used to introduce her men. She kept them separate from us kids. "Where are Vonna and Sienna?" I asked.

"Back with they people. Vonna's mama out of lockup and did her program, and Sienna's grandma out of the hospital. Apparently, she ain't going to die anytime soon after all." Janelle began to laugh. I had seen her drunk before, but not like this, not even the two times she went after me with that knife. It was like she was a different person inside Janelle's body.

"I'm sorry." She always loved the little ones. And she'd had Vonna for years. I hadn't thought I might never see Vonna again. I hadn't thought that much about Vonna these past few weeks, but now that I knew she was gone, I missed her. "I'm really sorry."

"You sorry?" Janelle stopped laughing. She waved her palm in my direction, as if she was waving away a gnat. "Yeah," she said. "It all because of you." I thought she was being sarcastic, but with the way she was acting, it was hard to tell.

I had the girls' room all to myself. It was strange to lie down in the dark without Vonna next to me in the other bed or Sienna or even another baby in the crib. I stared upside down at the white headboard, reaching up to trace my fingers around Vonna's stickers. Hearts and peace signs and rainbows and letters. A penguin and an umbrella and a banana bunch. It was strange to have sheets and a blanket. Even though this bed was more comfortable than the sleeping bag, my body hurt from the inside with wanting to be back at Daddy's. Wanting to be with Daddy. I couldn't stop from remembering every second we'd had. Him stroking me and kissing me and murmuring. His hands and his lips and his tongue all over my skin. His big, warm arms holding me tightly after. I traced those stickers, remembering Daddy, and that's how I got through the night.

Nobody was home the next morning. I still hadn't seen Jywon. I thought maybe he'd moved on too, like the little girls. I went to school, just like always. Nobody there knew my whole life had changed. Trevor was absent and Dawn was distracted with a makeup math test. I tried to help her study for it during lunch, but I was distracted too.

When I got back to Janelle's, she had piles of laundry to fold. Most of it was clothes that Vonna and Sienna wore. I guess they didn't need those old things where they were now. Sienna's grandmother and Vonna's mother must have wanted to buy their girls something brand-new. I guess Janelle had let the laundry pile up for a while. I folded little waffle shirts and tights and onesies and daydreamed about Daddy.

"Look who here," I heard. It was Jywon.

I handed him a pile of clean socks.

"Where you been?"

I shrugged.

"You staying?"

I shrugged again.

Janelle appeared. "Jywon, you went to school today?"

He tossed a ball of socks onto the folded pile. "I always go," he said. "Where else you think I go?"

"Liar," she told him. Then she looked at me. "You got homework?"

I nodded.

"Jy, you finish up this folding. She got to do her school-work." She was acting normal. Nicer than normal. It was confusing.

He raised his eyebrows. "I'm not folding no laundry," he said, and he walked out the door.

Janelle clucked her tongue. "Boys." She clucked again. "Can't do nothing with them."

Jywon showed up for meals a lot, but otherwise it was hard to know where he was. Earl and Janelle spent most of their time at the kitchen table and in front of the TV. They both drank her Booth's, but Janelle drank more. She got nasty to him sometimes, loud and mouthy, and he just sat there, taking it and sipping at his glass. She got nasty to me, too, but after three days I figured out that if I just cleaned up for her after school and didn't say a word, she would mostly leave me alone. The whole time, though—at school and at Janelle's—all I really thought about was Daddy. Not being back with him made me sick. I felt feverish and I couldn't eat and the inside of my chest ached, just the way they wrote about it in books when somebody ached for someone else.

On the fifth night, I woke up to the sound of angry voices and something breaking. My first thought was *Daddy*, because he was always my first thought. Then it took me a minute to remember where I was and another minute to remember that Sienna and Vonna weren't sleeping nearby. There was another crashing sound. I followed it into the kitchen. Janelle was swaying on her feet, standing barefoot in shards of glass. Earl was saying something to her but stopped when he saw me.

"That one," Janelle said, looking at me. Pointing. "That one think she special." She stepped toward me and tried to slap my face, but she was so drunk, she couldn't keep her palm straight, and her fingernails scratched my cheek, while her drink sloshed over the broken bottle on the floor. "Clean that up," she told me.

I glanced at Earl, who was frowning. When I moved past him to get something to wipe up the mess, I slipped on an empty, rolling underfoot. He caught my arm to steady me. Then he slid his palm across my chest, pressing on my small curves, and down to the middle of my legs, squeezing. It hurt, but the reason I gasped and pulled away was because Earl was everything Daddy wasn't and so soon after. And because of the way Janelle hissed, "Get away from my man."

I walked all the way back in the stinging air. It was late and dark and freezing and nobody was out on the streets. Nobody was home at Daddy's, either. I didn't have a key. I waited with my fancy bag on the hard stoop, shaking, the cold making my eyeballs hurt. What if he wouldn't take me? What if I had to go back to Janelle's? He wouldn't make me go back there after he heard about Earl, would he?

He came home alone. His head was bent, counting the cash I knew L.A. and Brandy had handed him out there somewhere. I didn't say anything. I just looked up at him.

He shoved his cash inside his coat and pulled me to my feet and to his chest. I held on tight. "All right, Beautiful," he said. "We figure it out. I'm a take care a you." He kissed my forehead and then my mouth. *Daddy.* "I'm a take care a you."

Chapter Thirteen

I WOULD WALK in from school, and he would take L.A. and Brandy to work, and then he would come back home to take me into his room.

I hadn't noticed any of it the first time, except for the slippery smoothness of the sheets. Now I knew they were black satin. He had thick white carpet and a king-size bed made of shiny black wood with a red leather headboard. There was a matching black bureau and shelves, all topped with what looked like genuine white marble. A television covered almost an entire wall. Eight speakers were mounted on all four sides, and there was an Xbox and a mini fridge. It was like a palace inside our apartment.

We always stayed in the bed. He would be so gentle, and if I got scared at something new, he would just kiss me and stroke me and tell me how special I was. Then I would try the new thing, partly because it wouldn't seem so scary anymore and partly because I loved how good I could make him feel. Once, a split second before we were about to fly, he slapped my cheek hard and then kissed me long, long, and I had already taken off, and it hurt, but it didn't. It felt good, but it didn't. And there was no time to think about it because I was flying so fast, so high. And afterward, he held me more tightly then he ever had and kissed my head and stroked my back, and we listened to each other breathing until it was time for him to go.

He was getting more tense, though. He began to tell me things while he curled himself around me.

"Owe my associate money," he said after another week. "Rent due in eight days. And my ride shooting smoke all out the tailpipe."

I backed my body into his as tightly as I could, and he brushed the back of my neck with his nose.

"You stay in school and do good," Daddy whispered. "Then after you graduate, you go to college. Then you get yourself a job and you can help me out. We can be a team taking care a things."

I loved the idea of being with him forever like that. I loved the idea that I could help him out, that we could be a team.

He pulled away and rolled onto his back. I rolled over

onto my stomach and propped my chin up on my hands so I could look at his face. "Only problem is my tailpipe can't wait no eight years."

I hated to see him so stressed.

"Rent not going to wait neither." He rubbed his face.

"I'll get a job as soon as I turn fourteen," I suggested. He would listen to me because I almost never spoke up, so when I did he knew it was important. "I can work after school and in summer and help out. Maybe selling clothes. Or at White Castle."

Daddy pulled me on top of him and smiled. "You a fool," he said. "Ain't no teenage jobs pay enough to put together nothing but a sandwich."

I hadn't known that. I thought those jobs paid something worthwhile.

"Thing is, Beautiful," he said, sitting us up. I scooted back to make room. "I'm a have to rent out that alcove."

Where would I sleep if he rented out the alcove?

He knew what I was thinking. He always knew what I was thinking. "Ain't no room for you on that couch with Brandy," he said. "And L.A. ain't going to share her room."

I thought of Janelle, speaking with me in that new ugly way she had, waving that knife, and I thought of her man, Earl, and the way he had touched me.

"Don't worry none, Beautiful," Daddy said. He leaned into me. "Don't worry. I'm a think a something."

I lifted up my backpack, and it was light. Too light. It was empty. No textbooks, no notebooks, no finished homework. No nothing.

"Brandy?" I looked down at her body on the couch, braided with the sheets and blanket. She was out. I nudged her foot. "Brandy? Have you seen my books?"

She didn't move. I went to the small bedroom.

"L.A.?" I stood over her mattress. "Have you seen my books anywhere? Did you put them somewhere?" She was too quiet.

"I need my books."

"Damn, girl." L.A. opened her eyes a slit. "Shut up." I knew she'd done it. I knew by the way her mouth pressed in. By the way she was pretending to be asleep.

I told Daddy as soon as he was out of his room, sitting at the kitchen table, eating his Lucky Charms dry and sipping at his glass of cranberry juice.

"L.A. took my books."

Daddy didn't look up from his phone. Maybe he hadn't heard me.

"L.A. took my books," I said again.

Now he looked up. He was so beautiful. The split eyebrow made him seem tough and tender both at the same time. "What?"

"For school. My books for school. L.A. took them."

Daddy smiled. His gold *D* flashed at me. "You know you special, right?" He spoke quietly so the others wouldn't hear.

"Yes." My skin and the muscles underneath and the blood all through did that hot jumpy thing.

"You know I got big plans for you?"

"Yes."

"You know I got respect for you staying in school?"

"Yes." I felt proud.

He stood and walked up to me. He kissed me on my mouth. It was his serious, openmouthed kiss.

"You want me like that all the time, don't you, Beautiful?" He was whispering.

It was too embarrassing. I couldn't look at him. "Yes."

"I want you, too."

The rushing inside never calmed down when he was near me. It made me smile now.

"But truth is"—he glanced toward the couch and L.A.'s room, still whispering—"L.A. and Brandy don't never get with me unless they bring home they quota."

I stopped smiling.

"Love you, Dime," Daddy breathed into my ear. "Love you best. But it going to cause issues around here if I keep taking you when you not bringing me nothing."

"When I turn fourteen, I'll get—"

"Square job ain't going to work," Daddy murmured. "Now I'm a find a way to keep you, but I can't be with you like that if you don't start contributing to the household. It up to you. You want to do what L.A. and Brandy do, you can earn your time with me. You choose not to, I'm a take care a you anyway. Just not in my bed."

He was still standing so near, I could smell his sugar breath and cranberries, and something else that was just his smell. I thought I would unzip right out of my skin with wanting him. Then he stepped away. He sat back down at the kitchen table and spooned cereal into his mouth.

I didn't think I could do what L.A. and Brandy did. Not with other men.

"L.A. bringing a associate by later to maybe move in, so clean up that alcove good, Beautiful." He was speaking at a regular volume now.

Where would I stay?

"We put you on the kitchen floor, if L.A.'s associate got coins for the alcove."

"How much is it?" I asked.

Daddy tipped his chair onto its back legs. "Couple a dates," he told me. "But that ain't for you. You said you ain't up for that."

I didn't want someone else in my alcove. And I didn't want to wait eight years before Daddy could take me into his bed again. How could I go eight years without him stroking me and holding me and telling me how special I was?

"Come here."

I went to him and he thunked the chair back on all fours to pull me onto his lap, the way he had done the first time we'd been together. He kissed me long. Long.

I couldn't think straight.

"Now listen," he whispered. "I don't want to know about no books. I don't want to hear no accusations on L.A. She your wifey. She the Bottom Bitch, and you under her. Don't speak out on her again, or I'll have to punish you. Understand?"

I didn't understand.

He pulled away. Slapped my face. It hurt, but it didn't. It felt good but it didn't. It was hard to think. I wanted to fly with him. "Answer me."

"I understand."

He slapped me again, then kissed me long, so long, just the way he did a few days ago tangled in those black sheets.

* * *

I had been hoping to reread *Macbeth* on the couch next to Daddy while he looked at his phone and the TV. So that I could keep up with class. I never did well in English anymore, like I did when I was little. But now I might not even pass. Now he had kissed me and slapped me and all I wanted to do was feel him wrapped around me in his bed. I would have to say all the books were lost. Would school ask me to pay for them? He had big plans for me. He loved me best.

"L.A."

She was brushing out her hair. It was after school, and Daddy already yelled at her for being late. Brandy was waiting on the cold steps outside. "What?"

"Where'd you put my books?"

"What books?"

"My books. The ones I asked about this morning. I need them."

She rolled her eyes. "You don't need books, Dime. What is books doing for you?"

"Where did you put them?"

"Didn't put them nowhere. Stop bothering me."

"L.A., I need them."

She reached out so fast, I didn't see it coming. The tears

sprang out of my eyes before I even knew I was hit. Then she did it again. My head felt five sizes too big and my neck buzzed.

I tried to slap her back. I aimed for her face, but something interrupted my hand. The next thing I knew I was on the ground. Daddy was stepping down on my arm, pinning it.

"What did I tell you about bothering anybody on those books?"

I began to cry.

L.A. sucked her teeth. "God, you is such a baby." She unbuttoned her top buttons and stepped over my body. She kissed Daddy good-bye and left. When she kissed him, she kissed him long, and he let her. She was showing off to make me feel worse.

Daddy lifted his foot off my arm. I tried to stop crying, but I couldn't. "Stop that fussing," he told me gently. I tried. "Stop, I said." He lifted me up.

He rested his forehead on mine. "I'm disappointed with you," he whispered. Then he left too.

I stayed that night because I kept hoping he would come into my alcove and say that I was the best and the smartest and hug me and kiss me and stroke my face and reach his hand up under my shirt onto my skin and then down inside my new jeans. I knew he loved me but was just mad at me for stressing him out. He was taking care of me. Buying me clothes and feeding me. Giving me a warm place to sleep and to be safe. Not letting anybody bother me. I felt guilty. He had to take care of all of us. He didn't need me whining all the time. He needed me to stay quiet and not make trouble for him. I mattered to him more than the others. He was proud of me for being in school. He had big plans for me. He nursed my head and cleaned up my mess and he put his big, warm hand in my back pocket when he took me out for hot chocolate. He made my body feel so good and he held me so close, like the way a father holds his baby.

The next day I went to school again without my books. I kept my face quiet, like I always did, but inside myself I was so mad and scared, I could hardly think. I must have been thinking, though, because after the last bell rang, I went back to Janelle's.

"Who are you?" Janelle asked. But she hugged me. I didn't smell any Booth's, and she seemed like her own self.

She handed Sienna over, and I took the baby like I'd never been gone. "You got her back?"

"Her grandma died."

We walked toward the couch and the TV, which was showing *Real Housewives*. "Where's your knapsack?"

"I left it in my locker." Sienna nudged her little mouth on my chin and sucked.

"Vonna home too." Janelle handed me the formula and held out a bag of Doritos. I took a few, popping them into my mouth over Sienna's soft head. "Her mama right back where she started."

I looked around for Vonna, wanting to give her a squeeze. Janelle saw me looking. "She around the block somewhere." Vonna was only nine. She shouldn't have been around the block anywhere.

Jywon walked in wearing nothing but his boxers and square-framed glasses. Holding a glass of Coke and a blue Booth's. "Where you been?"

I didn't answer. Sienna's baby gums were hard. I lifted my chin away and stuck the bottle in Sienna's mouth. Jywon handed over the drinks to Janelle. Then he brushed by me and laid his fat palm on my butt for a second in a way that Janelle couldn't see.

"Stick around until the fifteenth." She muted the TV and poured her gin. "Welfare coming to check up, and I can't have them keeping back your money. Sienna need a new coat and boots. Look at her. She growing fast."

How was welfare going to keep paying her to keep any children if they caught her drinking at three in the afternoon?

"Janelle!" I heard somebody call from the kitchen. "Nell!" It was Earl. I hadn't thought he would still be here. My body clenched, hearing his voice.

"You look like you doing all right." She eyed my boots and the sweater with the bell-shaped sleeves beneath my black puffy coat. I wasn't sure I understood. "Vonna got a school trip, and a tooth has to be pulled dental's not paying for." She didn't sound unkind. Only matter-of-fact. She sipped. "So we need that money coming in for you."

It was startling to realize I actually did understand. So startling that I guessed it was better not to think too much. Maybe not at all. I just kissed Sienna and put her and the bottle down on the floor. Then, for some reason, I hugged Janelle. Lightly, so as not to spill her drink. When I turned and walked out, we were both so surprised that neither of us said a word.

I went to the library until it closed. I looked around for Ms. McClenny, the way I always did in libraries, even though most of me knew that was foolish and even though I hadn't seen her since the last day of school in the third grade. I found a copy of *Macbeth*, but I couldn't concentrate. I couldn't stop thinking about Daddy. I left the library and walked to Dawn's, which was far. She hadn't ever invited me over, though, so I didn't have the courage to bang on her door.

Trevor once said she was embarrassed about her mother, but he didn't say why. He had never been inside her house either. Instead I walked up and down Dawn's block until it had been dark a while. I was thinking about Daddy the whole time. Nobody bothered me. It was a good block. I sat on Dawn's stoop and slept sitting up. I dreamed about him hugging me close and stroking my head and slapping my face. When daylight came, I walked back to school and around the block a few hours until the doors opened. I circled the hallways until classes began. I smelled.

"You want that alcove and my bed?" Daddy asked. He was wearing things I'd never seen that looked brand-new: a Polo T-shirt and bright Nikes.

L.A. and Brandy were sitting on the couch still in their sweats, pretending to watch *Dr. Phil*. I was standing with my head down, just barely inside the door.

"Can't do it, Beautiful, less you got coins."

I'd never given him anything in return for taking care of me, for feeding me and keeping me warm in his sleeping bag. I was embarrassed at how selfish I'd been.

"Ain't nobody live for free forever."

I lifted my face a little to see Daddy shake his head kindly. Brandy didn't move her eyes from the television, but

L.A. glanced over with a smirk on. He had even bought me all those new clothes and my first new warm coat.

"Don't worry about them clothes." He smiled a little, reading my mind, and letting me know he was glad to see me back. He had missed me. I knew he had. "Those was a gift."

I looked down at my jeans and gray sweater and soft T-shirt. I was so dirty now.

"L.A. and Brandy going to take you out later and show what you can do."

"She still going to school?" L.A. asked.

"Shut up," Daddy told her.

L.A. shut up.

"You got any questions?" Daddy asked me. "This the last time I'm a ask."

"Can we talk in private?"

He smiled. L.A. frowned. Brandy raised the TV volume.

He took me into his room.

"I know what you want." His voice was a soft rumble. He wasn't angry. He missed me.

I knew I needed a shower and to brush my teeth. I knew my hair was a mess. I was afraid to go too near him the way I was, so I just stared at him.

He came close and didn't even care what I smelled like or how I looked. He kissed me with those lips and with his tongue. Long. So long. "I wish I could give it to you right here, right now." His voice stayed quiet, and he kept his head close to mine while he talked. "But it ain't fair in the household. You got to bring in those coins first."

I didn't move, hoping he would kiss me like that again, hoping he would hold me. I knew I should have some questions, but I couldn't think of any over the hoping.

"Do what those bitches tell you to do," he whispered. "Make me my money."

He kissed me long again and sent me back to the alcove. My knapsack was on top of the sleeping bag. In it I found all the books. At first I was relieved. But then I thought to open them up. Torn paper. Old tea or coffee and raspberry jam staining the ink. Pages sticking together and pages missing.

Brandy came over, pretending to look for something lost. "I would have told you L.A. is not trustworthy for nothing." She spoke quietly with her back to me. "But L.A. the type you got to figure it out for yourself." She rummaged around, not looking at me on purpose. Which was kind.

Chapter Fourteen

I WAS DOLLED up in high-heeled silver boots I'd never seen before. L.A. said Satin used to wear them. They had me in the pale-pink bra and a white tank undershirt and a black miniskirt. It was late February, and I was cold in those clothes. Freezing. Daddy drove off in his gold Honda while darkness began to wrap itself around the air so it was hard to see the uneven sidewalk. I kept stumbling. The high heels or the dark or maybe all of it made me feel as if I was in chains.

The strangest thing was that, as I stumbled behind L.A. and Brandy, I had a memory. I don't know why. Maybe it was something about the clothes. Or the smell on these streets, which was different all of a sudden: old Doritos and cigarettes and beer. I'm not sure why the memory appeared like it did. Somehow, it was just ready to come out from hiding: the person who used to rock me and read to me wore a watch. Every time she turned the pages, that watch scratched my left shoulder a little. Not a hurt scratch, but a tickle scratch. Her watch would scratch me and her breath would be just behind my ear because my head was backed up into her chest, her chin resting on my hair. I could feel her softness. I could smell those barbecue chips.

"Here," L.A. told me. "Along here."

Remembering the watch, I had forgotten where I was for a minute: following L.A. and Brandy in clothes that made me feel like Halloween. It was a bad street. All broken lights. Abandoned lot here. Two low houses with plywood windows there. Three storefronts with the metal gates pulled down. One bodega lit up and open; a box of harsh glare in the middle of dark. One block, two blocks, three blocks, four blocks, then we crossed. And back again. Sometimes we walked in the street. Sometimes the sidewalk. The other girls I saw were dressed up like Brandy and L.A. and me. Short skirts. High heels. Halter tops or lowcut sleeveless, even though it was freezing out. Freezing. A few girls had coats with furry collars, but the coats were as short as the skirts. Cars were driving by. For such a rundown area, it was busy.

"What you got?" A man slowed down next to us, head out the window of a sports car I didn't know the name of.

"You take him," Brandy mumbled to L.A.

He heard her and laughed. "I want you."

Brandy spoke to L.A. "Twenty minutes."

"Hundred, minimum," L.A. answered.

"Yeah." Brandy nodded.

"What?" I said.

"Hi, baby." Brandy slid into the man's car. He drove away.

"Don't look so stupid," L.A. told me. For once she didn't sound mean. She sounded tired. "You got to keep moving," she explained. "Unless a john stop you. Then you talk fast, act fast. Daddy don't want us wasting time. They get out and you take them over there somewhere." She pointed over to the lot. "Or there." Around the corners of two brick buildings. "You can take them two blocks thataway. Room eleven is ours. But you got to be fast and come out quick. Faster not lying down. Cleaner, too."

Do I really have to? I should have asked. *Is there anything else I could do instead?* Maybe I could sleep on the kitchen floor. Maybe I could turn around and walk home and just being near him would be enough, even if he never held me again.

"Just do it," L.A. said. "Get the money, bring it to Daddy, and then keep walking and do it again."

I looked around. "Daddy's here?"

"He come around every little bit. You give him the coins. Nobody else."

Make me my money. That smile with the gold *D*. I wanted that smile from him. *I can't be with you like that if you don't start contributing to the household.* The feel of his arm on my shoulders and his hand in my back pocket. *You special.*

"Don't look at no pimp. Step off the curb onto the street if one of them come by: pimps up, hos down. It's only Whippet and George and Stone. Don't never get in a car with none of them. Don't speak to none of them. Whippet going to try, but you cross the street and keep your head down." She pulled something out of her bag. "Here." She held out her hand.

"What?"

"Rubbers, girl. Now get yourself together. God. You act like you don't know nothing."

I stared at them.

"If they won't wear them, you charge double. Daddy going to count those, so your math better be good." She counted them out. "Five. I'm giving you five. Right?"

I knew how they worked because Daddy used them most of the time.

"Right? Five."

I nodded.

Another girl walked by with her friend. L.A. nodded at them. They nodded back and kept walking.

"Those bitches is trouble," L.A. told me softly. "They Stone's. He keep them drunk and high. Daddy don't want none of us messing with that shit. You say hi to them and don't say nothing else. Just move on."

I could turn around and walk home and sleep on the kitchen floor and just be near Daddy. Without him taking me or holding me so close, so tight, afterward. "But I'm not doing this."

L.A. rolled her eyes. "Watch," she said.

Right after Brandy came back, they sent me with a white man in a Corolla with one window duct-taped together. *Go the other way right back to Janelle's,* I told myself. It was happening so fast, I didn't know how to make it not happen. *Daddy will forgive you and take you back later. Maybe not in a few days, but in a few weeks he'll take you back.* But what if Earl was still at Janelle's? *You got to bring in those coins,* was what Daddy had said. He had kissed my hands. *You can be one a mine.* I wanted so much to be his.

I half turned to L.A. to say *no*, or *wait*, or *I'm not doing this*, but it was too late.

For a quick moment I tried to imagine it was Daddy. But

there was no time for imagining, and this was nothing like being with Daddy. The man didn't bother with any feeling good but just opened my legs, and I was so surprised it was like watching it happening on TV to someone else. When he turned me around and pulled my bottom to him and did the next thing, it hurt so badly that I wanted to scream, but I didn't scream because I didn't think it was allowed. And when he finally stopped that and turned me around again and pushed me to my knees, making me open my mouth, I choked on him and then I think I suffocated and when I came back to life I was showing money to L.A., who was yelling at me because it wasn't enough, and there hadn't been any tunnel or light or angels singing, but I know that I had died.

They said Daddy was out on the street almost the whole time. I don't know how I didn't see him. When we came in, he was waiting. He ignored L.A. and Brandy and took me into his beautiful room. He undressed me so gently, and I wanted to want him, but my body hurt and I could hardly stay awake. He showed me how much he really loved me, though, because he put me in his shower and helped me wash, saying over and over, "You did real good, Beautiful. You did real good."

And then he laid me down in his soft, soft bed and held me close.

Chapter Fifteen

A MONTH AND a half ago, I never thought it would be this difficult to figure out how to write the note. I knew it wouldn't be easy exactly, the way it was for Celie, sewing pants after pants after pants, the colors and patterns and style just flowing out her fingertips. But I didn't expect it to be so hard, either. I didn't expect all the challenges that would accompany every idea.

For instance, it's occurring to me now that a big problem with writing the note as Sex is that the kind of people I need to pay attention might be uncomfortable. Because even though Sex is everywhere, regular people pretend it isn't. Regular people who aren't perverts, anyway. Squares. Real ones. Squares who might be compelled by Lollipop or entertained by Brandy or upset by L.A. or bored by me. They act like Sex doesn't exist half the time. Those people are the kind of people the note needs, but they're also the people who don't want to hear what Sex has to say. So I'm thinking about that a little bit, and I'm thinking, well . . . what about Sex's other cousin? Money.

Squares like Money as much as anybody does. Squares would be more comfortable listening to what Money has to say, at least at first. And if I write Money in the perfect way, squares might get just disgusted enough to refuse what Money suggests. And instead do what I actually want.

Come on now, Money could write. *Plenty of people love Sex, but plenty don't. Too old or too ugly or ladies who never liked Sex much in the first place. But me, I am the bomb. Everybody loves me. You can't deny it. Nobody ever gets tired of me. Nobody ever stops wanting me, me, me, and more of me.* Money would tell Lollipop's story more easily than Sex could, anyway. Money wouldn't be so mad about it. He would just be writing the note for his own ego. But squares would see through it all and be shocked and do the thing I want them to do. *Sex is going to bitch and moan about how he doesn't like working with children and it puts a stress on and all that bullshit. But I'm here to tell you that I am at my most powerful when children come into the picture.* It would be sickening to write, but I could make myself, knowing it might work. *Because I reproduce myself* faster than four rabbits in a barrel when there are kids around. Brandy and I couldn't figure out how much Daddy made off of Lollipop, but we knew it had to be a lot, because after she arrived things changed so much. *That Lollipop is one perfect example.* Money would grin. *I don't know how it all went on before the Internet, but that girl earned her hotel room one hundred times over putting her little body in front of that computer camera.* Brandy thought Daddy could get into a lot more trouble putting a little girl on a live feed than turning us teenagers out. She thought that the johns knew that, too, so that's how Daddy could charge so much more for Lollipop. *You wouldn't believe how much of me got paid for a look at her. And when she was old enough, which didn't take so long, I just exploded like a bomb.* Money would be downright gleeful. *All she had to do was live her life in whichever hotel or motel butt naked, doing her little girl things. That's it. And when she graduated to bigger girl, and top dollar was paid to visit her in person, that Uncle Ray was careful not to wear her out. All she needed was two or three a week to make him rich.* Lollipop even bragged to L.A. about this part. *Men ordered her up from around the country to get a piece of her. One took a plane. Five rode Amtrak. Yup. She must have lost her little virginity twenty times, and that costs pretty millions of pennies, if I don't say so myself. He loved me, Lollipop's uncle Ray did.* He would stop a minute to think over just how much of himself would be gotten if the right person read his note. *So you see,* he would continue, *if you and I work together, if you take this package, and you do what I'm trying to tell you is possible to do, then you are going to get more of me in one go than you ever imagined possible. That's right, my friend. Who doesn't want easy Money? Easy me?* I think it's called reverse psychology. I think it really could work.

Chapter Sixteen

I DIDN'T KNOW about reckless eyeballing until I got beat up for it. L.A. tried to tell me, but I guess I wasn't as smart as Daddy said. It was pretty soon after he turned me out onto the track. Not even a month. Still cold enough to ache my toes. Still not enough money for him to take me back into his room. *Almost,* he said.

I was getting out of a date's car around midnight. As I stepped up on the curb, Whippet was walking by. I walked around him.

He stopped. "What?"

None of them had talked to me before. I was scared. I looked at Whippet because Daddy had taught me to lift my eyes to Daddy's face, so I thought that's what I was supposed to do.

He was wearing a shiny coat zipped up to his chin. "The fuck you think you are?"

"I didn't—"

He shoved me into the street. L.A. was less than half a block away, and even though I could see her through the darkness, she acted like she didn't see us.

Whippet was taller even than Daddy. Standing over me with his neck inclined, he looked like a vulture. "Nobody taught you nothing?"

"I—"

"Pimps up, hos down, ho!" He slapped me. Not a tap, like Daddy. His hand hit my ear. Even in the icy air, it burned. I tried not to let the tears come.

"And you going to look at me too?" He slapped my other ear. Then he called out, "Whippet, yo! George. Stone!" He called out Daddy's name.

I hadn't seen Whippet or George or Stone all night. But now they were surrounding me. All of them.

"Don't you look at none a us," Daddy ordered. "Put your head down, ho."

My Daddy. My Daddy who loved me so much and took such good care of me. All I wanted was for him to let me back into his bed where he would stroke me and hold me and warm the back of my neck with his nose. *Ho.* That's when I started crying.

* * *

"They wouldn't of done it for just not stepping down when you still a new turnout," Brandy told me later. "It's because you was reckless eyeballing, too." She was under her blanket on the couch, and I was sitting on her feet, holding a bag of frozen corn to my throbbing face.

"What's reckless eyeballing?" My lip stung too. I could feel it swollen.

"Looking at a pimp," Brandy said. "Hos not allowed to look another pimp in the face. Not ever."

I moved the corn from one cheekbone to the other. What else was I supposed to know?

"Didn't L.A. educate you?"

I couldn't remember.

"She was supposed to . . ." She stopped because Daddy came in the front door. My heart sped up. I couldn't stand the way he had spoken to me out on the street. *Ho.*

"Dime, get in here."

I could tell by the way Brandy lowered her eyelids and tightened her lips that she felt bad for me. I left the corn and followed him to his room. I was shaking. My whole head ached. He sat on his bed, which wasn't made. His black silk sheets shone like oil. "You a mess."

I stayed quiet, trying to stop my arms and legs from

quivering. I was scared he was going to punch me again. Worse, I thought maybe he hated me now, and I didn't know what I would do if that was true.

"You going to have a hard time earning my money until your face heal."

"I'm sorry."

"You only been out three weeks."

I was fuzzy on the time. I was fuzzy on a lot of things.

"Three weeks not so long. You still green."

It didn't seem like he was going to hit me.

"But also, you going to school, so you not earning near quota."

I didn't want to quit school, even though I was so tired now. And even though I felt like a silhouette of the old me. A fuzzy silhouette, which didn't even make sense. The me before I died. My brain was like a silhouette of itself, and so was my body, except that right then it hurt.

Still, it didn't seem like he was mad, exactly.

"Pimps up, hos down. You look at somebody else, they can take my coins from you, they can teach you any kind of lesson. You lucky Whippet didn't tell you to break yourself."

"What's 'break yourself'?"

"When you give money to a pimp, and you his after that."

I didn't know anybody could do that. I wouldn't do that for anybody else, anyway. Only for Daddy.

"Whippet didn't want to bother with you cause you fresh work. You not making what you cost, and I'm doing you a favor even keeping you."

"I'm still trying to learn. . . ."

"I know, Beautiful." He lifted his right calf to rest on his left knee and slid off his shoe. "That's why I'm talking to you now and not giving you another beat-down for being out of pocket today." He slid off his other shoe. "Come here and take off my socks."

I did, thinking how Janie would understand. In *Their Eyes Were Watching God*, Tea Cake beat her because he had to show her and everybody who was boss. Janie let it be because they had the most pure love anybody could have.

"Now take off my jeans." He was looking at me with those puppy eyes and the gold *D* shining. I stopped shaking, remembering how Tea Cake was so sweet to Janie after he hurt her a little. Daddy and I had a love like them. My heart hopped even faster. I took the edges of his jeans and tugged. "You still want me like that?" He was leaning on his elbows and lifting his hips so that I could pull the pants all the way off.

The throb in my face melted down to other parts.

He could see that I had been trying hard to contribute, to behave. He forgave me. Just like I forgave him.

"Hard to smile with your lip busted." He took his pants from me and scrabbled his hand into the front pockets. "Let's see how much you made today." He turned his back, and I could tell he was peeling off bills, counting them fast. When he finished, he spread them flat on the marble-topped bureau, then turned back around and pulled me closer to him, his big palm on my bottom. Warm. He stared at my bleeding mouth. "I did that." He was proud. "That one from me." Then he was kissing my lip where it was cut. Long. Hard. It hurt. And it felt good. I tasted my own blood.

I braced myself for him to stop, to leave me desperate. But he didn't. I tried to ask while keeping my split lip on his. "Are we going to . . ."

He stopped kissing me long enough to answer. "You earned it, Beautiful. Now let me do you right."

Finally. It felt so good.

Chapter Seventeen

HERE'S HOW IT works, Money would explain to the squares reading my note. Money would think all his boasting about how much everybody focused on him would make the reader want him too. *L.A. earned the most of me and so she was the Bottom Bitch, in charge of the household after her Daddy.* He had been in a talkative mood once after I had made him happy trying something new in between those sheets. I heard a lot of things that afternoon. *He used to work his hos around the clock, but he changed that up back when Satin was with him due to multiple mishaps. He decided, rightly, that it was safer with all of them on the track together and then all of them going back home together. He decided it was safer and also more cost-effective, in the end.* But I would be the one writing Money, and maybe I could get the squares upset by him.

Upset enough to do the opposite of what Money would be suggesting. Upset enough to do the right thing instead. The more I think about it, the more I think this might be my best plan yet.

L.A. was unhappy because Dime going to school meant Dime worked less. Then again, L.A. was happy because it meant she was always going to earn more me than Dime. L.A. was thinking she would earn enough eventually to square up with her Daddy. She was certain he would take her down south and marry her, the two of them quitting the life and living large with every room of their house as fancy as Daddy's bedroom. L.A. was planning on having her Daddy's babies. He told her that, just like he told each of them the lies they wanted to hear. Daddy never told me anything about his lies. I figured out that part on my own. *L.A. was smart in some ways, but she was foolish, too, so she had her heart set on down south. She worked her tail off to bring me home to Daddy and make her dream come true.*

Now Brandy, on the other hand. Brandy didn't care that Dime was staying in school. Brandy had no interest in school. She wasn't trying to bring home the most of me and piss off L.A. by doing so. Brandy just wanted her couch and her food and her Daddy to always take care of her. That was all Brandy wanted. With what she went through after her grandmother died and before her Daddy scooped her up, she didn't want more than that: no trouble with L.A.

No trouble with Dime. Peace. Well, actually, Brandy did want a phone, and after Daddy once promised a trip to Disney World, she realized she wanted that, too. L.A. already earned a phone, even though she did not have a lot of minutes. Just enough minutes so that their Daddy could check up on her and the others. He said if Brandy brought home a certain amount of me, she would get a phone and a trip to Disney World. She was working on it: working hard. That's how Money would present himself. I am hoping if I compose the note just right, the squares will be outraged.

Things happen differently when you are in the life, even if you stay in school. The days and nights run into each other, and you only notice time passing by how the decorations and the light changes and by what's on TV. Red balloons and chocolate-box covers stapled to the hallway bulletin boards at school. Pastel heart-shaped candies on the coffee table. BE MINE, VALENTINE, I LOVE YOU. L.A. put them there. It began to stay light longer as the last traces of blackened snow finally melted. Kohl's commercials began showing women with diamond necklaces and fancy handbags: Mother's Day. Little American flags appeared in bunches at the corner newsstands: Memorial Day. Then it was warm and buggy, and it didn't get dark until you had turned five tricks, and there were more squads out, and George got into two shoving matches with a pimp from downtown, trying to move in on our track with his girls who looked like boys and boys dressed like girls. I'd seen that on HBO here and there, but I thought those were people made up for TV. Noticing a few of them not much older than I was bothered me, but everything was jumbled and spinning, and I couldn't slow it all down or think, and then it was the first day of June. A hot day. I turned fourteen.

"Guess what?" I said to Daddy when he was holding me.

He was surprised to hear me begin a conversation. "Huh?"

"It's my birth—"

His phone rang. He didn't have a song for his ring tone, like L.A. had, changing it just about every week. He just used the ascending notes that came programmed in already. He held it to his ear and unwrapped himself from my body, standing up and motioning for me to get up too. "Uh-huh," he said into the phone, and I had to take my clothes and leave.

I tried again on the way to the track. "Brandy." I stayed so quiet most of the time, I gave Brandy the heebie-jeebies. That's what she said once when she was doing my hair, but she said it like she thought I was funny, not aggravating.

Now she looked at me. "What?"

"It's my birthday today."

Brandy shook her head. "I tried to run you off the first night I laid eyes on you, Dime."

I remembered her serving herself the last of the rice, just after Daddy had asked if I wanted more.

"You should have went away right then." Brandy sighed. "Now you already growing up."

I wanted to ask her why it was okay for her to be there but not me. But I never did talk much.

Brandy sighed again. "I would have made you a cake."

I kept my head down and worked hard for Daddy's money, and he had no cause to beat me again. He wouldn't take us unless we made quota five days in a row. He took L.A. the most and then Brandy and then me. When he took me I was usually woozy tired, but I still wanted him so much I didn't care. He told me he loved me the best. He told me L.A. had to be kept happy and Brandy didn't turn him on like I do, plus neither of them were as smart as I was. He told me how I was so mature and how he had such big plans for me and he kissed me long, so long and held me tight after, and I wanted him to keep his arms wrapped around me forever.

Time passed, but with the fuzz and the silhouette it was hard to keep track, and it didn't matter anyway. I was with Daddy, and I wasn't going anywhere, so none of it mattered.

* * *

It was the last week of school. Trevor and Dawn didn't think I had worked up to potential.

"Didn't you used to be smart?" Trevor asked, raising his eyebrows at the grade on my last math test. *If one pizza palace makes ten thousand dollars in four days, and there are twenty pizza palaces, then how much does the entire franchise make in thirty-one days?*

I shrugged.

"She used to be smart in English, that Dominican girl told me," Dawn said. I hadn't known her and Trevor until the beginning of the school year. Dawn had moved here from Pennsylvania, and Trevor and I just never noticed each other. "Didn't you win the spelling bee in fourth grade?"

I had. A few days before that first baby after Vonna went home to its own family. Janelle took other babies, lots of them. It got hard to sleep with her crying every night after one left and before the next one came. I didn't win a spelling bee again.

Trevor drummed my head a few beats with his rolled-up test. "You're smart at reading."

"Too bad your English grades suck," Dawn told me. All of our grades sucked.

"At least we're passing." Dawn chewed her gum. "Look.

One point away from a C." I looked at the red *71* and the red *D* scrawled across the top of her paper, matching mine.

I thought of that gold *D* on Daddy's tooth.

"What are you smiling about?"

The scar splitting his eyebrow.

"What's the matter with you?" Trevor asked.

"I'm tired."

"You must be partying too much."

Dawn rolled her eyes. It was good they had no idea what I was. It was essential. But then again, I didn't like them making fun of me.

Trevor was set to work for his father installing carpets. Dawn was going to babysit her nieces for the summer. "We're doing basketball camp at the Y on Thursdays," she said. "You should sign up too."

"Maybe," I lied.

"What do you have going on, anyway?" Trevor asked.

I shrugged. "Reading, mostly." But I wasn't sure how I was going to read with no more school library; just the public ones, which would take away from my work hours if I wanted to go check out books.

Chapter Eighteen

IT WAS A steamy, slow night, almost dark, but not just yet. Brandy and I were walking the track up and down, up and down. She was telling me about her grandmother. "She had a picture of John F. Kennedy and Dr. Martin Luther King Junior and some lady on the living room wall."

"Who was the lady?"

Brandy shrugged. "I don't know. Some black lady."

"How long did you live with her?"

"And she had this crazy money. Silver dollar. Two-dollar bill. Bicentennial quarter." Brandy looked at me. "You know them?"

I shook my head.

"Dime, you looking fine," someone called out to me. At first I thought it was Whippet, because he was always chasing me or Brandy. But it wasn't. It was Stone. I hadn't seen him coming. He stepped up from the street he was crossing onto the curb.

"Turn around," Brandy whispered, but by now she didn't have to tell me. We spun and walked back down toward room eleven. It was just a run-down house. It didn't even have eleven rooms in it, but ours was next to an old kitchen and the number on the door said *11*.

"Get over here, bitch," Stone called. "I got something for you." He was up on our side now, taking fast steps with his short legs. I could almost feel him catching up to us.

"What do he want?" Brandy asked.

"I don't know." We walked faster. I wished L.A. would turn up. Stone was less likely to bother us if she was around.

"Dime!" Stone called. "You better stop and face me when I'm talking to you."

If Daddy saw him calling to us, even if our backs were turned, he might think we were associating with Stone, and then there would be a price to pay.

I was walking so fast, I was almost running. Brandy was keeping pace next to me. "Damn." I heard her stop.

When I turned around, she was skip-hopping because her thonged sandals had broken a strap. "Come on," I hissed. "Forget the sandal."

Stone was catching up to us. A car slowed down with two

johns inside. I ran to it, pulling Brandy with me. We jumped in without even naming a price. When I looked back, Stone was holding Brandy's shoe.

"Daddy not going to like this," L.A. said, shaking her head.

He took our coins as the sun came up and was out so fast we didn't have time to say anything to him. Now it was hot, late afternoon, but L.A. was making mashed potatoes anyway. Even with the windows open and the fans on, I was sweating at the small of my back and down my little cleavage. I kept adding ice to my water. Sometimes I would drink it, and sometimes I would drip it onto my skin.

"We have to tell him, L.A.," I made myself say. "Or else he's going to make up some other story when he sees Stone has her shoe."

"Leave it, I said." L.A. pointed the wooden spoon at me. "Stone ain't even going to remember any damn shoe, much less show it off to Daddy."

I looked at Brandy. She was crossing her arms, fingers up in her pits, in that way she did when she was feeling nervous.

"It wasn't even Brandy he was trying to talk to," I tried for the third time. "It was me." I had to speak up. I didn't want Daddy to hear about it and think we kept something a secret from him. He wouldn't like that.

"Well, if you didn't open your mouth to Stone, then what is you so worried for?"

"That girl, Shine," Brandy answered for me. "She said Stone been talking about Dime. He want to take Dime from Daddy."

"Please." L.A. sliced some butter off the stick into her pot. "Dime barely even making nothing for Daddy. What do he think he going to do with her?" She frowned. "Anyway, pimps don't be discussing they plans for a ho. They just do what they do. That bitch, Shine, a liar."

"I still think we should tell Daddy what happened." I looked at Brandy even though I was arguing with L.A. "People saw him chasing us down. Probably Whippet or George saw. Somebody is going to say it all wrong to Daddy."

L.A. pursed her lips at Brandy. "Stone trying to take you from Daddy with his junk?" She was thinking Stone was going to offer Brandy drugs for free. Except nothing is for free. L.A. was suspecting that Stone was going to make Brandy pick up again, get addicted, and then choose him over Daddy. I never thought of that.

"I been clean for over a year," Brandy said. She hadn't had any of those nightmares again in all this time. "Everybody know what Daddy did for me. Everybody know I'm not trying to use."

"Then why he chase you?"

"He was chasing me," I repeat.

"Dime right," Brandy said. "We should tell Daddy."

"You not telling," L.A. said. She dipped her finger in the hot potatoes and then licked it. "It's my say-so, and I'm saying he don't want to hear your petty shit. Leave it."

It was late July, and the days were getting hotter and hotter. The nights weren't much better. I sweated all the time, and the dates smelled fouler than ever. I wished so badly there was a way I could shower during work, but Daddy wouldn't let us leave the track with all those johns wandering around in the heat, ready to pay money to be hot in a way that felt good to them. At home I showered after L.A. and Brandy since they had seniority, and the water was freezing by the time it got to me. That should have felt good, and in the first second it did, but then I would begin to shiver and shake, and before I could get as clean as I wanted, I would be too cold, and I'd have to step out onto the tile. So each day I felt hotter and then colder and then dirtier and dirtier, and there was nothing I could do about it.

Every few weeks, after I earned my quota, Daddy would take me. His room had an air conditioner, which was like a taste of heaven. But his smell wasn't so good anymore, and I would be so tired. A few times I would say, "Could you just rest with me tonight?" Because even though at first I wanted him *like that* all the time, now I was so worn out. All I really wanted, maybe all I ever really wanted, was that being held tight to someone whose body was still and solid, who loved just being cuddled up to me, without wanting anything more. "Please?" I tried a few times. The first time he was quiet a split second and then he did things to me he thought I would like before he did things he liked, but I was hot and tired, so I guess I wasn't very good. He didn't hold me after, but sent me back to the alcove.

The second time I asked, he punched me with his fist in my belly, and I thought I would vomit from the pain. Then he told me he was sorry and that he hated to hurt me, but if I didn't appreciate being with him like that, it was a damn shame. He didn't send me back to the alcove, though. He spooned me close, instead. I tried to imagine the smell of barbecue potato chips, and I wondered for the first time ever, *Where is she? Where is that woman who rocked me in her lap and tickle-scraped my shoulder, whispering, "Goodnight stars, Goodnight air, Goodnight noises everywhere"?*

Two days after none of us said anything about Stone, Daddy came home holding Brandy's sandal by the broken strap. He marched right over to her and used it to pop the back of her head.

"The hell is this?"

"My shoe."

He shoe-popped her again. "You got something to tell me, ho?"

"No sir." I'd never heard her call him *sir* before.

"Stone say you been out of pocket."

"No sir."

I looked at L.A. She was the Bottom, and it was her job to set Daddy straight. But L.A. didn't say a word.

Daddy slapped the back of Brandy's head with his palm this time. "Explain yourself, bitch." I still wasn't used to it, but somehow, in the past few weeks, *bitch* was mostly how he referred to us.

"Stone was trying to talk to me." I hated speaking up, but it wasn't fair, otherwise.

Daddy turned around. "What?"

"The other day he was trying when I was out working with Brandy, and we were running away from him. Her shoe broke, and we left it and got in a car with some dates. We never talked to him. We never even looked at him."

Daddy eyed me for a long time. He dropped the sandal. "You expect me to believe that garbage?"

"It's the truth."

"Word," Brandy added.

"What do Stone want with you?" Daddy said. "You so fresh, you hardly know how to do nothing. You not making anybody's quota. I'm the only fool who keep you."

"Ask L.A.," I forced myself to say. Brandy crossed her arms and threw me a look to tell me to shut up. "We told her and she said not to tell you."

"What you knew?" Daddy asked L.A.

"I didn't know nothing," L.A. said. "Did I, Brandy?"

Brandy shrugged.

"Better not have known and not told," Daddy told L.A. "Or you in serious trouble."

"I didn't know shit," L.A. said. "Damn."

Daddy turned around and whomped Brandy again. She had to move her feet to keep from falling down, but she kept the tears in. "If I have cause to suspect you been out of pocket in any kind of way with Stone or anybody else, you better pray for your life."

He reached over and whomped me, too. "And that there for telling lies on Stone."

The back of my head hummed.

When he took me the next time, he was gentle. Gentle with his body and gentle with his voice. He held me close, using his remote to turn on slow, relaxing music and wrapping those liquidy sheets around us.

"You the best," he said. "You so fresh and beautiful. You smart and mature." He kissed my forehead in that way I loved. "You going to have a big place with me, Beautiful."

"What do you mean?" I looked at his split eyebrow scar, wondering how he got it. "You always say that, but what does that mean?"

He smiled because I almost never asked questions, and when I did he thought it was cute. He held me tighter, and that was all I ever wanted. "You going to see," he said. "You going to see."

There wasn't anything to read because Daddy wouldn't let me go to the library. I tried telling him that if I didn't do the assigned summer reading for school and failed the tests in September, somebody was going to come looking at Janelle's, and then there would be issues. I didn't think this was true, but I hoped Daddy wouldn't know. It didn't work, though, because he said he'd let me check out those books later, right before school, when they'd be sharper in my mind, anyway.

So after I woke in my sleeping bag, but before I slid out of it, I would try to remember a book I liked and read it again in my head.

Chapter Nineteen

L.A. GRABBED MY arm. "Come on," she said. "We going home."

It was only eleven thirty. We weren't even halfway into the night. "What for?"

"Shut up and walk."

Nobody was there when we got to the apartment. Sometimes Daddy picked one of us up early and took us home to be with him for a minute. But never this early.

"What happened?" I asked L.A. Where was Daddy? Where was Brandy?

L.A. put the stove on for her tea, even though it must have been ninety degrees. "Brandy got herself locked up. Daddy left out. I got to change and go get her."

"Can I come?"

"No."

"What did she do?"

L.A. actually stopped to stare at me. "You stupid?"

I guess I was. I knew girls were arrested. I saw it happen twice. And I saw them come back, too. I saw Stone and Whippet beat their girls for it. I saw George give one of his the day off. You never knew how your Daddy was going to react.

"Stay here, and don't go out," L.A. said. "Make some food for when we get back."

I made roast chicken just like that first night. That was a long time ago. I made a cold string bean salad and some macaroni salad too. I kept an eye on that back burner. I mopped the kitchen and changed everybody's sheets, except for Daddy's. I dusted. I straightened up all the clothes boxes and L.A.'s dresser drawers. I didn't touch Daddy's room since we weren't allowed in it unless invited.

Then I sat on the couch and waited. I wanted something real to read so much, but there was nothing but an old *People* magazine and an *Ebony* magazine. I wanted a book. Something fat and long.

When I finally heard the door, I jumped. It was Daddy. He was on the phone. ". . . got the other one coming soon. Going to have forty toes down. Nah. If that bitch rolls over,

I'll . . . What? Yup. Switch it to indoor is what I'm saying. New little one going to show . . . what?" He stopped talking long enough to motion to me to pack up some food. I packed it up quickly while he listened and then talked some more. "Russian bitches make you . . . That's what I'm saying. . . . North Carolina and then we changing . . ." He took the bag I held out and grunted something, then tapped off the phone.

"I'm out," he told me. "L.A. going to call me when Brandy back home. Nobody leave. Not until I get back. Only you go out for food. Tomorrow at four. I got eyes watching you. Shop and home under a hour. Get enough to last three, four days. Understand?" He handed me thirty dollars.

What about L.A.? "Why aren't you giving L.A. the money?"

"L.A. ain't here, is she?"

"No, but—"

He tap-slapped my cheek. "Don't give me no attitude. Just be happy I trust you and do what I say."

Brandy couldn't have gone back out to the track anyway. Her lip was swollen twice its size, and she had a black eye. She was walking funny too.

"Cop," she said. "Soon as we got in eleven, he put his

stupid handcuffs on me, told me I'm under arrest for solicitation, and then did it to me anyway." She shook her head. "Damn."

"Where Daddy?" L.A. asked me for the tenth time in under thirty minutes.

"I told you. I don't know. He said stay in three or four days and he'll be back."

"What about food?" L.A. opened the refrigerator. "We got hardly nothing."

I didn't want to answer that.

"We supposed to starve?"

Somehow Brandy knew. "He gave you coins?" she asked me. She spoke softly, but L.A. whipped around anyway.

"He said I should go at four." It was five thirty in the morning. Still dark out.

"He gave you his money?" L.A. tilted her head at me. "He gave it to you?"

I shrugged.

"How much?"

I showed her the three tens.

"Why he gave it to you?"

I didn't have an answer.

L.A. slammed her bedroom door behind her.

I made Brandy a plate of eggs. She examined her face in

her round makeup mirror. "I need a shower." She hadn't sat down since she got back.

"You okay?" She was standing strange. It hurt us sometimes, and I guessed with handcuffs on and a cop like that, probably it hurt more.

She didn't answer my question. "Why Daddy gave you the money?"

"I don't know."

"Where did he go?"

"I don't know."

"He mad at me?"

"I don't know." I trusted Brandy, but I didn't trust anybody enough to repeat things Daddy said to me in private. I wanted to tell her about that Brother Down South and the Russians, but I was afraid he would know if I told. Daddy had some sort of magic like that: He knew everything.

Instead I made myself eggs too. For Daddy's sake, I called out: "L.A.!" But she didn't answer or come out. So I didn't make her anything.

"This lady came," Brandy said quietly. But not too quietly. She didn't want L.A. to hear us whispering and think to listen, so she said it loud enough it was like regular conversation, but not so loud L.A. could hear the actual words. "A different cop brought me to her in some room. Cop was cool.

The lady say they could give me a program to get me out of the life instead of a regular court date."

"A place to stay?"

"Yeah. School. HIV test. A lawyer."

"A lawyer?"

Brandy was eating standing up. She was leaning against the counter. "They don't know, though. Daddy would find me. Probably kill me."

I thought about his guns. He had two. He said one of them was broken, but after George laughed so hard his beer sprayed out his nose over it, I thought Daddy just didn't like how that one looked. It had a pearl handle and was small enough that he could hide it in his palm. He kept it in one of the shiny black drawers in his bedroom. The other gun was always on him somewhere. It was black all over. I thought it was a glock, but I wasn't sure. He used it once to hit L.A., but I never knew what for. It left a bruise on her shoulder.

"Anyway, you wouldn't leave us, would you?" It would be hard without Brandy. Partly because she and I were cool together and partly because being the only other one with L.A. would be stressful.

Brandy shook her head. She put her plate down and pulled something out of her front pocket. A little rectangular card. She turned it around on the table so that I could read it. *Pamela Terrence, The North Star.* There was an 800 phone number and a different number to text. We heard L.A. opening her door. Brandy slid the card back into her pocket and picked up her plate again. She wasn't eating much. "I'd leave L.A. in half a heartbeat," she mumbled. "Not Daddy. He save my life every day." Her face got soft like I almost never saw it, underneath all that swelling and purple. "He take care of me."

What about me? I wanted to ask, but L.A. interrupted, appearing from her room.

She sat down and took my plate. "Get me a fork," she ordered Brandy.

Brandy got the fork. She moved slowly.

Now the interesting thing, Money would add to the note, *is that a ho is not supposed to handle me except for the time it takes to do her business and then drop me to her Daddy. Of course, the Bottom Bitch is sometime called on to take care of me when the Daddy is out hurt or, say, locked up. But for the most part, I don't touch a ho's fingertips more than a minute. It just doesn't look good and it's not wise practice. They better know me well, but hos are not meant to be the boss of me.*

We followed Daddy's instructions. We played poker for Fudge Stripes and watched some TV. I liked TV, but I wanted books. By midmorning, I closed my eyes against the heavy heat and reread what I could remember.

Alec, nearly drowning in the middle of the churning ocean, clinging to the black stallion in order to survive. Charlotte Doyle, desperate to prove herself to the pirates, climbing down the ship's ratlines, losing her footing and nearly dying. And that attic. Filled with handmade paper flowers and little Cory's deadness and Cathy, growing up hidden away, with hardly any sunlight to brighten her days.

When I ran out of book memories, I tried some of my own. Janelle's maple brown sugar turkey for Christmas dinner and then all of us singing carols as loudly as we could on the house's roof, looking for Santa, even Jywon, who brought the binoculars that got sent to us from Amazon by mistake and Janelle let us keep. Me going with my friend Angelica and her mother to buy her new pink boots, and her mother buying me a pair of pink socks, too. The man in the store thought we were sisters, and he gave us each a Dum Dum, which we hated, but we saved, and I gave them to Vonna later. Me, curled in a ball reading in the corner of the school library beneath a table and next to a cluster of three potted plants, and I was so inside my book, I couldn't hear them calling, and getting detention for causing trouble, and Ms. McClenny winking, saying, *She can serve it with me*, as if that were a punishment. The firefighters who came to our class-room and let us touch their breathing masks and taught us to stop, drop, and roll. Rocking inside of somebody soft and big who smelled like barbecue potato chips and whose watch scratched my left shoulder each time she turned a page.

We sat around. We were tired. It felt good to sit so much. Brandy didn't sit. She lay down. When L.A. made her get up so there was room on the couch, Brandy borrowed my sleep-ing bag to lie on the floor.

"At least take Advil for the pain," I told her. Advil was allowed.

"What pain?" She grimaced, her head resting on my blue pillow.

Daddy forbidding alcohol or drugs made him differ-ent from other pimps. Stone kept his girls in heroin, and Whippet and George gave theirs beer and liquor, too. Brandy said it felt good to be drunk or high most of the time. She knew about the feel of drinking because some-body who used to take care of her when she was small made sure she drank a lot. She said it made the work easier but living harder. They made her use smack later, which she loved more than anything ever except for Daddy. She said stopping cold for Daddy when he first found her was a million times worse than the worst trick she'd ever had to turn, but Daddy helped her do it. She said he was like a living angel.

"I can't take no Advil," Brandy told me now. "Daddy say that's like picking up. He say he can't trust a ho who's an addict."

"It's just Advil," I tried.

"I told you this before, Dime." Brandy sighed. "Daddy say the drink or the drug become a ho's God, and the ho going to choose that over her pimp any day. Daddy say junk makes hos stupid and not trustworthy."

"Do you miss it?"

"Used to." She pressed the heels of her hands into her eyes. "Felt like dying. And the dreams." She dropped her hands and shuddered. "Ugh." Then she rolled over onto her stomach, hiding her face, but I saw that it had gone pink. It embarrassed her, I guess, how much she loved him. "Daddy took such good care of me," she said quietly. "I was about to die. Daddy saved me." She rolled back over to face me again. "You ever mess with all that?"

I shook my head. Trevor and Dawn sometimes smoked weed. I smoked with them once or twice, but it just made me tired. I drank with them once or twice too, but I didn't like the taste. Janelle had offered me her gin, but after seeing what it did to her, I didn't want to touch it. Besides, I hated the smell.

"I'm getting you some Advil." Maybe if I was firm, she would take it.

"Advil ain't going to help the pain I got," Brandy said.

I looked at her.

She clicked her tongue. "I mean, if I even had any pain."

I wondered if that cop broke her ribs. Or broke something inside of her. I wondered what he had really done to her to make her not want to sit down, to make her walk awkwardly and gasp randomly, when she hadn't even seemed to move.

The only thing she did was shower. I showered too. Longer than I ever got to, and with hot water the entire time. With no work, I was going to stay clean after that shower, after I brushed my teeth. It was good to feel so clean in my mouth and in my underwear, knowing the clean would remain for two or even three more days.

But I missed Daddy. I kept hoping he would call and L.A. would have to give me the phone, but he didn't.

"What did you tell the cops?" L.A. asked Brandy after we ate lunch.

"I didn't say shit," Brandy said.

"Why he left out then?"

Brandy shrugged and reached for the remote. She wanted to watch *Bourne Identity*. "How should I know? He just being smart. He can't trust nobody, not even me. So he staying away."

"You know he down south, right?" L.A. said.

I kept quiet.

"I'm talking to you, bitch."

"I don't know."

L.A. looked at Brandy. "What does you know?"

Brandy shrugged. "He don't tell me anything."

I thought L.A. was going to jump both of us. She was big. I tried to decide whether to run or fight.

But instead L.A. laughed. "You bitches don't know shit," she said. "You know why he went down south?"

We shook our heads.

"He finding a place. He going to take me with him, and we relocating down there. And you, not neither one of you, coming."

"Whatever." I could tell Brandy thought it might be true. I could tell by the way her mouth turned down at the corners and by the way her face got more stiff than usual. And if Brandy thought it might be true, than it could be true. Why would he have lied to me, though, about a Brother and the Russians? Why would he have done that?

He still didn't call. I tried to take a nap, but I couldn't sleep, so I gave up. I showered again instead, just because I could, and got ready for grocery shopping. As I was about to walk out the door, L.A. tried to take Daddy's thirty dollars. I'd had it at my feet inside the sleeping bag during my nap, then folded in my underwear balanced on the sink's edge during my shower, and now it was steam damp in my pocket.

"Give it," L.A. said. It was three forty-five.

"Daddy told me to go."

"He meant you to give it to me."

"No, he didn't." I didn't care so much about getting out for the food. I wanted to get out for another reason.

"Give it to me or I'm going to pop you."

"Pop me then," I told her. "And then explain it to Daddy." I walked past her and out the door, half expecting a glass or a chair to fly through the air and knock me down.

Chapter Twenty

HE SAID HE had eyes watching me, and I didn't want to make him mad. But there was a library not too far from the store. I'd noticed it when Daddy drove us to work. He took different routes at different times, turning if a car in front of him was moving too slowly or if he just wasn't in the mood for the scenery. So I'd noticed that library. And if I went quickly now, I could get one book. Just one. And hide it in the grocery bag. And pretend I'd found it in my cardboard box later and have something to read.

It must have been strange to see a girl with a bag full of groceries walk into a library. But nobody seemed to mind. I didn't even glance around for Ms. McClenny. I just headed to the Ks and snatched a Stephen King I had already read and knew I loved. *Carrie.* I thought I could be in and out in five minutes. But then there was an issue.

"Your library card has expired," the librarian said, raising her eyes from her computer and looking right at me.

"Oh."

She was dark-skinned, with short, straightened hair. "It's not a problem. We can renew it. Do you have your school ID?"

"It's summer." I don't know what that was supposed to mean, but it was something to say.

She wore glasses just like librarians are supposed to. Thick black frames with an oval-shaped red jewel on each earpiece. "All right. Well. You can come back with it anytime."

Daddy made us give him all our IDs so he could hold them and keep them safe. He took my bus pass too. "I think I lost it."

She tapped on the keyboard, her eyeballs scanning her screen. "Do you still live on Crescent Avenue?"

That was Janelle's house. I nodded.

She looked at me straight on again. "Can you bring your mother by with some proof of address?"

"She's busy with the babies," I lied.

The librarian clicked her nails on the counter. The index fingernails were a pale blue, and the rest were silver. "That's not true, is it?" She said it kindly.

I was trying to picture what she saw. A skinny

fourteen-year-old with braided hair, jeans shorts, sneakers, a white tank top, and a pink bra strap striping her shoulders. Big eyes, pierced ears with huge fake gold hoops, and smooth skin. I knew I looked all right because I was clean and wearing square clothes. But maybe she knew what I was. Maybe hos weren't allowed to check out books. I wasn't sure, and the clock was ticking, and what if it was Whippet or Stone Daddy had watching me?

"I usually work over at the main branch." She wore a long necklace that had three pretty polished stones. Two white and one a cat's-eye. They clicked against one another as she moved, making the same sound her fingernails made on the keyboard and on the counter. "Daniel just left for the day, and I don't know how staff here handles this sort of thing. We are all supposed to go by the book." She sighed. "Of course you're welcome to stay and read if you have some time." She peered at me through her lenses. "But I just can't let you take anything without an up-to-date card."

I don't know why that was the thing that made me cry when so much for so long hadn't. But the silhouette and the fuzz cleared for long enough that I could feel certain ways I'd stopped feeling, and then the tears just came. I spun around, holding tightly to my grocery bag.

At the door, I felt something touch the back of my shoulder. She had come all the way out from behind her counter just to stop me. "Here." She handed me a thick paperback and the expired card. "Have you read *To Kill a Mockingbird*?"

I shook my head. It was almost impossible to push back the tears.

"It's presumptuous of me to give you a book you didn't choose," she told me in her steady, librarian voice. "But since I'm breaking the rules for you, I feel entitled."

I shifted the grocery bag to my hip and took the paperback from her. I would have rather had *Carrie*, but at least she gave me something.

"Just this once," she said, necklace clacking. She put her hand on my shoulder for a second. "And if that book is overdue, I'm going to Crescent Avenue myself to find it."

I almost couldn't get the words out. It took a few breaths. "Thank you."

Outside on the hot steps, I carefully put down the grocery bag on the sidewalk, removed the ramen noodles, turkey slices, grape tomatoes, Doritos, apples, bread, and the Coke. Then I slid the book inside and repacked. I held the bag with both arms, supporting the bottom on the fast walk home.

* * *

I made dinner, but when I fixed a plate for myself, L.A. took it from me. When I tried picking food up in my hand out of the refrigerator, she grabbed it away.

"Let her eat!" Brandy tried. "Damn, L.A. What is your problem?"

"Daddy told her to give me the money for food," L.A. insisted. "She lying to us, and we can't have no lying."

"Dime is not a liar," Brandy argued. "If she say Daddy gave her money, then he gave her money."

"Why he going to give her the coins?" L.A. nearly screamed. "I'm the Bottom Bitch! Not her!"

I was starving. It was the morning of the third day. Brandy's face wasn't looking any better. She was still lying down a lot too. And not doing a lot of walking.

"If you eat," L.A. told me. "Or you give her food," she told Brandy, "I'm telling Daddy Dime got a book."

L.A. had found it in two seconds. You can't really hide a book in a grocery bag.

"Daddy likes it that I read," I tried. "He doesn't care if I have a book."

"He say you could go get yourself a book?"

I wanted to lie, but Daddy would find out in two seconds.

"Uh-huh," L.A. said. "You don't eat. Not until Daddy home. And if you do eat, he going to know you went to get a book when he pacifically said nobody go out."

"Specifically."

"What?"

It was stupid, but I couldn't help it. "Specifically."

She smacked my head so hard I saw orange spots and couldn't get up off the floor the first two times I tried.

Sitting on the couch, clean, afraid to pull out my paperback that L.A. hadn't yet thought to take from me, staring at *American Idol*, starving, I tried not to think about what it all meant.

Was Daddy telling me lies to keep me happy while he was preparing to take L.A. with him down south and start up a new life? Or was he lying to L.A., and if he was lying to her, why would he? Why would he give me the money? Why didn't he tell me to give it to L.A. to tell her to go shopping? Was he testing me? Was he testing all of us? Was he really going to come back home? That last thought scared me. I didn't know what I would do if he never came back. I needed him to hold me. I needed him to take care of me.

L.A. finally went to bed, but she left her door open so she could stop me if I moved toward the kitchen. I thought

I would die from hunger at first, but then inside the sleeping bag, wrapped in two paper towels, I found a turkey-and-mustard sandwich, some grape tomatoes, and a Coke. I ate and drank as quietly as I could and then shoved the soda can to the bottom of the sleeping bag, because I didn't want L.A. finding it and going off on Brandy.

L.A.'s phone rang at two in the morning. I scooched out of my sleeping bag and went to sit on the couch. Brandy was horizontal but awake. She wasn't sleeping well, the way she used to. I heard her the last two nights, restless. Now we could hear L.A. talking, but we couldn't make out what she was saying. She sounded happy, which could be good or bad. Then she came out. "Here." She handed me the phone.

"Hi," I said.

"Beautiful."

Inside my chest, my heart warmed and things began to breathe after a long time of not. I waited.

"How you doing, Beautiful?"

"Good." I tried not to look at L.A. I could feel her steaming mad.

"Brandy?"

"She got beat up," I told him.

"I heard. Tell her she got to start over earning for that phone she want so bad."

"Okay."

He lowered his voice. "Don't forget I love you best."

"Okay." I was careful not to let my voice shift, not to let the joy seep in. I didn't want to hurt Brandy or make L.A. more bothered than she already was.

"Now give the phone back to L.A."

I handed it back, and she took it to her room.

I felt worried that he didn't ask to speak to Brandy, but I pretended I hadn't even noticed that. "He said you have to start over earning for the phone." I couldn't look at her.

"He didn't want to say nothing to me?"

"I guess he's mad you were locked up."

And now Daddy wouldn't even talk to her. She loved Daddy as much as I did. I didn't like that, but still. Daddy didn't have to be so cold. She crossed her arms over her chest and tucked her fingers into her armpits.

I found her feet through the blanket and rubbed them.

"Get off, pervert." Beads of sweat appeared on her upper lip.

"Daddy will come back soon," I told her.

I didn't stop rubbing, while she didn't stop shivering, trying not to cry.

Chapter Twenty-One

IT WAS NEARLY lunchtime on the fourth day of Daddy being gone. I decided to risk reading in front of L.A. I just couldn't wait any longer, and I was hoping starving me to death was enough for her without taking my book, too. When Daddy walked in, I had just reached the part where Scout realizes somebody slipped a blanket over her shoulders during the fire.

"How my bitches?" He was wearing new Seven jeans and new orange-and-blue high-tops and a new leather coat. I let *To Kill a Mockingbird* collapse closed.

Brandy had finally started sitting down again, but now she stood fast and went right to him. "I'm sorry," she said. "I'm real sorry. It was—"

He interrupted her with a hug and whispered something

in her ear. He held her close like that for a long time and kissed her mouth tenderly before letting her go. It was hard to watch because I got so jealous, but I was glad Daddy had decided to forgive her.

"Come here," Daddy ordered L.A., releasing Brandy.

Brandy went to the armchair while L.A. glared at him from the couch. "Why you gave Dime money?"

"You mad." His gold *D* was shinier than ever. "Get over here and trust your Daddy always got a good reason."

She thought about that. "What good reason?"

"Get over here."

She stood without touching him, her arms by her sides, while he whispered to her. She crossed her arms when he was done, but leaned into his chest.

He looked at me. "Where my change?" I got up shakily and pulled three dollars and fifty-three cents out of my pocket. "You sick?" He let go of L.A. to look at me more closely.

I was starving. "No." He caught me as I started to fall. His arms were huge and hard.

"Maybe some toast," Brandy suggested, cutting her eyes at me.

"She sick?" Daddy asked L.A.

She shrugged.

He pulled me into him and whispered into my ear now. "I missed you, Beautiful. My big plans coming soon."

He let me go so I could sit at the kitchen table. Brandy started pulling food out of the refrigerator for me, Daddy walked over to the open window. "Check it out."

"What?" L.A. peered through. "Nuh-uh," she said. "That yours?"

"That ours." Daddy grinned.

Brandy left the food to look. "The ride out there?"

I picked up the cheese, turkey, and two pieces of bread and made a sandwich as fast as I could. "What is it?" I asked with my mouth full.

"Escalade," Brandy answered. "White."

"Why you got white?" That was L.A. "White cheap-looking. You should have gotten black."

"Shut up." But Daddy was in a good mood. He spanked L.A. on her behind.

"Where's the Honda?" Brandy asked.

Daddy chuckled. "Passaic River."

I went, wobbly, by the refrigerator, pulling more food out. More cheese and bread, a fistful of grape tomatoes, three more slices of turkey, sweet pickles. I sank back down, already planning what to eat after.

"We going indoor," Daddy announced.

"For real?" L.A. sounded surprised, and it wasn't easy to surprise her.

"Indoor?" Brandy said. "Where at?"

Now once we go from the track to indoor, Money would explain in the note, *a lot more of me can be had. First of all, a john has a room with a bathroom and a bed in it. That right there allows you to charge more of me than when all you have to offer is an empty lot or a car. It's true that now you have to pay out to keep the room. That's a con. But on the pro side—no pun intended—you can keep an eye on your hos better, and in some ways you are better protected from the police. This Daddy with the D on his tooth was ambitious. And he had a good mind in a lot of ways. He was going to move himself and his stable up by moving indoor. He could have done it too, if circumstances hadn't interfered. But that's not your problem. In fact, you don't have a problem.* I'm counting on any square reading Money's note to be horrified. *What you have here is a golden opportunity.*

"You bitches going to earn me back my money I lost these past days," Daddy told us. "Then we taking us a road trip."

"Where we going?" L.A. asked.

I was eating everything left in the refrigerator.

"Down south." Daddy gazed out at his Escalade. "Getting a prize, and then back here for indoor."

"Indoor where?" Brandy asked at the same time L.A. said, "What prize?"

"Indoor like room eleven?" Brandy wanted to know. "Because eleven don't even count as indoor. That's just a room in a rotted-out house."

"Shut up," L.A. said. She turned to Daddy. "What prize?"

Would we go to the track anymore? I was thinking about Whippet and Stone and how hot or cold it could get. I was thinking how it would be good not to have to go back there. Daddy knew what I was thinking. He always did.

"Next few days out on the track," Daddy said. "Then, you do right by me down south, we done with the street."

Their Daddy was a go-getter, Money would elaborate. *He could have chosen to become something important, some kind of respectable business owner or an accountant. Maybe even a lawyer. But this Daddy wasn't interested in living a square life. Instead he used his good mind and his ambition for something more to his liking. If his Lollipop worked out the way he hoped, he would have more of me than ever. And as soon as enough more of me got dropped into his pocket, he was going to run an indoor scheme down south with some Russian bitches. He would travel back and forth, and that would be the beginning of his franchise.*

But in order for his grand plan to succeed, this Daddy needed a lot of me at the front end. So he had to toughen up. His bitches weren't going to like that, but the boss sets the rules and the employees must live by those rules. It's not as if those hos were chained to him. They worked of their own free will. If they wanted to try and make enough of me on their own somehow to eat and sleep and stay warm in the cold and cool in the heat, well, as you know, it's a free country. Anybody with a little get-up-and-go, like her Daddy, can pull herself up and make more of me than she even needs. This Daddy's hos didn't choose to do that. And of course you will never be in such a position. Especially because you—I would write Money to be so repulsive—you in fact have a windfall: You don't even need to be a go-getter. Dumb luck has brought you a gift.

Daddy didn't take any of us for over a week. He had us working practically all day and all night. "Whoever make the most money by Thursday get to lie down in the back," Daddy promised. He'd told us the trip down south would take a few weeks; half driving, half working, so that meant whoever was lying down would sleep more comfortably than the others. We all wanted sleep.

"That's fifty," I told a date. It was usually forty-five, but I was so hot and tired. L.A. and Brandy both would be angry if they knew I was changing prices, but I didn't care.

"Fifty?" the date said. "Since when is that fifty?"

I shrugged and pretended I was going to walk away. Sweat glazed my body. I could see my own skin shining with it. We were in the alley between the two far brick buildings. I always went to the spot where there was one gray brick in the middle of all the red ones. It was eye level if I was bracing my forehead on my forearms, and I liked to look at it and try and get lost in the gray whenever I could. I pretended it was a dusk sky or the skin of an elephant or a magic panel that would open up and pull me into somewhere beautiful, some alternate spectacular universe. Oz. Or Never-Never Land.

"Wait," the date said, pulling at my shoulder. "Fine. Fifty. You better be good."

"I'm the best." I said it the way Brandy had coached me way back at the beginning of the summer. The first time I practiced saying such a thing with such a surprising tone of voice, she laughed enough that she almost choked on a blueberry muffin. *Damn!* She sputtered, *Where that come from?* They pay you more when you tell them you're worth more. That's what Brandy said. Also if you smile while you turn your trick and act like you love it. All of it. That's what Brandy told me, and she was right. It's difficult to show with your face and your body and what you do that you love something you actually despise, but if you practice enough and you have already died, you can learn.

I must have been good, because he made me get on my knees to do some extra things, and I got another five.

I guess I wasn't the only one making up new prices, though, because Daddy said L.A. won. Brandy sat up in the front seat, and I sat up in the back with boxes of clothing and supplies loaded beside me and *Mockingbird* on my lap. L.A. had tried to tell Daddy how I had sneaked away to get it, but he ignored her, saying he didn't want to hear about our petty shit. If I weren't so scared of L.A., I would have laughed in her face.

He worked us twelve hours straight before we got in the car. He let us shower, but then he told us to dress in clean working clothes for the car ride. The Escalade's air-conditioning was like Daddy's room and Christmas. Even sitting up reading, pleased that Scout was finally beating up Francis in the pages of my paperback, I fell asleep so fast, I didn't notice the city disappear behind us.

It only felt like a minute, but it must have been hours, because when I woke up to the car stopped and the back door opening into the dusk and me stepping out onto gravel, I didn't recognize anything: small roads with wide, short houses, a church off in the distance, and a bodega next to a gas station next to a motel. Daddy handed me a cardboard box, and I followed L.A. and Brandy along a covered sidewalk to the door of room five. We three waited while Daddy swiped a card through a slot to unlock our door and then walked down the covered sidewalk to swipe room six. When we all walked inside, I saw the two rooms were connected by another door. I'd never been in a motel. I liked the way it looked like an apartment. Two double beds, a chair, a desk, and a bathroom. Heavy dark curtains, which moved together and apart on chains made of tiny metal beads. It smelled like bleach and mold and like old Doritos and stale smoke and beer. It smelled like the track.

I put the box on the desk while L.A. sat down on the bed. Daddy came through the adjoining door.

"Get up off that bed, L.A. Get them boxes in my room and then we going out."

"Where are we?" Brandy asked.

"Don't matter," Daddy said. "Get the boxes out the car."

When we finished unloading, he let us go to the bathroom. I was the first one, and when I lifted the closed toilet seat, I broke a plain piece of paper wrapped around it, like an oversize ribbon. I wasn't sure what that paper was for, but my bladder was about to burst, so I didn't spend much time wondering about it.

He had us back in the car without any food, and I felt shaky and crampy from having slept sitting up and being hungry. I stepped on my book by accident. I picked it up and wiped it off with the back of my hand.

As we drove away from the motel into the evening, a word popped into my head: *portico*. That covered sidewalk was a portico. I tried to remember what books I'd seen the word in. I pictured rounded red tiles and white columns and maybe even green vines, bright in morning sun. Not a strip of concrete covered by a dark ledge, lit up by vibrating fluorescent glare.

Daddy dropped us on a stretch of road behind the highway. In the soft darkness I saw three or four other shapes of girls off in the distance. Other than that, it was just high grass, broken bottles, a plastic baby swing half-stuck in a patch of dirt, and gravel under our feet. There was no pavement anywhere, and I kept turning my ankles on the unsteady ground.

"Go make me my money." Daddy drove the Escalade down the road and over a low slope, so that when it stopped on the shoulder, I could barely see it.

It was different. Almost no johns came at first. We walked up and down just out of boredom, sweating through our tank tops. We tried to sit, but the ground was prickly and uncomfortable, so we walked slowly and chitchatted. Mainly

L.A. did the chitchatting. I didn't say a word, and Brandy only spoke back to L.A. once in a while. L.A. didn't seem to notice. She liked the sound of her own voice.

Then, after another hour, everything happened in fits and starts. First there would be no johns at all, and the girls would just slouch around. Then three or five vehicles would arrive almost at the same time, their headlights blinding us for a minute. Most of the dates wanted to stay in their cars, so we didn't have to walk to the Escalade. But twice I led a john down the road. I was nervous Daddy would be there in the front seat while I worked, which would have been mortifying. But I didn't see him at all. He must have gotten out to walk and text or talk on the phone. The second time, though, Brandy was there. I didn't realize it until I opened my eyes to look into the Escalade through the window, since my date didn't seem to want to wait but just leaned me face-forward on the car. When I looked, Brandy was below, facing up from the backseat while her john had his head buried in her shoulder. She was yawning. When I saw that, I started to laugh, and when I laughed she jumped and yelped, and her john must have thought he was something special because even from the outside, I could hear him saying, "Yeah, feel that, feel that, feel that." And then Brandy was laughing, and then I was laughing harder, and then I stopped laughing because I was afraid my date wouldn't like it, but he did. "That's a good time, huh?" he said into my ear.

I had little bug bites all around my ankles and on my feet. They itched like crazy.

"Why we couldn't do indoor right now?" L.A. whined. "Why we had to work like that out on a farm road?"

"You ain't seen farm yet," Daddy said. "We not even close."

"Whatever," L.A. said. "My legs itching."

"You all shower and eat something. More work coming."

It was late. Four, maybe five in the morning. Daddy had some kind of bucket chicken on the table and a package of Fudge Stripes. I thought I would fall over from hunger and fatigue.

"Can we sleep?" Brandy asked. "I'm tired."

"Got to make up all that money we lost," Daddy said. "Get yourselfs clean and eat if you hungry and then put the food mess back in my room. Be ready in forty-five minutes. You going to work in here now."

On the street I sometimes had to work with Brandy busy not three feet away. I even had to do three-ways sometimes with her. It was embarrassing. Brandy acted like she didn't care, but she didn't like it either, when we had to do it like that. We pretended with our smiles and giggles because you had to, but we never really looked at each other. Now I was nervous. It seemed like we were going to have to work all day in the room on the two beds. How were we supposed to manage the space? How were the dates going to feel about not having privacy? When things didn't go the way they liked, some of them got rough.

"We worked a lot already." I made a point of never complaining. I never spoke much, anyway, but somehow I was speaking now. "Can't we rest a little?"

"I'm surprised with you, Dime." Daddy pointed his finger at me and then waved it at the others. "You all had three days' vacation. You going to stress me when I got us a new car and we out taking a trip all together?"

"We're just tired." I wanted to go back home to my alcove and read my book all at once, without interruptions, in peace. I wanted to get past the part with Mrs. Dubose fighting her drug habit and dying so slowly in front of Jem. I wanted to catch another glimpse of pale Boo Radley and watch Jem take a dare from Dill.

Mostly, I wanted to stop working, even though I knew that was part of being with Daddy. For the first time since my first steps on the track back home, it occurred to me that maybe I should just tell him I didn't want to do it anymore. But I was too tired to think much about that.

"L.A.?" Daddy said. "You tired?"

"Please." L.A. rolled her eyes.

Daddy kissed her, long. I didn't even care. Then he left.

L.A. took the first shower, using up twenty of our forty-five minutes. I didn't mind because I was so hungry, and it gave me a chance to eat in peace. But she told Brandy to go next. When it was finally my turn, just like at home, there was no hot water. Also, there was mold all along the shower stall walls and around the faucets and the handles in the sink, and there were no towels. L.A. had used the only one. It was only a little bit bigger than a washcloth. So I had to dry myself with toilet paper, which is practically impossible. It kept falling apart and clumping in white bits. I was freezing from the water and from the cold damp I couldn't get all the way off.

I was barely dressed again when Daddy came back with the johns. There were five of them. Four were black and one was white. I thought the white one would go with Brandy, but he wanted L.A. All the other johns wanted Brandy, but they all wanted to go right away. There was nearly a fight, but Daddy said something to them, and they calmed down and two agreed to go with me.

Daddy put me to work in the bathroom. Which was good because at least it wasn't with L.A. or Brandy right next to me, watching. And because I could find a way to rinse just a second right before or after a date. But bad because it was small, and I kept banging into corners. And because it meant Daddy couldn't charge the men as much. So I couldn't make as much money as the others, which meant Daddy would be annoyed with me, even though it wasn't my fault he put me in the bathroom.

Over the next few hours, I could hear the men arriving and leaving. A lot of them complained at the door when they saw the way Daddy had us set up. They all had to wait to come in and pee until I was finished with whatever job I was doing. Some of them grinned when the door opened and I came spilling out of it with another man. Some of them cursed.

Then one of them punched me. I think he was aiming for my face, but he hit the very front center of my neck, taking all my air, painfully, and making me cough a long time. Daddy spun that one around and pounded him so hard, I could hardly believe it. The first hit sounded the way a car must sound hitting a tree. Over at the beds, L.A. and Brandy's dates jumped up fast.

Daddy hauled the one who hit me toward the door,

glaring at the other two over his shoulder. "You better leave me my money."

Then he disappeared while the dates hopped into their clothes, threw cash onto the dresser, and practically ran out the door. Daddy walked in right after, blood on his shirt. He pulled it off with one swoop, revealing his chest, slick with sweat. He strode over to me. "You okay?"

"Yes," I sputtered inside his hug, his hot wet skin, my heart pounding with pleasure at how he'd just defended me.

He straightened to speak to all of us. "Ain't nobody messing with my bitches." He stroked my neck with his big hand. "See?" he whispered to me. "See how I take care a you?"

The fingers on my neck were the ones I was used to loving. The same ones that touched me so gently in all the right places and cupped my bottom and my face when he whispered how special I was. They had just beaten off someone who hurt me. I leaned in to hug Daddy again, so grateful and happy at how he took care of me. But Daddy stiff-armed me, holding me away.

"Get off." He glanced at his watch. "We got three more coming in ten minutes."

Oh. I swallowed back disappointment. I hadn't thought he would put me back to work.

* * *

I worked and I worked. I don't know how Daddy got so many men to come to our crowded motel room in the middle of nowhere, but it was a steady stream the whole day long. When daylight began to ease away from the bathroom window, Daddy came to get me.

"Get in that shower and get clean," he said. "You did good."

That meant he was going to take me. After all those johns and my throat hurting from being punched and being so dead tired. I took a shower. I had hot water, and I was thankful for that.

Daddy led me to his room. The sheets were clean. It was quiet. I tried to be thankful for that, too. He began by kissing my neck, where it hurt. "Daddy," I started. He was kissing up to the underside of my chin. Usually I loved the warm tickle, but now it bothered me. "I don't like being with dates," I whispered. I said it so quietly, I wasn't sure he heard.

But he paused and then mumbled through his kisses as he kept on. "Where you going to be without me?" He was making circles on my skin with his lips. Usually I loved that. Usually it just made me melt. "Living with that bitch keeping you home from school, making you take care a all them kids, beating on you for no good reason, her pervert taking it from you hard and for free." He switched to using his tongue. It felt too wet, too big. "Or you out sitting on some bus stop bench, and some do gooder notice you and send your ass to a home or say you crazy and lock you up."

It was true. I had nowhere else to go. And he didn't have to take care of me. He took me when nobody else wanted me. He punched anybody who punched me.

"I don't like turning tricks," I tried, while he left my chin and neck and began to lick toward my belly button.

"What?" He sat up and back and then pressed himself on my stomach. "You like it just fine when you with me."

"Feels good with you," I told him, trying to remember the truth of that. "But all those dates . . ."

"Yeah?" He sat up. "Nobody forcing you," he told me. "Go ahead. Get dressed. Send Brandy in. Then, soon as we home, you go on back to your Janelle."

"What? That wasn't what I meant. I don't want to . . ."

He had his jeans on already. "You said you don't like it here, then leave."

I sat up too. "I don't want to leave. Don't make me leave."

He picked up his phone and thumbed it. "Beef me again, and you out."

I didn't want to leave Daddy. But I didn't want to be a ho, either.

It was like he had read my mind. "Once a ho, always a ho." He didn't even bother to look up from his phone. "That's what you is. Ain't nothing else for you now. You go out there without me and somebody likely to kill you or lock you up or put you in a crazy hospital. You want to live out your little life in jail?"

I shook my head, but he didn't see me.

"You want to be strapped down to a bed next to somebody think she Jesus?"

I shook my head again. He glanced up.

"You want to break yourself to Whippet? And him gorilla you nine times a week?"

I knew I didn't want to be beat up or worse every day. "I didn't mean that I—"

"You better get straight what you mean," Daddy said, tossing aside his phone and unzipping his jeans again. With his pants half on, he pressed me back flat again and slid his palm from my sore neck all the way down. "Get it straight, Beautiful," he whispered, "or we done."

Chapter Twenty-Two

MRS. DUBOSE FINALLY died, right as Daddy pulled off the highway by a rest area sign.

"Get up," Daddy said. I tried to picture him reading to Brandy longer and longer each day the way Jem read to Mrs. Dubose, weaning her off her drug. How did Daddy help Brandy get clean? I couldn't imagine it.

"I said, get up."

I closed my paperback.

On the near side of the diner and the 7-11 were rows and rows of gas pumps. On the far side there were rows and rows of trucks. In the dark, it looked fake somehow, like a painting in a book, or the way I imagined the set of a movie.

Brandy lifted her head from the hammock of her shoulder

belt. I saw her wipe drool off her cheek with her palm. She unbuckled. "I'm hungry."

"L.A.!" When nothing came from the backseat, he flung an empty cranberry juice bottle. I had to dodge sideways so it didn't hit my face.

I heard it *thwap* L.A., who made a noise and sat up. "Damn," she said. "Stop it."

"Move your ass."

I thought he meant to the diner so we could eat and use the bathroom, but he didn't.

"Brandy, you middle. L.A., you at the back end, and Dime, you there where the front at." He was pointing through the window at that parking lot of trucks.

"You bugging?" L.A. asked him when she figured out what he meant.

I didn't like the idea. It was one thing to go with dates in Daddy's territory, but this wasn't Daddy's territory, and what if the rules were different here?

"You want us to go inside those things?" Brandy was eyeing the huge trucks all lined up, sleeping in the dim-lit dark.

"Whatever it take," Daddy said. "Inside, outside. Just make me my money."

"May I go to the bathroom first, please?" I asked as politely as I could manage.

Daddy tilted his head toward the ground. "Squat and take care of it."

L.A. sucked her teeth. "Why you being so savage, all of a sudden?"

"Savage." Daddy smiled, flashing his *D.* "You got that right."

I looked across to the sleeping trailers and wondered why he wasn't worried about us. He knew what I was thinking, like always. "You need something, you scream loud. Enough people around here, someone going to hear you, and your date know it. You scream loud enough, it remind him to treat you nice."

Brandy glanced at me from the front seat, twisting her head.

Even L.A. was worried. "Easy for you to say," she told Daddy.

He tapped her cheek. "None of you eating," he declared, "until I see some coins."

I wasn't sure if I was supposed to get up on one of those giant steps and knock, or if I was just supposed to walk around or what. L.A. and Brandy weren't saying a word, so I didn't ask. But L.A. chewed on her fingertips all the way until we fanned out. It wasn't pitch-black dark because lights from the diner and the 7-11 and the gas station and the traffic and even some of the trucks lit the air. But it was still night, and we tripped over each other a little.

Brandy shook her head at me as she peeled off, as if to say, *Is this for real?*

I went to pee first, because my bladder was about to explode. I went near the mass of trees on the far side of all the trucks. It was darker there, and I was glad because I didn't want anybody to see me squatting. A girl climbed down from a tanker near me. I pulled up my panties and adjusted my miniskirt and watched. She was white with blond hair and a halter top and jeans and Uggs, which seemed strange in all this heat. A white man helped with the huge step. Then she picked her way through the narrow alleys of the trucks. Her purse swung and patted her behind gently as she went.

The man caught me watching. He jumped at first. "Lot lizards every damn where," he muttered. I didn't know what he meant. I started to turn away. "I'm worn out," he called to me softly. "But my friend will be glad to see you." He pointed somewhere down the line. "He likes pretty brown girls." He began texting something. "I'm telling him you're on your way now." I looked to where he was pointing and saw headlights flash. "That's him."

I didn't want to, but I was starving. I looked around for

L.A. and Brandy. I couldn't see them anywhere. Then I saw Daddy, talking on his phone in front of the diner while looking out at the trucks. That made me feel better, to know that he might see which one I was climbing into. So I went.

It was different because the two pimps I saw were white and most of the johns were white and so were two of the other three girls. If the girls weren't climbing up or down from the trucks, they were wandering around or in their cars: two in a van that looked maroon in the night and the other in an Escalade, a black one. They disappeared before it got light out. Daddy allowed us into the diner all together after the sun came up. He let us eat whatever we wanted. I ordered an omelet and chocolate chip pancakes. I watched Brandy. She was keeping her head down, just looking at her eggs and home fries. I hadn't wondered for a long time about her not being black. I had even forgotten about it a little bit. But after seeing those other white hos, it felt strange. She seemed different all of a sudden. More white.

"Nice-looking bitches around here," Daddy told Brandy. She just kept chewing.

"What's the damn prize?" L.A. asked for the thousandth time. "Why we doing this?" She glared at Daddy over her waffles. "I do not like this shit. Some crazy man going to drive us away and chop us up."

"Nobody going to hurt you." Daddy shoved a cheeseburger into his mouth.

I saw a new family walk in. A white Daddy with a dark Bottom leading three dark girls. When they got closer, I saw they weren't Puerto Rican or Dominican or black or even dark white. Also I saw they were tiny skinny.

"Chinese hos," Daddy said. "See that." There were some Asian girls back home. George had two. Stone used to have one and another one stabled with Whippet. But I think their girls were all a little mixed.

These were pure-looking. Korean, maybe. Or Chinese. I wasn't too sure. They glanced at us and then glanced away when their Daddy said something. They sat down, and I heard them speaking softly to one another in a fast, whining language. He said something again, louder, and they stopped talking.

Daddy left cash pinned beneath his plate and then walked us out to the car. When we passed their table, the youngest one, about my age, glanced at her Daddy ordering more coffee and then quickly at the back of the Bottom walking away—probably to the bathroom—and then at Brandy. Just at Brandy. The Asian girl whispered something

I couldn't understand. "Hep. Heppeese. Stowen."

Daddy didn't hear, but L.A. did and so did Brandy. She slowed down, then sped up. L.A. started to laugh, and when she laughed I pictured myself picking up a ketchup bottle and slamming it into the back of her head. I didn't really know then what that Asian ho said. Or why I was so especially mad at L.A. for laughing.

I didn't figure it out until later, when I closed my eyes in the Escalade, Brandy asleep in the front, and L.A. stretched out behind me. I was so tired I could hardly hold on to it in my brain when I realized that what the girl had said was, *Help. Help, please. Stolen.*

You might wonder, Money would write, *what kind of ho makes more of me. That is an interesting question without an answer everybody will agree on.* I had heard Stone and George debate it at our kitchen table. *Some say that the ho who is most foreign to the man makes the most of me. Others will swear that most men prefer white bitches, the more blue-eyed and blond-haired, the better. Hos of Eastern European descent and Asian bitches are said to bring in more of me than anyone, depending on where in this free country the transaction is occurring. Then again, there are always exceptions to a rule.* Mostly Daddy claimed he had no interest in associating with his competition, especially such ignorant competition.

But other times he chitchatted with them just like a girl. *Some men will only purchase black hos. Others won't look at a black bitch. It all depends. Knowing the rule and then knowing the exceptions to that rule is a moneymaker, a me maker.*

This Daddy intended to make a lot of me off of knowing these kinds of things. Why not use his northern associates to bring some "Russians" down south? Stone said Daddy didn't know a Moldavian from a Czech from a Russian. Daddy had said he didn't have to know bullshit details because all those types of bitches were the same to dates. *He knew business, and he knew his particular down south could use some fresh cuts of meat. He knew me.*

Daddy let us sleep in the motel beds for four hours and then he had us up again.

"You back in the bathroom," he told me, right before he went out to find some business.

"Daddy." I wasn't sure what I wanted to say, and I was afraid of saying anything to him, but I couldn't help it. And he knew, the way he always knew everything.

He walked in with me and closed the door behind him. "I know I'm working you hard, Beautiful." He pulled me close to him. "I know you tired. We going back to something better after we get us our prize and get home."

"I just don't—"

"Shh." He rubbed my back. The bathroom was so small he had to hold me close anyway. It felt so good to be held like that, but the sink was jabbing into my spine. "I got a big plan," he told me. "You going to be real happy when it get done. Just keep that complaining mouth quiet and trust you Daddy."

"I don't mean to complain," I tried. "It's just that I—"

Daddy thunked his fist on the side of my head, and the jolt exploded my skull and jabbed at my back, from the lip of the sink.

"I told you shut your complaining."

I stood still, not making a sound.

He looked at me, disgusted, and for a part of a second I knew I hated him, and then he pulled me close again and pushed me away a little and kissed me long. "Don't make me hurt you, Beautiful," he whispered. I tried not to cry, but the tears came. I was so tired. Then he kissed me some more. "You know you my best. Don't make me hurt you. I hate to hurt you." He wrapped his arms around me and held me again, and I felt bad for making him feel so sorry.

About ten minutes after we packed up and drove away, in the daylight, I saw those Asian girls. They were getting out of a white van, walking in a row, like dark little ducklings, into a low, flat-roofed building that had MASSAGE painted in red on its front. Their Daddy and the Bottom Bitch were arguing about something behind them, but the girls never turned to look. They kept their shiny black heads tilted down and walked quickly, disappearing through the door. Something about the way they walked made me realize they weren't as old as they had looked in the diner. They were young. Younger even than me.

Chapter Twenty-Three

I WAS COMING out of a dream where my mouth was filled with chewing gum, but it tasted nasty and was choking me. When I woke all the way up, I was drooling morning-breath drool. I sat up fast to wipe it away. Brandy was still sleeping, her head lolling. And L.A.'s feet were two inches from my face, where she'd somehow hooked them from the backseat across and over to my row. Daddy was outside pumping gas.

I looked beyond him and saw a highway. I looked opposite and saw a massive strip mall rest area with vehicles and people and dogs everywhere. I noticed a lot of vehicles had boats hooked up to trailers. I opened the door to humid air tinged with the taste of fuel and salt. Seagulls flapped against the wind in the sky, screeching.

"May I go to the bathroom, please?" I called to Daddy.

"Fast," he told me. "Don't speak to nobody."

I could leave, I thought. *I could disappear until he gives up trying to find me.* Would he give up or would he keep looking? If he kept looking and found me, would he beat me, or would he put his arms around me? Probably both. Where would I go, anyway? Maybe instead I could find an official somebody and tell them. But what would I tell them? *Would you ask my boyfriend to let me stop working?* And who would I tell? I was nothing but a ho.

I stared across the way at all the people and food windows and tables and chairs. A little brown girl perched on a fat woman's lap. She was eating school-bus-colored crackers from a Baggie and leaning her head back against the fat woman's doughy chest. The fat woman rested her cheek on the girl's head. Maybe I could find the woman who smelled like barbecue potato chips, who tickle-scratched my shoulder, who read to me. Had she been my mother? My grandmother? Where would I look for her?

There was a spinning rack of paperbacks in the store next to the ladies' room. I spun it, reading titles, watching them blur by. About a week ago in the Escalade, I came across the word *chifforobe.* I thought that might be some sort of dresser or bureau, but I wasn't too sure. I wanted to figure it out, and more importantly, to find out what had really gone on between Tom Robinson and Mayella. I wished I could read *Mockingbird* in the motel, but there was too much work. We had been staying in this one—our second—for five days now. This time I was in a bed and Brandy was in the bathroom; a bigger bathroom than the first one. I wondered if Daddy was planning to take us to another soon or to pick up our prize, whatever that was. I wondered what would happen if I didn't go back to the Escalade. Just stayed wandering around the pretzel stand and the book rack and in and out of the ladies' room. Probably I would be arrested and put away for good. In jail or in a mental hospital. I spun the rack and spun it again. It was whirring around so fast, I thought it might topple over, but I kept spinning it anyway.

"Daddy looking for you," I heard L.A. say in my ear, and she was there, grabbing my shoulder.

"Books," she told Daddy, as we climbed into the car. "She was looking at books again."

Daddy's *D* glittered. "Told you she wouldn't never step out on us."

Brandy was still asleep, the seat belt still hammocking her head. I slid into the middle seat, looking around.

"You want this?" L.A., popping gum, handed me my paperback. With a hot-pink wad stuck between the middle pages and another caked onto the back cover.

I tried to hand it back. My fingers were still somehow, but my heart was shaking. "Clean it up." Inside my head I apologized. *Sorry*, I said to Scout and Jem and to their daddy, Atticus Finch. *I'm sorry*, I said silently to Dill and Boo Radley and Tom Robinson.

"You funny, Dime," L.A. said, as if she heard me apologizing, and then she blew a bubble.

I glanced at Daddy up in the driver's seat. I could see the right side of his face. His angled eye cut a dark slash. I knew better than to say anything else after what happened last time when L.A. messed up my books. But I was so mad I thought if I could get my hands on Daddy's gun, I could kill somebody.

When I don't have anything to read, I feel like a tortoise without a shell or a boat without an anchor. There is nothing to hide under. Nowhere to stop and rest. When I don't have a book, there is nowhere good or interesting to be, there is nobody to care about, nothing to hope for, and nothing to puzzle over. When I do have something to read, it keeps me breathing. It's the reward for all the other things. It's the thing to look forward to, the reason for doing my day.

When I was little and living with Janelle, I knew that after the beds were made and the dishes were washed and dried and the floor was mopped and the toilet was cleaned and the laundry sorted into piles by color, I could go sit on my pillow in the corner behind the TV and read myself into other places and other times and other clothes and hair and words and people. I could melt through a page and out the other side, where nobody could find me or touch me because I was floating on a boat inside my shell, and I could just gently rock with the wavelets of the phrases.

About fifteen minutes after Daddy got back on the highway, Brandy woke up. She glanced back at me. "You crying?"

I shook my head.

Brandy wiped her mouth and her eyes. She picked up her Poland Spring from its little round cubby by her seat and took a lot of sips. Then she glanced back at me again. "L.A!" she called past me. "You mess with Dime?"

"Who you talking to?" L.A. called back. She didn't even sit up.

"You: Bitch," Brandy said.

Daddy's hand struck like a snake as he popped Brandy's ear. It must have stung, but Brandy ignored the pop and looked at me again. I hadn't even known I was crying until Brandy asked. "What happened?"

I shook my head again and pressed my fingertips on my

eyes. Sometimes you can push the tears back in. But sometimes is not all the time.

"This is bullshit," Brandy said to Daddy. She said it with the kind of attitude only L.A. ever gave.

"Shut up," Daddy told her, and he popped her again. The Escalade swerved.

"You got to let us rest!" Brandy yelled at him. "Look at her!" She meant me. "She's nothing but a baby, and you working her to death! You working all of us to death! We tired!"

"See what you did." L.A. was sitting up, and now she popped my head.

"Get off her!" Brandy yelled. "Damn!"

Daddy yanked the wheel and the car over three lanes and screeched onto the shoulder. The other cars and trucks whizzed past us, making zooming noises just like in cartoons. Daddy opened his door and stepped out. He gazed out at the traffic for a second and then opened the back door. He grabbed Brandy and hauled her out and then hauled me out, too. He shoved both of us down. Then he kicked us all over our hips and behinds. The next thing I knew, he hauled L.A. out of the car too and punched straight into the side of her jaw, as hard as if she was a man. Blood gushed out of her mouth. She spit the blood and spit again, and one of her teeth landed on the back of my hand and skittered off.

"I am just about sick a all you all," Daddy said. The traffic kept whizzing by. "We a mile from picking up our prize, and let me tell you, she going to be a breath of fresh air. She called Lollipop, and you, every single one a you, going to treat her like she a goddamn queen. Now get your asses back in my ride, and if I hear so much as a swallow out of any bitch, I'm throwing you out the window while we driving, and I am not playing."

So we stood up and got our asses back into the car.

Chapter Twenty-Four

DADDY LET US out one at a time to use the bathroom. As usual, I went last. The house was wood frame, peeling yellow paint, at the end of a sandy dirt road. Tiny bits of broken-up shells, and a few bigger swirly chunks, were mixed in with the sandy soil all over the ground. They gleamed in the sunlight. Inside, I could hear the ocean all around, but I couldn't see it. It sounded a little bit like a highway, only deeper and with more rhythm. The soap dish on the sink was actually a clamshell turned on its back. It made me think of Mandy: She had an entire cottage room made of seashells.

As I washed my hands and splashed cold water on my face, I heard men's voices speaking a language I'd only heard on TV and from the father and son who sold bagels and doughnuts from the truck across the street from school. The words were fast and harsh with a lot of consonants and *ch* sounds. It must have been Russian. I listened, wondering if it would be possible to guess the meaning of a word, but I couldn't even figure out when one word ended and another one began.

When I stepped out of the bathroom, I saw three females who hadn't been there minutes earlier. Two looked about eighteen or nineteen years old. They were white and sat straight on a sky-blue couch, their pretty knees nearly touching a wooden coffee table. Except for the shadows beneath their light eyes, these two girls were more beautiful and perfect than any real person I had ever seen. Their backs were straight as ladders, and their faces had no expression at all. They were like mannequins. Opposite them on a matching couch was an amber-skinned man sitting next to one of Daddy's cardboard boxes, and Daddy, who ignored me completely. He was looking at the girls. It didn't seem like he could look away. I tried to notice if I cared or if I felt jealous, but I couldn't understand what I felt. All I could think about was L.A.'s tooth skittering off the back of my hand and when Daddy washed me himself the night he turned me out and the way his voice sounded when he shut himself in his room and spoke on the phone.

Standing behind the white girls were two other men.

White men; one huge and bald and the other medium-size with shiny black curls.

The third female was a cute little maybe-white girl with sandy-colored skin and pretty hair and a glow. She was sitting at a bar stool, up at the counter, spinning slightly right and then left, holding Daddy's cell phone, playing Angry Birds. I knew by the sounds. She was dressed in spotless pink-and-white sneakers, pink shorts, and a T-shirt with silver glitter letters that said FRESH.

"This Dime," Daddy told the girl. She looked up. "Take them bags and go on out to the car." He looked at me. "This Lollipop." The prize.

"Where's Uncle Ray?" Lollipop asked Daddy.

"He driving up separate," Daddy told her. "We going to meet him in a few days."

"Okay." Lollipop picked up a pink suitcase and a white suitcase by the handles, one with each hand. "Hi," she said to me. She looked at the beautiful white girls. "Bye," she said. They looked back at her blankly. One of them said something to the other in the same language the men had been using. The other one shrugged. Then Lollipop looked at the three men. "Bye," she told them, sliding off the stool. The two Russians laughed, and it seemed like they laughed in English, but then they muttered something back and forth and that was in Russian. The amber-skinned man nodded slightly to Lollipop. He had a skinny nose and full lips. He looked more Native American than he looked black, but he looked black, too.

I led her out the door and carried one of her bags to the car: the white one, since it would get dirtier than the pink. She realized pretty fast how sandy and dusty her pink would get if she continued to pull it on its wheels, so she stopped rolling and lifted it instead. "Uncle Ray carried it in for me before," she explained.

With her bags in the back, nobody could lie down now. L.A. wasn't happy about moving to the front seat. But L.A. wasn't happy about anything right then.

"What happened to your face?" Lollipop asked her, climbing in to sit with me and Brandy.

"Shut the fuck up," L.A. told her. Even though her mouth was swollen unrecognizably, I could still see the new black gap on the top front.

Lollipop blinked. "Oh," she said. "Well, I can run back in and get ice," she offered.

"Ice?" L.A. asked. "Ice?"

I don't know what they said next because Daddy was calling me, and I had to get back out of the car and go see what he wanted.

"This my brother," Daddy told me, while I stood by the bar stool where Lollipop was just sitting. "Bird, this Dime."

Daddy was dark and Bird was amber and their features didn't look at all alike, but I was wise enough by then not to say so. "Nice to meet you."

"See?" Daddy smiled. "She polite."

"She skinny," Bird said.

"She going to grow. Also, she look better bare-assed."

Bird laughed. "That right?"

"She smart. And she obedient," Daddy said.

One of the Russian girls said something, and the enormous bald man said something back. Then he spoke to Bird, or to Daddy, or maybe to both.

"These girls believe they will owe to you nothing after they earn and pay to you two thousand dollars." He spoke with that accent.

Daddy's gold *D* flashed, and Bird smiled too. His teeth were tiny, and his gums were big. Like the way the mouths of some small children look. "That's real entertaining," Daddy said.

The Russian man shrugged.

Daddy watched the shrug, seeming to think about something for a quick minute. Then his face froze over the way it did sometimes when he was mad on the phone or at L.A. "They was supposed to come turned out already."

The bald one shrugged again and spoke over the other one, who was jabbering in Russian to the girls, who were jabbering back. "You don't want, I sell to someone else."

Daddy sat back, staring. "Well, you ain't getting what got guaranteed, then." He pulled up one flap of the cardboard box sitting between him and Bird and pulled out cash. Handfuls of cash. I was shocked to see him handle money in front of me. Was it everything we had earned? Three girls and we'd been working every day for eight days. Each of us earned close to a thousand dollars a day, so was that twenty-four thousand dollars' worth of cash?

He gathered the cash into his lap, guarding it with his palms domed over the pile. Then he nodded at the cardboard box. "You want to count it, go ahead. Going to take you a while."

The black-haired man threw a warning look at his friend and then walked over to pick up the box. "We will count," he said, and they both went into another room, closing the door behind them.

The Russian girls began talking rapidly again, to each other, to Daddy and Bird, to me. I didn't have to understand their language to know they were worried.

"Ten grand." I heard Daddy mumble to Bird, ignoring the beautiful girls.

"Word?" Bird seemed impressed.

"Twenty and . . ." Daddy lowered his voice so I couldn't hear what else he was saying.

If ten grand was in the box, where was the rest? Where was Daddy keeping fourteen grand? Or was there twenty in the box? If so, where was the other four?

"You break them in and train them up correct, they going to bring us ten times that." Daddy eyed them while they tried to tell us or ask us something. "You ever seen hos so fine?"

"Nah," Bird said. He glanced over at me. "What she staring at?" I guess Daddy forgot I was standing there.

"Shit, Dime," he said.

I was quiet. Now the girls were, too. We—all three of us— were nervous. They were nervous because the truth was hovering in the salt air, and they could taste it and almost see it. I was nervous because Daddy could read my mind, and even though I wasn't planning to take any of his money, it wouldn't be good if he knew I was even thinking about his money.

Daddy laughed. He looked at the Russian girls and at Bird. "She love me," he told them, pointing his thumb at me as if he were hitch-hiking. "This bitch here looooove me."

It was a belly punch. Leaving my gut seared and empty. Because all of a sudden I knew it wasn't true anymore. It hadn't been true for days, maybe even for weeks. I hadn't known it a minute ago, or maybe it was that I had, back on the shoulder of the highway, or even before that, only I hadn't let myself admit it. But then, now Daddy said, *This bitch here looooove me*, in that ugly way he had of speaking to me or about me, and it was like I woke up or I opened my eyes or my heart started beating again. My belly burned. *He doesn't love me.* Scorched. *He never loved me.* Hot lava and laser beams. *I have nobody.*

I used the internal tricks Brandy had taught me about how to make my face lie. Because I was scared of what might happen if Daddy realized my insides had just imploded.

"Don't tell L.A. or any of them nothing you heard just now," Daddy warned me. "You tell them I had you unpacking shit before we left out a here."

"Don't tell them I met your brother?" I asked. *That's not his brother.* It didn't matter. *He doesn't love me.* It didn't matter.

"Don't tell them I got a brother."

I wanted to fall down, but I had to show him the same self he thought he knew.

"You my best," Daddy said. "Why I'm going to tell anybody but my best all my business?"

He never loved me. "But isn't L.A. . . . ." *I have nobody.* "I mean. . . ."

"L.A. staying back home," Daddy said. "You the one coming down here. After we get Lollipop and indoor set, you coming down here to run my down south Russian stable." He looked at the Russian girls and then back at me, grinning. "You got your work cut out for you if you going to earn more than these bitches and stay my Bottom." He chuckled, smirking with Bird. "Better find you some game."

I thought I heard him wrong.

He could tell. "L.A. going to be my Bottom Bitch up north. You going to be my Bottom Bitch down south. When I'm gone, Bird going to be your Uncle. You answer to him."

Two stables? Two Bottoms? An Uncle instead of Daddy? *I have nobody.* My stomach was melting nails. I looked at the new girls. "But they're older than I am." *I have nothing.*

"You more seasoned. You going to make more money." He grinned. "Until you don't. Then you might just find your ass replaced."

Atticus Finch spoke to me then from inside my gummy paperback, lying on the floor of the Escalade, parked on thousand-year-old seashells. *"Courage is not a man with a gun in his hand. It's knowing that you're licked before you begin but you begin anyway and you see it through no matter what."*

"Two thousand," the girl with the brown eyes told Daddy. She looked at him with her chin held high. I half expected him to punch her.

Daddy shook his head. "Sorry, sister," he told her. "I don't know why your man wasn't straight with you, but it ain't no two thousand. It ain't like that."

"Two thousand," the other girl said. "We clean house many house many day, we earn two thousand, we pay to you for that airplanes ticket, we pay to you for sleep and for finding job, then we continue clean house, we hold money, we have American life, we finish you, we do not give to you more."

I stayed still and quiet, hoping Daddy could not hear the heat screaming inside my belly. *He never saw me.*

The Russian men returned from the other room with the cardboard box. How much of the money L.A. and Brandy and I made was in that box?

"What bullshit you told them?" Daddy asked the men.

"Money good," the black-haired man said, ignoring the question.

"You better communicate to these bitches on what they in now." Daddy was getting agitated. I could tell by the way his eyes angled downward more. By the way the scar got covered over by the two unharmed halves of his eyebrow. By the way he started breathing through his nose, his nostrils flaring. *He never saw me. He never loved me.*

The bald man sighed. The black-haired man shook his head at the girls.

Suddenly I wondered what was happening in the car outside. L.A. and Brandy must have opened the doors for a breeze. Maybe with Lollipop they even scattered out of the car to stretch their legs. L.A. could have already popped Lollipop a few times. It was even possible they were picking up sparkling bits of shells or walking toward the smell of the southern ocean.

"Courage is not a man with a gun."

The black-haired man kept shaking his head as he explained something that took a long minute. The girls began yelling. They stood up. They were not mannequins anymore. They were angry girls, like any angry girls anywhere. They were scared girls, like any scared girls anywhere. They were panicked girls.

"Mine mother!" the gray-eyed one screamed at the Russians and at Daddy and Bird. "Mine mother!"

And the blue-eyed one was crying and shaking her finger, just like we did, we black girls back in Newark, New Jersey. "No!" she shouted, slicing the air. "No, *nyet*, no! We will not!"

"This how you do business?" Daddy yelled over them, to the Russian men. "Bitches was supposed to come broken in!"

The black-haired one shrugged. "Give to us the money you removed, and we will break them for you," he offered. "We do here now. Few hours. Finish."

"Shit," Daddy said. "Fuck." He shook his head at Bird, nostrils wide. Then he handed over his pile of bills.

The black-haired Russian added the money to his cardboard box and then punched each beautiful, angry girl on the side of her head, almost faster than I could see. They fell quiet and down, caught by the sky couch and by the coffee table. The bald Russian yanked the blue-eyed girl around and then tore her shirt.

"I'm out," Daddy muttered to Bird. "I ain't watching this shit. Text me when it done."

Bird grinned at how the black-haired Russian dragged the gray-eyed girl by the hair. "I'm in."

Chapter Twenty-Five

DADDY DIDN'T WORK us the same on the way home as he did on the way down south. We drove straight through. It took us two long days and one night in a motel where we actually were allowed to sleep. I shared a bed with Brandy and Lollipop. Daddy shared the other bed with L.A.

I didn't know how to keep on being without Daddy's loving me, without me loving him. I didn't know anything anymore.

Savage, I thought to myself all night, holding as still and as straight as possible so I wouldn't roll over the edge of the crowded mattress. *Savage* was what L.A. had called him. And he had liked it.

L.A. and me and Brandy. We all chose him. The shame was hot coals inside my belly. Because despite everything, that's what I still believed. That I chose Daddy. *But those girls didn't choose.* The Asian ones from the truck stop. *Hepeese. Stowen.* And the beautiful ones. *They were played.* I didn't want to remember what I saw Bird and the Russian men perpetrating on those two in that house with the seashell soap dish. *They didn't even choose,* I thought, while Lollipop's small body made mine sticky with her sleep sweat.

And Daddy was going to make me be their Bottom. He didn't even love me. *He never loved me.*

"Could we pull over, please?" Lollipop asked as we crossed the Chesapeake Bay Bridge-Tunnel. It was early, and she was squirming next to me. "I think I might be sick."

I scrunched away from her, pressing up against Brandy. "Look the other way," Brandy ordered. "Throw up on me and you not going to live to see Newark."

Daddy pulled over in a spot where you could see the gray-green water chopping below at splayed bridge columns, like giants' teeth. Lollipop jumped out of the car, leaned over, and vomited more neatly than I'd ever seen. So neatly it made me admire her. I handed over a crushed napkin from the car seat, and she uncrushed it and wiped her mouth clean.

"Thank you," she said, to all of us, buckling herself back in.

Daddy was silent. A bad silence. Angry and impatient.

I was never beautiful. My belly burned.

He pulled back onto the bridge road. A minute or two after it dipped into a tunnel, he spoke to us in the dark. "When we home," he told us, "I'm setting up a computer in L.A.'s room. Lollipop going to spend her first days in there. L.A., you going back into the living room. Share that couch with Brandy."

L.A.'s face flattened, but she kept her swollen mouth shut. Daddy drove us uphill onto more bridge and thumbed his phone at the same time. A car honked and slid past us.

"Did you know you're not supposed to text and drive?" Lollipop said. "The TV says it's more dangerous than drunk driving."

"You got an attitude, little girl," Brandy muttered. Then she poked me. "That one need to get a piece of afraid." I nodded, trying to act regular, the way I'd been trying to act for days. It was hard, with my insides burning up.

"I was just saying," Lollipop said. "I wasn't sure he knew."

Nobody spoke. She was looking anxiously at the back of Daddy's head. "Uncle Ray said you two are just setting me up in a new spot up north. Uncle Ray says it's good to travel to new spots."

Lollipop spoke like I did. *Standard English,* Ms. McClenny

explained to us once. *It's not the only way. It's just the standard way. But like it or not, it will get you further in life. And that is something worth considering.* It made me wonder about who Lollipop grew up around. About Lollipop's uncle Ray. Did he love her the way she seemed to love him? *Daddy. Never. Loved me.*

"Who is Uncle Ray supposed to be?" Brandy asked quietly.

"You're going to see him," Lollipop explained. "He's driving right now to meet us, right?"

Daddy didn't answer.

"What am I supposed to call him?" Lollipop asked me. I looked at the back of Daddy's head too. It was square. I never noticed that before. He had finally put his phone down and had one hand on the steering wheel and the other resting on his crotch. A part of me wanted him to turn around and flash his gold *D* at me. But if he did, it would only be a lie.

"Daddy," I told her. I tried not to choke.

She smiled. "That's what all the dates tell me to call them," she tittered. "Uncle Ray is the only one I never call Daddy."

She was so young to be turned out already. To be talking about dates already. It was hard enough to know that now I was nothing but a *ho*. Somehow, it was harder to think of her as one. *I chose.*

"Daddy," Lollipop said in a louder voice. "Uncle Ray is meeting us as soon as we get to New York, right?"

"Newark," Brandy said. "New York the next one up."

"Nah," Daddy called back to Lollipop. "Your uncle Ray going to visit you some other time." Lies.

I was never his best. I was never his anything.

Lollipop's forehead wrinkled, and she pressed her lips together. "You said he was meeting me up in New"—she glanced at Brandy—"Newark."

"Plans changed," Daddy said. "He got business."

I watched Lollipop's face become a wall. A pretty little sandy-colored wall.

"Ohhh," L.A. said suddenly. She smiled at Daddy, her lip fat and her gap black and big in her mouth. It made her seem silly, if you forgot a minute that she was L.A. "You going to put me indoor in my own motel room, huh?"

Brandy and I looked at each other. Was that it? Were we all going to our own rooms in a motel somewhere? While in the apartment Lollipop pranced around naked in front of the computer camera?

Indoor or outdoor, I thought. *It doesn't matter. There are no big plans for me. I'm not special. I never was.*

"Shut it, all a you," Daddy said. "You going to see when you see."

Chapter Twenty-Six

IT'S BEEN ABOUT a month and a half since I understood what I'm going to have to do. Over these past few days I've been settled on using Money. But the more I write in my head, the more I worry Money might disgust readers so much that they would turn away from my note almost as soon as they begin it. And then my plan would fail.

So I start all over, looking at the problem every possible way, trying as hard as I can to come up with a better idea. What voice could I borrow? What could work that I haven't already considered? Maybe I should go back to the idea of using an actual person instead of a concept. But I can't think who. I wish I could somehow be inside *The Color Purple* and write a letter to Nettie: *As you can see,* I could say, *I need to make this note perfect, and I would very much appreciate your advice. . . .* I ruminate on it while I'm in the shower and while I'm eating and lying or standing or crouching under or over or sideways whatever john happens to be there. I think and think some more while I'm riding in the back of the Escalade, and while L.A. and Brandy snap at me to pay attention, to stop spacing out.

Then, finally, driving by the track, seeing Whippet up on the curb screaming at a new turnout down in the street, it comes to me: Truth. Doesn't the Bible, or Atticus Finch, or somebody else important say, *The truth shall set you free?* If I do it right, it could be perfect.

I respect the fact that you might not like me, Truth could begin. *But I'm hoping you are the kind of person who wouldn't want to ignore me either. Please hear me out. I will try to be quick. I know it's too late for the girls involved, but I still need to tell you some of me about their lives.* It's a pattern I think I've noticed. And the more of the pattern I realize is there, the more important it seems.

The one called Brandy had a grandmother in the very beginning. After that grandmother died, Brandy lived in seven homes over eleven years. Most of those places were just training for the street. The ones that weren't couldn't keep her long for one reason or another. At twelve they shot her up with heroin. After that she got lost in the life, chasing that high. She chose up or was sold from pimp to pimp until she was saved by her Daddy.

L.A. was raised by her own family. By now I think Brandy had told me everything there was to know about L.A. *Everybody in L.A.'s family was messed up worse than you can imagine. She was confused and scared and bruised and sore and mad all the time. At fourteen L.A. ran away. She survived the only way she knew how—by sex. At sixteen she was rescued by the Daddy she'll never willingly leave.*

The girl who attached this note, Truth would explain about me, *did live at first with someone who loved her. But she mainly remembers only a worn-out foster mother. During those nine or ten years, she slapped off boys inside her own home and also two school security guards, two bodega owners, and one neighbor. She was already lonely and cold often, but when her foster mother began to drink, this girl felt scared, too.*

In many ways, these girls were different from each other, Truth would say—because that's true. *But the things they wanted made them the same.* I've been noticing this ever since down south. Noticing the pattern and how it makes us the same even though we are all different. *The things they wanted led them to the same household, to the same life inside the life. The things they wanted were not what they got, regardless of what these girls believed. But they were things other people had and seemed worth hoping for.*

To be touched gently.
To be seen clearly.
To be part of a family.
To be fed regularly.
To be protected.
To be loved for free.
   *I know it must be hard to listen to me. And as I've said, I
know I'm not all that likable. But I am Truth. And this is impor-
tant information for you to have. Maybe it will convince you to do
what I am asking.*

Things happened so quickly after we arrived home. Lollipop
got the bedroom. Daddy made us take everything out of it
except for the bed and a lamp and the chest of drawers. He
made us put Lollipop's clothes—and she had a lot—in those
drawers. In the living room, we piled cardboard boxes filled
with our clothes and with soap and shampoo and razors.
Underneath the coffee table became where we could find
our hair product, extra toilet paper, makeup, and smaller
clothes like socks and panties and bras.

   The other boxes with our shirts and skirts and jeans
and sweats were lined up along the hallway by the front
door and also bookended the head and feet of my sleeping
bag in the alcove.

Lollipop kept asking when Uncle Ray was coming, but it was the bald-headed Russian from down south who arrived instead. He just walked in with Daddy three days after we got home and went right to work on Lollipop's brand-new computer. Daddy called him Eagle. He spent a day and a half in Lollipop's room, swearing in Russian and asking Daddy for new passwords every hour. I guess displaying a naked little girl on a live feed must be much more complicated than just setting up a regular camera.

The rest of us were banned from that room completely. "Can't have no recognizing nothing in there. No people. Blank wall. That's it." Daddy even painted over in white so there weren't marks anywhere somebody could identify in the future.

Once the computer was ready, Lollipop was not allowed out all day except for an hour on the front steps after schools let out. Daddy wasn't worried about the neighbors. Nobody asked anybody questions much anyway, and people were used to seeing nieces and girl cousins or family friends come and go. *She shy,* he told us he was planning to say if he had to. *Real shy, so we homeschooling that one.*

Even for peeing, Lollipop had to squat over a bowl in her room, in front of the camera. She was supposed to empty and wash it herself the next morning.

When Brandy heard that, she clicked her tongue with disgust. "Perverts want to see you pee?" she asked.

Lollipop shrugged. "I don't know," she said. "I just go when I have to go."

"Your room going to stink."

"I don't usually pee much anyway." Lollipop shrugged.

"Don't you get sick of being stuck in there?" Brandy asked when the four of us were eating breakfast together the second morning after Lollipop's computer was set up. Daddy was out.

"Somebody might snatch me if I go out," Lollipop said. "One of my fans might."

I flipped my spoon over and over. My insides hadn't unclenched since down south. The hot fists in my belly made it hard to eat, and the truth made it hard to think.

"Your fans?" L.A. said. "You serious?" Her lip was almost down to normal size now. She poked her tongue in the space where her tooth used to be. It was a new habit of hers.

The locks on the doors turned and Daddy walked in. L.A. looked at him. "What about school for her?"

"I don't go to school," Lollipop answered.

"They going to come looking," Brandy said.

"Shut your mouths." Daddy sat at the table. L.A. poured Lucky Charms for him. I noticed a new chain around his neck and a watch I'd never seen on his wrist. They weren't extra large or flashy, but L.A. once showed me platinum on a date during a three-way we had to do, and I'm pretty sure Daddy's new jewelry was platinum too.

"She only ten," L.A. pointed out. "They going to come looking for a ten-year-old."

"Actually, I'm eleven," Lollipop said.

I tried to keep my expression normal, the way I had been trying for days. It was difficult not to let my face crumple every second for wishing the truth wasn't true. *I have nothing.*

"Nobody know nothing about Lollipop." Daddy poured his own milk when he wasn't eating his cereal dry. It had to be just the right amount, and none of us could ever do it correctly for him. While he poured, his watch caught the sun from the windows and threw jerking lines of light onto the ceiling. "Quit nagging at me."

L.A. looked at Lollipop. "Where your family?"

"Just Uncle Ray as long as I can remember."

I flipped my spoon over and over, stopping every now and then to sift Special K.

"This messed up," Brandy muttered.

"She fucked already?" L.A. asked Daddy.

I daydreamed about shoving the spoon handle in L.A.'s eye.

"Or just do what she do in front of the computer by herself?"

"Don't make me tell you shut up again." He said it with his full. Then he nodded my way. "Why you not eating?"

I slid some cereal into my mouth and chewed. I made myself keep chewing. Daddy winked at me, and when I faked a smile back at him, the fists unclenched and became smoldering spikes.

Lollipop was nodding. "Yes." She spoke earnestly, but with a little bit of swagger, as if it was important to her that we were impressed. "I was so good on the Internet Uncle Ray said my fans could start visiting me in person as soon as I turned eleven."

Brandy bugged her eyes at Daddy. "This is messed up," she said. "This is serious messed up."

"Don't make me tell you again neither." He texted something and spoke next to Lollipop. "You talk too much."

"It's funny, right?" Lollipop whispered to us girls as if Daddy couldn't hear. "All the things the men like to do. Only some of them like to pet you gently. I like that, but not the rest. But Uncle Ray said it's worth the money, and I agree because then I get everything I want pink and purple."

I forced myself to swallow, hoping the mush of milk and cereal wouldn't come spraying back up and out.

Brandy pushed her bowl into the center of the table, leaned back, and glared at Daddy.

"I'm really good at it, you know." Lollipop smiled. "Uncle Ray taught me if you pretend the parts that hurt don't hurt and that it all feels good and you like it, they give you even more money."

I swiveled my head at Brandy, who'd taught me the very same thing so well. She was eyeing laser beams at Daddy. "Your uncle Ray sound like a piece of work," she said.

Even L.A. looked gray in the face. But in a second I could see it wasn't for the right reasons. "You going to give her dates?" she asked Daddy.

"Dime." Daddy ignored her and pointed to my bowl. "Why you not eating?"

I kept my face regular and scooped more flakes into my mouth. He had always been so good at reading my mind. *You never loved me.* I couldn't let him read my mind then. I was afraid of what he might do. Put me out. Sell me. *Ho.*

"You going to give Lollipop dates?" L.A. asked again.

I thought he might reach over and swat her hard, but he grinned down at his phone. "She going to make us rich."

I swallowed back another gag.

L.A. stood from her chair, gap flashing, hands on her

hips. "You going to make a ten-year-old the Bottom next, she going to earn you so much coins?"

"Sit down, bitch," Daddy said. "I'm not making no little girl Bottom."

"I'm not ten." Lollipop slurped up her pink hearts and purple moon marshmallows, which she must have been saving for last. "I'm eleven."

Forgive me, Truth would request. *But I must continue. You won't like the story of the newest and youngest. However, you must hear me out and believe me. I am, after all, Truth.*

Chapter Twenty-Seven

BRANDY WAS HAVING her period, so maybe that's what was adding to her bad mood. L.A. was always telling her she should just go on Depo so she wouldn't bleed as often, but Brandy said Depo gave her side effects. Daddy didn't care what method we chose from the clinic as long as we didn't get pregnant and made him his money. Brandy's problem was that even though she wouldn't go on Depo, she hated doing the other things johns always insisted on if it was her time of month.

That day she decided she was furious that Lollipop got the entire second bedroom all to herself. "Perverts got to watch her sleep, too?" Brandy said, outraged. It had been like this for a few weeks. She always was more audacious with Daddy on her period, but ever since she saw me crying in the car right before we picked up Lollipop, she had been bolder than ever. "Pee and sleep?"

"Shut up," Daddy warned. When he glanced at his new watch, I noticed an even newer ring on his finger. A thick gold band that looked real with a flat top edged in tiny diamonds. Real. All of it real. It was the first ring I ever saw him wear. It looked good. Solid and serious. How much did a ring like that cost? How many dates' worth? My insides were still fists clenched and unclenched, spikes, and lava.

"Nice, right?" Daddy asked me quietly. He had noticed my glance.

Pretend. "It's really nice."

"Sometimes I don't sleep," Lollipop was explaining. "Sometimes they call in for a live show. Then I have to wake up and do stuff."

Brandy wrinkled her nose. "That's disgusting."

"You looking run out," Daddy murmured to me. "Since down south." The spikes in my belly burned. "You getting skinny."

"I'm good," I lied. *Don't let him read your mind.* Where would I go?

"I'm a get you a ring like this," he whispered. "Cheer you up, Beautiful."

I ducked my face the way I guess I always did. I tried

to look shy the way I guess I always did too. He kissed my forehead and whispered again. "Brandy a complaining little bitch." His breath was warm on my ear. "She do good to learn from you."

I made my face do what it must have always done before when he was close, talking to me like that, like I was his beautiful best. But the searing in my belly felt nothing like the slow melt that used to feel so good.

"Her in the bedroom means you off the track, ho," Daddy told Brandy. "Stop sweating me when I'm making life better for you."

Daddy and Eagle drove us to work. Eagle drove a black Lincoln town car and Daddy still had the Escalade. He paid for two hotel rooms next to each other inside a big hotel that had bulletproof glass at the front desk and a little store with T-shirts and candy. We switched off locations—outdoor or indoor—depending on things only Daddy understood.

I didn't know where Eagle stayed, but now he also drove us to outcalls at indoor locations other than the main hotel: apartments and other hotels and motels. Sometimes to a room in an office building. At parties the men were louder and ruder and showed off more. It was harder to smile and pretend you enjoyed it. There was never a safe moment to allow your face to arrange itself naturally and get the disgust out. It was tiring always having to pretend without any love anywhere, and it made it hard for me to think, hard for me to make a plan, to remember that maybe I needed a plan.

I didn't like Eagle, either. Mostly I didn't like him because I was afraid of him. In the down south house, I'd seen a minute of what he could do and what he seemed to enjoy doing, and I didn't want to be alone with him in a car or anywhere. But I had no say. So far, he hadn't given me more than a glance. He never spoke to me or to any of us, unless he had to. I don't know where he lived, unless maybe it was in the town car. I couldn't tell if Daddy paid Eagle or if it was the other way around. Daddy must have been texting him and talking to him on the phone, because Eagle always knew when to pick us up and where to drive.

I saw things I'd never seen, driving around Newark. The huge courthouses with their wide lawns, like parks. So many churches built out of gray or wine-colored stones, like castles. Twice, at dusk, a pair of girl-boys walking a track for their pimp. The train station with its curved, decorated entrance. The river beneath all those bridges sparkling in a winding band. And a group of greened statues halfway up the front of a building, guarding a massive arched doorway. I'd noticed them a few times before I noticed the letters below: FREE

PUBLIC LIBRARY. It was the main branch—the one where that librarian had said she usually worked.

I saw a lot driving to outcalls, but I would rather have stayed in the hotel room. It was comfortable with a real bed and air-conditioning and a bathroom. And a lot of the time, I could shower between tricks. And I could sit or lie down instead of walk and walk and walk. Whippet and Stone weren't around to stress me out, and I usually only had one client at a time. The hotel wasn't far from the airport, for the johns. I could hear the planes all the time. I liked hearing those planes. I liked imagining where all the people on them were going, where they were from. Imagining that distracted me from myself, from the panic of having nothing. Imagining cooled down the constant fire in my gut.

Best of all, though. Best about being indoor was that sometimes, between dates, I could read. And when I read, I could be inside my shell on a boat, far away.

I had cleaned *To Kill a Mockingbird* so well that you could hardly see what L.A. had done to it with her pink gum. Five pages had torn, but I taped them with the Scotch tape I smuggled into the hotel room from the bottom kitchen drawer at home. And the day I sat next to Scout in the courtroom, falling asleep and then waking to Tom Robinson being found guilty, I was so upset that I begged Eagle to send my next date elsewhere and text Daddy that I was too sick to work.

"You do not look sick," Eagle had said.

I tried to keep back the tears, hating what Maycomb County had done to Tom Robinson, hating how unfair it all was.

But Eagle sent in my john anyway, and I knew he texted Daddy.

When I finished the book, it was back home, inside my sleeping bag with the flashlight. My head was aching from the pounding Daddy had given me for mouthing off to Eagle and trying to skip dates. My empty stomach simmered. I turned to page one and began to read it all over again. It was as good as anything by Stephen King or Suzanne Collins. Better.

Daddy had more money than ever. He wore a new outfit almost every day now, including shoes. He never took off that flat-topped ring, but now he had a different watch for each day, and he switched out his chain and earring almost every day too. He didn't overdo it like pimps in the movies. He never chose anything too big or wore too much at once. But everything on him was real. You didn't have to be an expert to see that.

He bought us all new work clothes too. We got to pick what we liked and not share anymore. He let us get our hair done properly. And our nails. He gave us each a fourteen-karat gold chain with the letter *D* on it, to match his tooth. Mine matched my name, too—before down south I would have thought he planned that out for me somehow. We looked better than we ever had. We smelled better.

But we still lived in the same apartment. I had it best, except for Lollipop. Because the alcove, especially with the cardboard boxes for a headboard and footboard, was a little bit private, and private meant you could read or imagine yourself anywhere else. Maybe L.A. wasn't acting as mad as Brandy those days, because she had the couch and Brandy was back on the floor, nose to nose with the box of tampons. L.A. thought the couch was the best, since she was up off the floor. I wasn't going to argue. It was better if L.A. thought she was getting more than I was. She'd be mad enough when she found out I was going to be a Bottom Bitch too. Even if it was down south.

"This such bullshit," Brandy said. "I don't even have no phone yet."

"Keep fussing and you not getting no phone," Daddy told her.

"L.A. fusses all the damn time, and she got a phone."

"L.A. Bottom Bitch, and she been got her phone, so shut up about the goddamn phone." Then he winked at me when Brandy couldn't see, as if to say, *Don't worry. When you get down south, you going to have you own phone.* It made the heat in my stomach lurch up into my mouth, a sour, burning clump.

The first time that clump came up was when he had taken me earlier that day. He had been tender, and I tried to look at him the way I used to, and I faked flying, hoping he wouldn't be able to tell. It was harder—much harder—than pretending with dates. I was afraid of what Daddy would do if he realized. If he put me out, George and Whippet might take me for theirs. I didn't want to have to drink and stay high for George, and I didn't want to have to pick a specialty for Whippet, the way he made his girls do. I didn't want to have to be a ho anymore. But I chose it, so now that's all there was for me.

Brandy was looking at Daddy with her face twisted into an expression I'd never seen on her before. "You got enough coins to get me a stupid phone," she said. "You just a asshole."

Even L.A. got still.

"Brandy!" I hissed. If Daddy decided to beat her to death, I wouldn't have one friend left in the world.

She ignored me. "You a motherfucking dog." Her voice

was quiet, but her chin was up, under her twisted face, like that Russian girl's had been down south.

Daddy kicked her right in the middle of that twist. Out of the corner of my eye, I saw Lollipop go statue while Brandy went down. Daddy kicked her again. I looked away to see L.A. smirking.

Daddy stopped as suddenly as he had started. "Get back to work," he told Lollipop. "Take care a her," he told me, meaning take care of Brandy. "Come on," he told L.A. "You going on a outcall. Overnight."

L.A. beamed, flashing her gap the way Daddy flashed his gold *D*. She loved overnights. She liked how easy she thought they were. Truthfully, L.A. seemed to like the sex sometimes. Not on the street on a long, hot day, and not when we were down south. But there were times since we'd been indoor, or before when I'd had to do three-ways with her in the alley, when it didn't seem like she was pretending. Not that a date would know the difference. But I might.

I'd been on two overnight outcalls, and I hated them. One john tried to talk to me about normal things, like where did I grow up, and what was my favorite color. He had another girl there too. She was white, and she said she worked for herself with no daddy. She said she kept all her money and lived with her cousin in their own apartment. She said they were paying for college doing outcalls. She didn't want to three-way with me, maybe because I was black or maybe because it was obvious I had a Daddy and wasn't going to college. But the john offered her more money to cooperate, so she did. That might be the date I hated the most in all my time working.

The other outcall that went all night tied me up. When he finished, he left me trussed up for hours before he came back. The only good thing about that one was he left the TV on and I got to see the entire documentary about those elephants.

"Eagle driving me?" L.A. asked.

"You mess with Eagle, and I will kill you." Daddy didn't want anybody getting anything for free from one of his bitches. And he didn't want any of us catching feelings for anybody but him and then making any mad moves.

I gathered ice, a few Ziploc bags, and some paper towels. Lollipop went back to her room quietly, her face staying so still. Daddy and L.A. left. I helped Brandy onto the couch.

"Better not let me bleed all over L.A.'s pillow," she told me.

"When did you get so uppity?" I was hoping to make her laugh. *Uppity* was L.A.'s word.

She didn't laugh. "I'm not uppity," she said. "I'm just wore out. Getting locked up wore me out. That cop wore me out. Down south wore me out."

I slid my fingers along the edge of a Ziploc bag, sealing in ice. Then I wrapped it in a paper towel. I lay the ice bag down on her right ribs as best I could.

She winced. "You going down south and I'm stuck up here with L.A. and I ain't never going to Disney World."

I dropped the other ice bag. It burst, sending ice everywhere. How did she know? Had Daddy told her? "Disneywhat?"

She tried to shrug, but winced again instead. "You heard me."

"He's taking you to Florida?" I knew I shouldn't let the ice melt into cold puddles, but I couldn't look away from Brandy.

"He's not taking me to shit," Brandy said. "He said if I brang home fifteen hundred every night for two weeks straight, he would, and I was almost there."

I was thinking fast to follow what she was saying. She knew Daddy was planning on sending me down south. Did that mean that L.A. knew too?

"But now he about to have two stables to run, and I can't earn for days until I heal up, and I'm going to be stuck up here with L.A. behind all of that."

"Daddy told you?"

She shook her head. "I heard him and Eagle talking

outside the hotel door when I was with a trick." She eyed me. "How long you knew?"

"Since the day we picked up Lollipop." I couldn't look at her, so I got on my knees to clean up the wet spots.

"Why didn't you say nothing?"

Because even though I trusted her the most, it wasn't enough? Because I was afraid Daddy would find out I'd told her, and if he found out I disobeyed him, I might get beaten, or worse? I wiped up the mess as best as I could and finally looked at Brandy again.

She rolled her eyes, which must have been difficult, because one was swollen shut. "I probably wouldn't have said nothing neither." The cut over her eye started oozing again, so I dabbed at it with the wet paper towel. "He wasn't taking me to no Disney World anyway," Brandy said. "Daddy full of shit." Then her one good eye filled up, spilling over.

"You want ice for your eye?" It was the same one the cop got that time. She nodded.

While I put it together, she said, "I still got that card." At first I didn't know what she was talking about. "It fit perfect underneath my powder. The powder dish part come right out."

I could picture it. The circle of face powder lifting off its rectangular base. The card from when she got arrested, tucked away. The one with the lady from that place that say they get girls out of the life. *Pamela Terrence. The North Star.* I could borrow L.A.'s phone when she was in the shower. Or I could ask to use somebody's phone. A john's phone. I couldn't text Pamela Terrence from someone else's phone, but I could call. Only who was Pamela Terrence, anyway, and how did I know she wasn't going to lock me up?

"You still want him like that?" Brandy asked.

I couldn't believe I'd ever wanted him the way I'd wanted him. It made me feel like a true ho. The shame of it hurt worse than my scorched insides.

Brandy nodded as if I'd said something she agreed with, even though I hadn't said anything. "I'm not using no card," she said. "My place with Daddy." She glanced at me with her one good eye and then glanced away. "He save my life." I tried to think if that was true, but it was so hard to think sometimes. "He love me," Brandy said. "Only one who ever did." She touched her swollen eyelid. "I piss him off is all."

I stayed quiet, wondering what was true and who got to decide. If I told Brandy that Daddy didn't love her, would I be right? And if I was right, would she believe it? For her sake, I didn't want to be right. I wanted him to love her, even though the idea of him loving her and not me made the burning spread upward from my belly into my heart, and it hurt.

"It under my powder. Stupid card. The little round part come right out. Don't forget."

I stayed silent.

"You got to watch out for L.A.," Brandy warned. "She lost that tooth and look all ugly and now she getting crazier than ever."

I thought she looked ugly. But I guessed a lot of dates liked her mouth freaky like that.

We heard vomiting sounds coming from Lollipop's room. We were forbidden to open the door. We listened, and it stopped. But later, at lunch, she came out with a stinking bowl full of puke. She cleaned it out in the bathroom without a word.

Nobody was sure where she came from, Truth would write. Lollipop had some guesses, and once I got her talking a little, it was hard to shut her up. *Maybe she was sold by her mother or by someone else without her mother's permission, or kidnapped. Her beginning is muddy, but Uncle Ray is clear. He never let her go to school. She lived in apartments and motel rooms, not allowed out of them during school hours. In the summers she played outside in parks and playgrounds with Ray, and sometimes with his friends. Lollipop liked her life with Ray, enjoying the best food from the best chains, plenty of toys and clothes, and television.*

At first she thought all girls at home in their rooms played naked with their uncles in front of a computer camera. When Ray began to tell her this was not the way it was and that she was special, living a special life, she believed it. She felt special. When Lollipop told me that part, she didn't even realize what she was saying. She just puffed up her little body and smirked, like she was some sort of celebrity. *When Ray began asking her to do unpleasant and sometimes painful things and to smile and pretend she liked and wanted those things, she learned fast. She had to because he punished her by taking away meals and TV and sometimes punching her for refusing or crying or looking scared. He gave her prizes for doing a good job: pretty headbands and bracelets, pink ponies and princesses and fairies and glitter glue and unicorn puzzles and shiny beads and cute sweatpants with words written on the backside in black cursive letters she couldn't read.*

By the time Ray began to allow Lollipop's "fans" to visit in person, she knew exactly how to do the things Ray had taught her. She had also found a way to keep her face still, but friendly, like a kind statue, so that nobody would punish her. Ray was extra nice after she did a good job with fans in person. He made her brownies and painted her fingernails pink, adding sparkles to her thumbs.

When Lollipop went to live with her new Daddy and his stable, she thought it was temporary, that Ray was coming back for her. She missed Ray like crazy and was afraid of Daddy and the two older girls. She had laughed when she said she wasn't afraid of me because I was too sad to be scary. Which made me feel mad and weak, both at the same time. *But she had learned to hide her afraid part, to show only the kind statue face. For such a silly little girl, she was strong.* Then Truth would apologize. *I'm sorry to upset you with all of this,* Truth would say. *But please. Please keep reading.*

Chapter Twenty-Eight

WHEN I FIRST understood what I was going to do, I expected to write the note as Lollipop. But in the six weeks since then, I've had to face the facts. Lollipop has lived in front of one screen or another her whole life, possesses the vocabulary of a four-year-old, can't read, and thinks a cheeseburger and a new pair of glitter panties are things to get excited about. Using her is just a poor idea.

Back in August, Daddy assigned Lollipop to me, saying, *You school her.* I must have been doing a good job hiding my insides from him, or he wouldn't have. L.A. was still the only one of us who touched the money. If she were to find out, it would be the second time she would learn about Daddy asking me to hold coins. Which would only make things worse than they already were.

Lollipop didn't know the difference between a twenty and a one. "What's that?" She held out her hands, nails trimmed neatly and painted little-girl pink. She was polite, even if she was stupid. "May I touch it, please?"

"Nobody touches the money but Daddy."

"Listen to you," Brandy said from the couch where she was dabbing Polysporin on the cut over her eye that was taking so long to heal. "Cat gave back your tongue?"

"You're touching the money now," Lollipop said. She leaned her head in close to get the best look she could. Then she sniffed. At the one first. Then the twenty. "It stinks."

"Stop," I told her. "Money is dirty. You don't know where it's been. Don't put your nose on it."

Brandy grunted. "That there the funniest thing I heard all week." She didn't sound amused.

I pointed. "That's a two." I pointed again. "That's a zero. That's twenty."

"I know that says twenty." Lollipop pretended to be offended. She was obviously lying. "What's that one?"

"A one next to a zero is ten. You didn't even learn any of this from TV?"

"They have numbers on *Sesame Street* all the time," Lollipop said. "And *Little Einsteins. Mickey Mouse Clubhouse.* They have it on a bunch of stuff. So I know them, but I never paid attention to what's more. Only I know a hundred is a lot and a thousand is even more than that. A thousand keeps me pretty in pink."

"Do you know letters?" I asked.

Lollipop nodded. "Yeah," she said. "TV and Uncle Ray taught me those."

Brandy grunted again. "I bet he did."

"Do you know how to read?"

"Some signs." Lollipop scrunched up her face, thinking. "*Exit.*"

I waited.

"*Ladies.* Um. *Ice.*"

I waited some more.

"Maybe that's all the signs I know. But I can read two books."

That didn't seem likely. "Which ones?"

"'In the great green room, there was a telephone and a red balloon . . .'"

Some kind of a hiss or a gasp or the sound of a punctured lung came out of Brandy.

"'. . . and a picture of the cow jumping over the moon.'"

Brandy flew off the couch as much as anybody still limping can and smacked Lollipop so hard that Lollipop fell, a perfect handprint seeping onto her cheek. She didn't cry out a sound. Not a whimper, not a squeak. She just got still, like a statue knocked over. You have to respect an eleven-year-old who gets smacked like that for no good reason and keeps quiet. That Uncle Ray trained her well.

"Brandy!" I stepped between the two of them. Brandy wasn't weak, but this. This was a whole side of her I never knew existed.

Her face was twisted up again the way it had been the other day with Daddy, only now it was beat up from him, fat lip and bruised eyes.

"What was that?" Brandy asked Lollipop. Her cut seeped blood right through the shiny Polysporin. "What was that?"

Lollipop answered as plain as she could manage. She didn't move any part of herself but her mouth. "*Goodnight Moon.*"

"Get off the floor."

"Brandy." Those flames that were lit in my belly the day we took Lollipop rose up, flaring. Was Brandy going to turn vicious now, on top of everything with Daddy? But Lollipop was standing, calm as anything.

"Don't you ever say those words again." Brandy smacked Lollipop's other cheek. Lollipop went down. This time tears oozed like rain dribbling down a wall.

"Daddy's going to kill you," I told Brandy. Even saying

Daddy made me want to slide through the floor and die, but there was nowhere to slide to and no way to die, so somehow I just kept on.

Brandy slipped around the corner to the alcove where my sleeping bag was. I heard her zipping into it. *L.A.'s going to kill you!* I wanted to shout, but the cat took back my tongue again. Anyway, probably Daddy was getting home before L.A., who was doing an outcall. So Daddy would get to Brandy first.

I hauled Lollipop up and propped her on the couch. I made sure the bills we had been studying were in my back pocket. Then I wrapped ice in a paper towel and held it to both sides of her face. She had white features and good, light-brown hair. Her skin was the color of wet sand. Mostly she seemed white, but with that color, it was confusing. She was prettier than the rest of us. Baby-faced.

"What's the other book you know?" I asked her. "Whisper." I didn't want Brandy hearing anything else that might make her charge back out here. But it had been a long time since anybody could talk to me about any kind of book.

"'Be still,'" Lollipop whispered. "It's monsters. There's more, but I can't remember it right now."

I had never been in the front seat of the Escalade. The streets looked different with a view through a windshield instead of just a side window. I liked feeling so high up. I thought maybe if Daddy drove fast—maybe fifty miles an hour—I could open the door and throw myself out and die. But the traffic was thick and slow, and if I didn't die and just got hurt, Daddy would be furious. And I didn't really want to die. I wasn't ready. I still needed to touch an elephant one day.

We weren't going toward the hotel. We weren't headed toward the track, either. It was a half hour after my start time for working. I was more nervous than my usual since-down-south nervous, except Daddy wasn't acting mad. He was acting kind. I wanted to ask where we were going, but I figured I'd find out soon enough.

"Why you don't want to eat no more?" Daddy asked as we drove along Broad.

I shrugged, then remembered to speak. "I don't know."

"You too skinny to be pregnant, so I know it ain't that."

He reached his hand out and rested it on my knee, heavy and familiar. It was upsetting how badly I wanted to forget what I knew and just slide into his old warmth I used to live for. And it was strange how I couldn't un-know, how the warmth was gone, replaced by that burning that made me want to swallow back sour clumps so much of the time.

We passed by the train station. "Bet you wondering where we going."

"Yeah."

He squeezed. "We not going nowhere. Just driving."

I stayed quiet.

"Worried about you, Beautiful." He turned off, away from the river.

"I'm good." Cars and people and buildings flashed by. Men and women pushing strollers and carrying babies. Couples with the men's hands slid into their bitches' back shorts pockets.

"You crying?"

Flocks of girls with big gold earrings and small spray bottles to damp down the heat.

"No," I said, wiping away a tear. It was like that time on the highway just before we got to the house with the upside-down seashell. Maybe cars just made me cry.

We passed an open hydrant, and the little kids' bodies running and jumping were shiny wet and sharp on my eyes, reflecting the sun. Daddy pulled over down the block from an ice cream truck and another open hydrant. "Look at me," he said.

I pressed on my eyes to push the tears back. Then I looked at him.

"You know I don't got no feeling for Lollipop."

It took me a minute, which actually helped.

"It ain't like she going to take your place."

I stared at him, and when it hit me, I smiled. It wasn't a fake smile. It was real. He thought I was jealous. Of Lollipop.

He grinned back, flashing his gold *D*. "This whole time," he said, "you been thinking that little girl something special to me?"

I started to giggle. I couldn't remember the last time I had giggled. It felt sideways somehow, a little insane. But I couldn't help it. *He thinks I'm jealous of Lollipop. He thinks I'm jealous.* I couldn't stop giggling. The word *lovesick* came to my mind. *He thinks I'm lovesick,* and I had been that for him, but now the idea was crazy.

He was still smiling. "Girl, pull yourself together."

I nodded and snorted. I wiped my eyes with the backs of my hands and watched the shiny kids play in the stream in the middle of the street. I calmed myself down, pushing a bubble of laughter back every time the thought of being jealous of his feelings for Lollipop rose up. It was difficult not to collapse altogether.

"Now listen." Daddy unbuckled his seat belt and turned his body toward mine. "Lollipop don't know it, but she going to start seeing dates in person."

He could tell from my face that bothered me, but he wasn't reading my mind at all. Maybe he wasn't as good at reading my mind as I used to think. "Yeah. She going to earn ten times what you earn, but don't pay that no mind."

I knew Lollipop wasn't a virgin, but still. Just because a little girl has had sex, doesn't make it right to make her have it again before she's grown up more.

Daddy was still talking. "My plan the same it always been for you. Few more weeks and you going down south to be Bottom." He scooted close and put his forehead on mine. "You my best," he murmured. "You my smartest. I'm a miss you, but I'm a come down two times every month. I'm not trying to have Lollipop in my bed."

He kissed my mouth, and I tried so hard to kiss him back the way I used to. The laughter, the craziness from before was gone. My insides boiled. He pulled away, groaning. Did he just need sex all the time, and the groaning was real? Or did he fake it for all of us to get us to do what he wanted? "You turn me on more than any of those other bitches." *Liar.* He pulled away, as the sweat popped out all over my body, from the scalding shame. He wrapped his thumb and finger around my slippery wrist and wagged my hand. "But you got to eat." He let go and straightened up behind the steering wheel. "Dates don't want no skin and bones. And I need my money."

"Okay," I said. *You don't love me.*

He put the car in drive and turned it around. "We going to get some fries right now."

It was too hot for fries. I wanted a fire hydrant and ice cream. "Thank you, Daddy," I said. *You never loved me.*

"Then after I watch you eat, I'm a cheer you up but good."

I choked down the fries and a Coke at McDonald's and listened to him complain about how L.A. was a pain in the ass and about how Brandy was getting too much attitude and how johns who went for Lollipop were perverts and deserved to give up every goddamn penny they paid for her.

Then he drove me home and took me into his room. Into those oily sheets. He was as gentle as he ever was and I pretended as much as I ever had, not knowing what else to do or how to make any of it end.

Uncle Ray had been good at keeping Lollipop babyish. L.A. thought it was a front.

"That little girl is not as dumb as she act," L.A. said, after Lollipop nearly set the place on fire.

We warned her about the back burner not working properly, but Lollipop left it stuck on. When L.A. turned the dial for under the saucepan, flame banged out a circle with a loud *thwack* and then somehow skipped through air to a paper bag of apples resting nearby. One second the bag was just sitting there as peaceful as you please, the next second it was crackling blue and orange.

L.A. nearly hit the ceiling, she jumped so high. But she had the presence of mind to pour that saucepan water over the crisping bag, and that was enough to put the fire out. I wished she could pour water into my belly.

"Stupid fool," she told Lollipop.

"I never cooked before," Lollipop tried to say. Even if she forgot to turn back the dial and check the flame, it wasn't all her fault.

L.A. smacked the top of Lollipop's head. "Don't even try to mess with me," she warned. "You could have blown us all up."

"I always got food from out," Lollipop explained. She was strong for such a little thing. "And I'm not a fool."

"Stupid fool. And a liar." L.A. smacked her hair again. "You start a fire in here, you better off dying in it than letting Daddy find out it was your fool self."

"McDonald's," Lollipop argued. Those tears squeezed out again, but at the same time, her face was all wall. "Taco Bell."

"Clean up the mess," L.A. told her. "And shut your mouth." She refilled the saucepan and fired up the back burner again. "What is you staring at?" she asked me.

I shrugged and looked away.

Brandy raised her eyebrows in my direction from the kitchen table, where she was eating a breakfast bar. "Every night?" she mouthed silently. I could tell she didn't believe it. But Lollipop had bragged about McDonald's and all the rest before to me. She wasn't a liar. I think she really never turned on a stove before. I think she had McDonald's or Taco Bell every day of her life that she ate anything. Maybe White Castle, too. Domino's. Who knows? I didn't really care. It didn't matter. Nothing mattered.

A few weeks later school was about to begin, and I was pretty sure Daddy wasn't going to let me go back. But if I went, I wouldn't have to work as many hours. I hated the johns' bodies inside of mine. I hated the way they pushed me this way and that way, onto my knees, onto my stomach, against a wall, on all fours. I hated the ones stupid enough to think they were kind and the ones who squeezed too hard or smelled so bad or did everything rough just to make it hurt. I hated smiling and agreeing and pretending. I had to go back to school.

And then Daddy got stabbed.

I was lying on the hotel bed, halfway through my third reading of *Mockingbird*, when the door opened. I put down the book and sat up fast, expecting it to be a trick. It was L.A. She was supposed to be working a party.

"Daddy got cut. He in the hospital. Eagle out there waiting to take us home."

My body got loud around the fire pit in my center. Shaking and pounding and whirring. It was a volcano inside of me, while we waited until Brandy's date left her room so we could go get her. When Brandy heard, her face went whiter than a piece of spearmint Chiclets. "How bad?" she asked L.A. I hadn't thought to ask that at all. "Who cut him?"

"Whippet. By his lung or something. He in the ICU."

Brandy started sobbing. She sobbed all the way home in the back of the Lincoln town car. I was too scared to cry. Eagle and I stayed quiet.

"Shut up," L.A. kept telling her.

If Daddy died, who would take me? Eagle? Bird? L.A.? I didn't want to imagine any of that. Maybe I could go back to Janelle. But I could never go back to Janelle. *I have nobody.* If I tried to run away, maybe I could go . . . where? *I have nowhere.*

If Daddy died, I wouldn't have to be a ho anymore. Except that even if I tried not to be, I always would be. *Once a ho, always a ho.* I would get arrested for all the tricks I'd turned, for being a criminal all that time. The police might rape me the way they did Brandy. And if I tried to explain, they would never understand: *I just wanted to make him happy. He loved me—at least I thought he loved me—and he took care of me, and I wanted to stay with him, so I did what he said.* But it would come out all wrong. I would sound disgusting. They would lock me up. I wanted him to die. But I was scared of him dying. *It fit perfect underneath my powder.* Maybe Brandy and I could get that card and call that lady.

But back at home, Brandy was still falling to pieces. "He going to be okay, right, Dime?" she kept asking, her brown eyes as round and wide as open manholes beneath the scabbed cuts.

"Yeah," I kept telling her. I knew he would. Nothing could hurt him.

"Word?" She was barely healed from the beating he had given to her two weeks ago. But all she cared about was that he was going to be okay.

"I'm sure." I didn't know if it would be worse if he lived or died.

Me and my Daddy, Brandy might say. *Maybe I'm not his only. But he take care of me so good. Nobody else never done nothing for me since my grandmother. My Daddy save my life every day. He got me clean, he give me food, he give me a couch to sleep, a place to stay, and clothes. He the only one who ever love me.*

If he did die, maybe it would just be me, searching beneath her powder.

Chapter Twenty-Nine

EAGLE DROVE L.A. to visit Daddy. After, she told us Daddy said we had to go back out to the track. I didn't believe her. I was under the impression that Daddy couldn't even talk yet. But I knew he would want us to make money, and I knew he didn't trust Eagle or even L.A. to keep things running smoothly indoor. Anyway, L.A. was the Bottom Bitch, and I had to do what she said.

"He gave up our rooms?" Brandy asked. Her face was healed enough that makeup covered what was left.

L.A. shrugged. "How do I know? All I know is we ain't supposed to be in them. We supposed to go back out to the track."

"What about Lollipop?" Brandy asked. "Lollipop can't go out there."

L.A. sighed and looked disgusted. "Lollipop stay working in her room."

Lollipop bit at her pink ribbon tying up one of her pigtails. She was too old for ribbons, but Daddy said she had to wear them.

"You was supposed to start getting your first dates at the hotel this week," L.A. informed Lollipop. Her baby face didn't shift a muscle. But L.A. looked annoyed. "Now it's going to be me taking calls for your little shows."

Lollipop stayed a pretty blank wall. I couldn't tell what she was thinking. Was she disappointed? Relieved? She looked carefully at L.A. and shrugged. "Whatever Daddy says I'm supposed to do."

"Oh," L.A. added. "Also. Your Uncle Ray? He ain't never coming back."

I saw it in a flicker when she glanced at me and Brandy. We had nothing different to tell her, and she could see that we didn't, so she looked back at L.A., who was smirking. That was when I saw Lollipop's real face. Anguish is what I saw. Then she went wall again and stepped back into her room.

That was Friday. I went to the track that night, Saturday, Sunday, and Monday, which was Labor Day. We all stayed as far away from Whippet as we could. We didn't know what the beef was between him and Daddy, but we were scared he might try to cut us, too. I heard him call my name a few times, but I was far enough down the block to pretend I couldn't hear.

Hello, I said to that gray brick. *It's been a while. How have you been?* It didn't answer me back. While the dates did what they did to me, I would sneak a tap on it, just in case it would open up into Narnia. Or Number Twelve Grimmauld Place. *Welcome,* Aslan would say. Or Professor Dumbledore. *We have been waiting for you.*

Eagle watched us. It was different to have another man under a Daddy instead of just having the Bottom Bitch handle things. But I guessed Daddy didn't trust L.A. Also he needed Eagle for taking calls for live, customized shows from Lollipop when L.A. was out working, which was most of the time. From what I could tell, passwords were constantly changing, and Eagle had to type different things into her computer and into his iPad every few days, setting up different pages or sites or whatever he had to do to make sure Daddy didn't get busted.

I never saw a sign of him going into Daddy's room. I think he mostly sat on the couch watching TV, tapping his iPad, and answering the phone when he was inside our apartment. He watched us on the track, too. I caught glimpses of the Lincoln town car, cruising, of him leaning against it. We handed our money to L.A., and I saw L.A. hand it over to Eagle.

Tuesday morning L.A. was still out from an overnight. Even though I didn't have my school ID, even though Eagle was sitting on the couch, I had to try. I dressed in school clothes and went to the first day of ninth grade. In the front office I filled out paperwork with lies for a new ID, and I ended up in the same homeroom as Dawn and Trevor. Trevor had grown about three inches and looked like some kind of basketball player now. Dawn had extensions and a boyfriend also in our homeroom.

Trevor looked down at me. "What the hell?" he clucked. "You look like you haven't slept or ate all summer."

I shrugged. "I'm good."

"This is Brian," Dawn told me. She gave me a hug. "You lost weight. Where have you been?"

"Down south." Her hug made me feel more ashamed. "Carolinas."

"My aunt lives in Greenville," Brian told me.

"Were you in Greenville?" Dawn asked.

I shook my head, got quiet again, and stayed quiet for the rest of the day.

When I got home, my chest was pounding above the

heat in my gut. Eagle wasn't there, but L.A. was. I thought she might kill me for having gone to school, but she didn't touch me. I guess she knew now was not the time to piss off Daddy. Also, if I got marked up or hurt now, she would have to earn more money to make up for what I would lose.

"Get your funky ass dressed and go make Daddy's coins," she hissed instead. "You wasn't supposed to go to no school."

"I'm not like Lollipop." I made myself speak up, loudly. "I'm in the system and until I'm sixteen, they're going to come looking for me, and we both know Daddy doesn't want that."

"Daddy had a plan for you, and now you messed it up."

What plan? What had he told her?

"He was going to send you down south." L.A. stuck her tongue in her gap. "You was supposed to go tomorrow."

"What for?" He couldn't have told her I was supposed to be the Bottom Bitch down there for Russian girls. I didn't think L.A. even knew about the Russian girls.

"You was going to work for Eagle's brother down there. Dude called Bird. Daddy was going to sell you to Bird, since if you in school up here you can't make enough and if you up here, you got to go to school. But if you down south, Bird can make you disappear, just like Lollipop. Then nobody come looking. Daddy make some money off you, finally."

What L.A. was saying might be true. Daddy had me believe he was going to make me the Bottom to those Russian girls down south, but maybe he was lying. Maybe he was just going to sell me to Bird, and believing Daddy's lies, I would go quietly until it was too late.

I couldn't back down now. I had to keep going to school. It was hours and hours I wouldn't have to turn tricks. "Well, he never told me that and you never told me that," I said. "And now they have a record of me in school just like I'm supposed to be. So Daddy's going to have to change his plans."

"You a little nothing skinny bitch," L.A. said. "Now get your ass moving." Her cell rang. She picked it up. "Password?" I heard her say, as I went to my alcove. "All right. Second password?" She listened. "Yeah. You good. What you want?" Another pause. "All right. She going to start in five minutes." There was a silence, and then I heard her call into Lollipop's room. "You got a show!"

There was no answer. I had to come back out for panties from under the coffee table. "Answer me when I'm talking to you!" Still nothing. I watched L.A. open up Lollipop's door. Lollipop was fast asleep on her bed, belly down, with her head to the side and her thumb in her mouth. She was naked, except for little-girl panties, pink with purple hearts on them. And purple ribbons in her hair. L.A. didn't walk in.

She threw a tissue box instead. It hit Lollipop on her shoulder. She barely moved. "What?"

"You got a show in two minutes," L.A. whispered, from the doorway. "Get your shit together."

"I'm so tired." Lollipop yawned.

"Get the fuck up," L.A. whispered fiercely. Then she slammed the door.

Room eleven was hotter than outside, hot like summer, even though it was already an autumn sixty degrees most days. You got to room eleven by walking through the house entrance and down a short, dark hallway with a sticky tile floor. It had no door, and the bed was just a platform with a mattress. The floor was uneven since some of the tiles were torn or gone. There were hooks all over the walls. Colorful balls of glass at the end of curved metal. *Who put those beautiful hooks on these old walls?* was what I thought about when I was working in there. They were blue and red and orange and green and yellow. The dust covered any brightness, but they were still so cheerful to look at. *Who bought them and hammered them in? Who was trying to make it pretty in here?* Sometimes there was a towel or two hanging on the hooks and a fresh sheet on the mattress, and I would feel better about working in there. But then they would disappear. It was cleaner out in the open air in the alley or between two parked cars. It was cleaner inside the dates' cars. But when someone asked to go inside, Daddy said we had to take them into room eleven.

This time, after I finished my date and followed him out into the cooler air, Eagle took my elbow.

"Hospital," he told me.

"But I have to give the coins to L.A."

He held out his hand. L.A. would be mad. She had said all the money had to be given to her so she could personally hand it to Daddy. But I'd seen her give cash to Eagle, too. I hesitated. He pulled the coins out of my fingers, then pushed at my back to guide me toward the Lincoln town car. I saw L.A. up the street negotiating with a date. She glanced at us and didn't seem surprised. That reassured me. Maybe it was okay. Maybe he really was taking me to the hospital. On the other hand, if he was taking me to Daddy, what for? Was this good-bye before I went down south? Was Daddy furious with me for going to school?

He was sitting up in a bed. There were three other people in the same room, but two were lying down, sleeping, and one had the curtains closed. I could hear that one murmuring in that tone people use when they're on the phone. Daddy was wearing a hospital gown and had an IV in each arm. There was a bandage on his chest peeking behind the ties of his gown.

He looked smaller than I'd ever seen him, which was surprising. But other than that, he seemed the same.

A nurse was doing something with one of his IVs when Eagle and I walked in.

"Hi," I said. I wasn't sure if I was supposed to call him Daddy in front of squares, so I didn't. He flashed his *D* at me.

"Hi, Beautiful," he said. There was a rolling tray over his lap. His cell phone was on it, along with a pitcher of water and a cup of ice and the remote control for the TV attached over our heads on the wall.

"This is your other niece?" the nurse asked.

"This her," Daddy said, winking at me.

"Nice to meet you," I said. I knew L.A. visited Daddy almost every day. I guess the nurse thought she was his niece too. Who did she think Eagle was, then? But she walked away without saying anything else, so maybe she wasn't all that interested.

"You earning my money?" Daddy asked. The man on the phone behind the curtain had gotten loud enough that Daddy didn't need to be too quiet.

"Yes," I said.

Eagle handed Daddy the cash I'd earned so far that day and then stepped out. Daddy counted the bills. "Not bad," he said. "But not good, neither."

The volume behind the curtain increased. It sounded like the man was arguing with somebody, but it was a language I didn't know, so I couldn't understand the actual words.

"You miss me?" Daddy asked.

"Yes." I nodded.

"Well I'm a come home in two days, they promising."

I tried to make my face look happy or shy or something he would like.

"I ain't had time to plan out school with you." Daddy glanced around, but the other two weren't moving in their beds. "L.A. say you went ahead and went."

"Yes." I tried to sound sincere. "You always tell me how it makes you proud that I'm smart, so I thought that was the right thing to do." I tried to look *lovestruck*. "That was the right thing, right, Daddy?"

He frowned. "You going down south soon, anyhow," he said.

I could tell he hadn't wanted me to go back to school. I knew it. Maybe I could read his mind a little now. The idea cooled my belly just the tiniest bit.

"Now it going to make some things more complicated."

I waited, trying to think over the sound of the man behind the curtain shouting the same phrase over and over.

"But it ain't the worst. Keep people from poking they nosy heads all up in our business."

He took a sip of water from the ice cup. Then he shook ice into his mouth and chewed.

"Your wifeys behaving?"

I nodded. "Yes."

"L.A. beating on any a you?"

"No."

"How you like being back on the track?"

"Wherever you need me, Daddy."

It was silent all of a sudden, and I realized the man behind the curtain must have ended his call. Daddy lowered his voice again.

"You go home after school, you change, you get out working by three thirty every day. You don't come home until you got quota. Understand?"

I nodded. "Yes."

"You don't got quota, you don't come home. Understand?"

I nodded again. How was I going to stay awake in class if I worked the whole night? Because it would take the whole night to earn my quota. When was I supposed to sleep?

"You going to be busy, Beautiful," Daddy said. He

crunched on his ice. "But it ain't for long, since you going down south soon." He spit back into his cup. "And life down south slower."

The next day they announced the school library caught bed-bugs and was closed until further notice.

"How does that happen?" Dawn asked. "There aren't any beds in libraries."

"Guess we don't have to read any more this year," Brian said.

Dawn rolled her eyes.

Trevor looked down at me. "You're going to the one by the hospital, right?"

I nodded my head, but it was a lie. I met that librarian I liked at the other branch, the one near the store we used, over on Bergen. I would tell Daddy the school said I had to. That if I couldn't go to the library to study the books I needed to keep up my grades, official people would definitely notice and come poking their noses up in our business.

I doubted that was true. I doubted Daddy would think it was true. He was planning to send me down south so soon that I doubted he would care. But I had to try.

Chapter Thirty

WE SAW IT the same day Eagle was bringing Daddy home from the hospital.

Lollipop came to breakfast naked, except for her panties. Black with orange glitter pumpkins for Halloween, even though Halloween wasn't for another month. But nobody was looking at her panties.

"Jesus," Brandy said. "Sweet Jesus."

L.A. and I just stared. *What?* I thought. Even though I could see. Even though I knew. *What?*

Lollipop looked up from her Special K. "What? I was hot, and I have to go back in for a show anyway. It's okay to eat without all your clothes on, you know."

L.A. and me and Brandy all looked at each other. Then we looked back at Lollipop. *What?*

"You had your period already?" Brandy asked.

"My who?"

"Your bleeding," L.A. said. "Your period."

Lollipop didn't understand.

"You know what a period is?" Brandy asked.

Lollipop shook her head. The rest of us looked at each other again.

"She didn't have no boobies when we picked her up," L.A. said. That was less than a month ago. "Now look."

Lollipop looked down at herself. "I'm getting fat. Is Daddy going to be mad?"

"How many times you bled from your stuff?" Brandy asked.

Lollipop shrugged. "I don't know."

"Try to know," L.A. said.

"Maybe two or three times? From the dates, I think."

"How long ago was the last time?"

Lollipop thought about it. "A couple of months before I came here. It was just getting real hot. June maybe? Uncle Ray didn't like it. He said I couldn't give full service if I was bleeding." *What?*

"Oh. My. God," L.A. said. "Little girl. You is pregnant."

* * *

At first it didn't seem possible or real, and I wanted to laugh, even though nothing was funny. But in about five seconds wanting to laugh stopped. Lollipop looked down at her body and grinned and began talking about what clothes she would ask Daddy to buy for the baby. L.A. seemed more than happy to explain the birds and the bees, immediately lecturing on everything she knew. Except she got some things wrong, like when she said men had a bone in their penis that made it get hard. She used the word Lollipop used for penis, *wiener*, and that word used to amuse me, but now nothing was amusing even though a few minutes ago I'd wanted to laugh. Brandy sat still for a long time with her spoon balancing in her hand. I guess I was sitting still too, but my mind was busy with questions. Is the body of an eleven-year-old big enough to birth a baby? Is it against the law to get pregnant when you're eleven? Will the hospital arrest Lollipop? Will Daddy be glad to have a baby or will he be mad because of how much babies cost? Will Daddy know to buy diapers and powder and formula and wipes and booties? Will he send L.A. to do it? What if Lollipop dies while she's trying to give birth?

"Then the sperm swim all up through your tubes and hit a egg right where your belly button at and then you pregnant and that baby growing get all its food from your umbiblical cord," L.A. was saying.

Brandy unstilled herself to cross her arms and tuck fingertips under her armpits. She wasn't making a sound, so it took me a few seconds to see that she was crying. Her eyes were shiny and blinking. There were three wet tear tracks lining her cheeks.

What?

I was terrified.

Daddy was like the devil. A weak devil, but the devil. He threw things at us constantly. He didn't lift his arm all the way, and his throws were feeble and he winced every time. But he hurled whatever he could reach: forties not even empty, plates, the remote control, boxes of gauze pads, a comb, a vanilla-scented candle. He stayed on the couch because it was hard for him to get off it, and he wanted to watch us. L.A. and Brandy got his bedroom, and I stayed in the alcove and waited on him.

What? It was all I could think. I did what I had to do each day, and everyone saw the same Dime they always saw, but inside I wasn't me. I was just, *what?*

Daddy didn't eat much at once but a little bit all day long. He held his gun in his hand all the time. Before, he used to keep it hidden inside his pants somewhere.

"I'm a kill that motherfucker," he kept saying that first

week. He was talking about Uncle Ray. "I'm a blow up his ass."

Then he got a visit from George, who talked sense to him. My body was right there, bringing chips and salsa and taking away their empties, but my brain was lost.

"Dudes out there paying mad money for a look at that?" George asked, tilting his head toward Lollipop's room.

Daddy nodded from where he was lying down on the couch. "Bunch of perverts out there."

"Perverts going to travel for it too," George added.

What?

"Travel to get some of that in person. You got you some months. But you best get rid of the little bitch before any baby come. What you going to do with her?"

"I'm a make my money first," Daddy said. "And then I'm a send her back down south."

What?

"You giving up a boy?" George asked. "You giving up a son?"

"Ain't mine." Daddy shook his head. "I never hit that."

George looked surprised. "Baby ain't yours?"

Daddy shook his head. "Lollipop a little girl," he said. "Damn. I ain't no pervert."

What?

He shook his head again. "She came pregnant."

"Huh," George said. "She might be having a bitch, anyway."

Daddy threw his bottle of Advil at me and winced. The bottle hit my arm and fell onto the floor. "Open that up."

I untwisted the cap. "Give me four," Daddy said. "Then get out. Eagle waiting on you."

What what what. I was stuck, frozen, trapped. No more hot coals and lava and searing volcano inside my belly. No nothing but stone cold *what?*

I came in last just as the sun was rising. Two and a half hours before first period was going to begin. L.A. and Brandy were on either side of Daddy on the couch, still in their work clothes. He was sitting up straight. In the past few days, he hadn't been taking so much Advil, and he didn't seem feeble anymore when he moved around. He'd gone back into his own room and had mostly stopped throwing things at us.

I could hear Lollipop through her door, talking to some john on the computer. I could hear her giggling. *What?* Daddy was drinking cranberry juice from a glass. I hung up my coat in the closet and then waited until he put the juice down on the coffee table before I gave him his money.

I was cold in my miniskirt and high boots and short sweater with no bra.

"Sit down," Daddy told me.

I sat on the cloth armchair.

"Bitch," Daddy said to me. "Looks like you going to be real useful right about now."

What?

L.A. poked at her tooth gap with her tongue and tapped her foot fast on the coffee table. Brandy's eyelids were drooped so low, I thought she was asleep, except she would never disrespect Daddy like that. All I wanted to do was lie down inside my sleeping bag and warm up. I forced myself not to slump.

"All you all listen good." He glanced down at his phone. "We got a new plan."

L.A. spiraled her tongue in the gap. Brandy lifted her head a fraction.

"Dime. You been wanting to go to the liberry so much, now you going."

What?

"Take you a hour one time a week after school and educate yourself on birthing babies."

Brandy opened her eyes.

"She ain't working no more?" L.A. asked.

"Shut up," Daddy said. "I never said she ain't working."

I didn't want to go to the library for Daddy. The library

wasn't his. It wasn't for him. It was for me. It was mine. Daddy didn't belong there. He wasn't allowed there. And I didn't want to read about how to deliver a baby. That wasn't what I wanted to read. That wasn't anything.

"You not taking Lollipop to a hospital when it her time?" Brandy asked.

"Hell no," Daddy said. "My grandma say ain't nobody had they babies in no hospitals back in the day."

"You got a grandma?" Brandy asked. "Stop."

What? I closed my eyes for longer than a blink. It didn't make me feel warmer or help me to disappear.

"Hospital for dying," Daddy said. He flashed his *D.* "Or beating down dying, just like I done."

"Nurse said you wasn't going to die, anyway," L.A. muttered.

"Shut up, I said."

"Where Lollipop having her baby, then?" Brandy asked.

"In the hotel room," Daddy said. "Dime, you going to be the main doctor. You going to educate yourself everything about it." He looked at Brandy. "You going to be Dime's nurse."

What?

"I know you not asking me to help deliver no baby," L.A. said.

Daddy threw a bag of Cheetos at her head. "You got that right," he said. "Because I know you ain't no doctor."

"You off the track again," he told the three of us. "Brandy and Dime back to the hotel. L.A., you on outcalls and overnights." She smiled.

"Lollipop moving into the hotel. She going in, and she ain't coming out until after that baby here." He stood up. He could stand now without wincing. He was getting stronger. "Come on, now," he said to me. He glanced at Brandy and L.A. "You two dismissed."

He took me into his room. He let me shower, and the water was warm but I kept shivering anyway. He tucked the sheets around me tenderly, just the way he did the very first time he turned me out. When he crawled into bed wearing nothing but his boxers, I could see how much he really had recovered. His bandage was fresh and small, and his body had bulked back up a lot.

"You going to do good, Beautiful," he whispered to me, stroking my back. "I'm counting on you to do good." He kept stroking. "You get that baby out and we going to send it straight back to Uncle Ray."

What?

Daddy stopped stroking to turn me around. He sat up and pulled me with him. He leaned his face close to mine.

"You tell anybody and I'm a rip your fingernails off and beat your teeth out. Understand?" He slowly took a fistful of my hair and then suddenly yanked so hard it was like he'd set my scalp on fire.

What?

"Understand?" He yanked again and then again and then pulled my face the last inch closer until he was kissing me. I couldn't breathe.

After a second, he let go, pressed me down, and spooned me again, like it was nothing. My head burned. "Don't tell nobody, but we getting a sweet price."

What?

"Dime, we getting a sweet price. And with that baby money, I'm a buy you some nice new clothes and a diamond none a the other bitches going to get, plus a phone." He rubbed his nose on the back of my neck. "You get that baby out safe and it going to be the best thing ever happened for all a us."

There's only so much one brain can take. There are only so many thoughts one brain can have at any one time. The body is different, though. The body knows things instantly that the brain can't understand so fast. When a brain has all it can handle, it just thinks *what?* But while the brain is thinking *what*, the body is like an entire planet exploding or becoming. My brain was thinking *what what what what what what what?*

But my body already knew I was going to get that baby a decent life, if that was the last thing I ever did with mine.

The icy slam at my chest and the slushy freeze in my blood knew right away, knew underneath all the *what?*

I was going to use courage and write the best note ever written. *What?*

I was going to have to kill myself after, but that wouldn't matter, and the note I was going to write wouldn't even be about that or for me. *What? What? What?*

The note would be for the baby. Only for that baby.

She must have remembered who I was, because she greeted me when I walked by her desk. I watched myself greet her back quietly and then duck away so that I could find what I needed. Then I watched myself sit at a corner table and pretend to do homework. I was hunched over a childbirth guide, my gray sweater nearby to cover it up fast if anybody came near. *What?* I read. *What?*

When I had fifteen minutes left, I made sure to return the book to the spot where I'd found it so that nobody could see what I'd been reading. Then, without meaning to, I was in front of the stacks for *Mockingbird*. There were only fresh copies on the shelf. She didn't usually work at this branch, so maybe she never saw the taped pages on the one I'd returned back in August.

When I slid one of the fresh copies over the counter to her along with my school ID, she took it like it was nothing and began conversation as if it hadn't been any time at all since she last saw me. "So you enjoyed this, then?"

I tried to think. *What?* I nodded. I was inside myself and not watching myself now. I wished I could lie down.

"What stood out in it for you?" she asked, swiping its bar code beneath the red beam and adjusting her jeweled glasses. "What did you like about it?"

I liked so many things about it, I suddenly thought to say. *I loved so many things about it.* It was a relief to have a new thought, something other than *what?* Even though I didn't speak.

She didn't seem to mind, but just slid *Mockingbird* back over to me and then drew her index finger along a line of books standing upright next to her computer. "I got my love of books from my father," she continued as if we were having a conversation. "What about you?"

I was still just barely thinking, and not well enough to answer, so I stared at a black clump of gum stuck to the blue carpet.

When I lifted my head, she was pulling a different title out from the row she had been searching next to her computer. *The Color Purple.* She opened it up and swiped it beneath the red beam too. She handed it over to me, along with my school ID. Her necklace clacked. "Maybe we'll run into each other again the next time I'm covering here."

One thing I liked was that everybody thought Boo Radley was a shameful criminal and not a respectable person, I realized I wanted to say. *But all along, he was actually a hero.*

Walking back home, somehow I unfroze.

Lollipop was pregnant, and there was going to be a baby, and I was going to deliver it. Lollipop was pregnant, and there was going to be a baby, and I was going to deliver it.

There was going to be a baby.

I thought about the babies I'd known. Vonna, and Sienna, a little bit. And the other ones. There were a lot. Eight. Maybe nine. I couldn't remember all of their names. I just remembered holding them, tiny bundles tipped over my shoulder. Tilting bottles at just the right angle so they didn't drown and they didn't suck in air. I remembered their hard gums on my chin, and their fists tangled in my hair. Their drool soaking their onesies and the way their two front teeth glistened inside their mouths. I remembered how when they started to walk, they lurched around as if they were drunk. How they played with my ears and how they loved bowls and feathers and tape and watching things drop onto the floor.

I had to stay unfrozen now. I had to form a thought more than *what?* My body had understood and prepared a plan while my brain had been stuck in *what*. Now I had to stay unstuck and leave *what* behind. I had to keep my brain caught up to my body. I had to concentrate.

It had to be me because there was nobody else. Not L.A. Not Eagle. Not Bird or any of the Russians or Uncle Ray. Not the johns. Not Daddy. Not even Brandy. I had to get that baby out alive, and I had to come up with a note so good that its reader would do the right thing and keep on doing the right thing until that baby was grown.

Daddy and L.A. and Eagle and George would kill me slowly if they found me alive. I couldn't let that happen. But more importantly, I had to make the note perfect.

Chapter Thirty-One

THAT WAS SIX weeks ago, and all the time since then seems so slow and so fast, both at once. It seems like a book I read a long time ago and I can't remember the title or the ending. There are parts I do remember, clearly, and other parts that don't make any sense.

When I came home from school four days a week and from the library one day an hour later, I had to change clothes and then let Eagle drive me to work the hotel room next to Lollipop's. Lollipop did her thing in front of the camera there and sometimes with a live date. Daddy moved her in on a Saturday with all of us so that things wouldn't seem suspicious. He took the hotel comforter off her bed and made sure no identifying furniture was in the camera's view. L.A. said he paid somebody at the hotel not to send in the cleaning people, so the only ones who ever went in and out were him, Eagle, and dates. Lollipop cleaned up after herself, and L.A. or I took her sheets home to wash.

Daddy was strong, all the way back to his old self, and he was driving again. When Lollipop had live dates, he circled the block until they left. Then he double-parked around the corner from the hotel, put on his flashers, and went up to check on her.

Otherwise, Eagle was around the hotel most, working in his Lincoln town car as if it was his office. Eagle was still in charge of the computer part of things. According to Lollipop, the passwords would never stop having to be changed, and there were always different things that had to be typed in every few days. Eagle had his own gun. It was bigger than Daddy's and black. He kept it sitting on the seat beside him, like it was nothing. Eagle also had an iPad. He watched a lot of YouTube on it. But mostly it was for managing Lollipop's website and also using Backpage and Craigslist and DateHookup ads to attract johns looking for dates with little girls.

He usually drove me back home around two in the morning. I was making quota by then most nights, since Daddy lowered it after he assigned me to deliver the baby. I guess Daddy realized I had to rest sometime. So I was able to sleep four or five hours most nights, which helped. I was still tired, but not as tired. My brain seemed to be working better. I forced it to work better. I was thinking about the baby all the time, every minute, except when I was reading. *I have to get this baby born alive,* I kept thinking. *And then I have to save it. Nobody else will. It has to be me.*

Eagle pulled up in front of our stoop, and I stepped out without either of us saying anything. We never spoke. I walked up the steps and knocked on the door. Daddy let me in.

I handed him the money and kicked off my heels. They didn't bother me as much as they had on the track, because it was only sometimes that a date asked me to put them on, and that was never for walking anywhere.

It wasn't until my heels were off that I noticed L.A. sitting on the couch. And three parallel scratches on Daddy's cheek. L.A. was wearing sweats. Lollipop's pink suitcase and white suitcase stood ready by the door. Daddy was holding a forty and his eyebrow was scrunched tight, hiding its scar.

He barely seemed to notice me. He took the money and counted it, but then he turned to L.A. I walked straight to the alcove and didn't even look at her. I didn't know what was going on, but I knew I better disappear. Right as I was trying, something whipped past me, crashed against the wall, and fell to the floor. Before I had a chance to see what it was, I could hear Daddy walk across the apartment. I waited for a thud or a thwack, but there was silence and then he was laughing. I was afraid to peek. Instead I looked for what L.A. had thrown. It was the remote control, lying in the alcove corner. The battery lid had come off, and the rectangular battery was dangling by short red and yellow and black wires.

"You do that again, bitch," Daddy said to L.A., "and I will kill you." He sounded cheerful.

Now I peeked. Daddy was pointing his gun straight at L.A.'s jaw. He didn't look like a man who got stabbed anymore. He looked just like his old self.

"You said we was getting married," L.A. said. She looked sadder than I'd ever seen her. She looked weak.

Daddy held the gun steady. "And we going to. But we can't get married if you dead."

"You keep saying six months and it ain't never six months and now you sending me down there without you?" She was crying.

Daddy lowered his gun and softened his voice. "I'm a come soon as I can. You stupid?"

L.A. poked her gap with her tongue, sniffing. "You know I ain't stupid."

"Then you know plans change. You supposed to be

Bottom means I rely on you. I need your ass down south, then you get your ass down south. You don't throw no fit and scratch up my face."

He leaned down to kiss her and kissed her long. Then he grabbed a fistful of her hair and wrapped it around his fist. He yanked her head down to one side hard. Then he yanked it down to the other side hard. She gasped from the pain. He did it again. "I would shoot you in the rest of them teeth right now for this bullshit lack of cooperation." His voice was like he was stroking her instead of hurting her: whispery and tender. "I would shoot you right now except you my Bottom." He kissed her long again. "And I'm a marry you just like I said." He unwrapped himself. "Get up."

She stood up, wobbly.

His voice was regular again. "Take your shit and go. Eagle out there waiting. He going to drive you."

L.A. hesitated a second, but Daddy raised his gun again, and this time he wasn't laughing or kissing her or looking soft. She left.

Daddy nodded at me. "Plans changed," he said. "You not going down south until after that baby born. L.A. going to be my Bottom Bitch down there."

Who was Bottom Bitch here now? Lollipop was making the most money, but she was only eleven and never left the hotel room. Brandy made more than me because she was out working more hours. But Brandy didn't even want to be the Bottom Bitch.

"I got to go to the hotel," Daddy told me. He tucked his gun away. "Eagle going to be gone a few days. Don't open the door for nobody."

Before he pulled the door closed, he winked and flashed his *D*. "I ain't marrying that bitch," he told me. "She too stupid."

Even though I wasn't pregnant and I was too old for the johns who saw Lollipop, Daddy thought I was young enough that having her and me next door to each other would bring in more johns and make us more money. I was tired of worrying about Lollipop's baby, but it was hard not to. A few times, between dates, I pulled *The Color Purple* out from underneath the bed, but I was too distracted to begin reading. Instead I stared at the cover, trying to guess what the bottom half of a woman in a dress, the hindquarters of a dog, and purple flowers might be about.

Brandy still had to work the street. She still didn't have a phone. She didn't care. She was just glad L.A. was gone. It made her different, or maybe being worn out was finally making her different. More quiet and less attitude. She was sort of the Bottom Bitch, but Daddy had it all set up so strangely, it was hard to tell. I heard George and Stone making fun of him.

"You a simp," I heard them say when I was in my alcove, changing from school clothes into work clothes and trying to review in my head what I had learned about breech births.

"Yeah?" Daddy said. "Who making more coins? I'm a forward thinker. You want to stay on top of the game, you got to think outside the box."

George and Stone snickered like a couple of little boys. *"Box."* Stone giggled.

I heard front chair legs thump back down on the kitchen floor. "Life give you a lemon," Daddy said, "you make lemonade."

I just want to be clear, Truth would continue. *Lollipop got pregnant in May by the second or third fan who ever visited her.* Brandy and I questioned her closely until we figured it out as best we could. Until we put together a picture of how things must have happened. *Uncle Ray probably never even knew. By chance, Lollipop's first blood came after her first date. Uncle Ray thought the blood was from that date. She had no other signs: no nubs on her chest, no hair. Nothing but a slim little-girl body. Uncle Ray didn't realize what that first blood was until her second period, when she had not been visited in person by anyone.*

Ray never touched Lollipop again. *And it wasn't long before he was telling her all about the adventure he was going to arrange. While he was setting it up, Ray made himself more money from two previously and carefully arranged in-person dates. He wasn't thinking about Lollipop getting pregnant, and Lollipop didn't know she could.*

Chapter Thirty-Two

"HOW MUCH I got to throw down for some of that?" Jywon asked, sliding his fingers across my butt.

I slapped him away. "Get off."

I had been up for most of my sleeping time—two thirty to seven thirty—reading *The Color Purple* inside my sleeping bag. I was so exhausted from working and from worrying about the baby and the note, that I thought I only had the wherewithal to peek at the first paragraph. Just to distract my tired brain. But Celie starting out writing directly to God about what was happening to her made me want to crawl inside the ink, grab her hand, and hold on. And when you feel like that in a book, you don't stop turning its pages. A few hours later, when Celie finally tells off Mr. ___ at the dinner table in front of Shug and Sofia and Squeak and

Harpo and everybody, I knew I was going to march over to Crescent Avenue to demand what was mine. If I was going to get Lollipop's baby out alive and then make sure it got what it needed, I had to have coins Daddy wasn't going to provide—not for some baby not even his own.

Janelle came to the door, holding a tiny newborn, swaddled in a flannel pink-and-blue hospital blanket. Sienna toddled behind her legs, hiding. She got so big. Jywon scooped her up, making her cry. I wanted to kill him, but I forced myself to look at Janelle instead.

"Hi," I said.

"You all right?" She moved back to let me step inside, but neither one of us closed the door. She didn't seem drunk. "Vonna miss you." She fussed with the newborn's ear while Sienna squirmed in Jywon's arms.

"Where is Vonna?" I had this idea that maybe I would take her for a walk and try to tell her some things. Things about life.

Janelle shrugged. "She around."

I couldn't let myself think too much about Vonna right now. I had to stay focused. "I need to start getting some of my DYFS money." Janelle's hands went still. "Every month."

Jywon put Sienna down, and she went running to huddle behind Janelle's legs. "We heard you making your own money."

He used his thumb knuckle to push his glasses higher. Maybe he had seen me once on the track or one of my dates was someone who knew him. Maybe he was just guessing.

"You still staying at that friend's?" Janelle asked. Sienna peeked around to get a good look at me. She was still cute as anything.

"Yeah," I said. "But what I'm saying is if you want to keep on taking my DYFS money, I need some of it too from now on."

"Listen to you." Janelle shifted the bundle to her other shoulder. "You speaking up."

I waited, glancing around to see if there were any blue Booth's bottles anywhere.

"Well, you know it ain't easy as that. Comes in stamps and vouchers. Ain't no cash."

"You have cash."

"Glad to see you got some get-up-and-go now. You was always so quiet."

"Get-up-and-go for damn sure," Jywon said.

"Shut up," Janelle snapped at him. She tucked the new-born under one arm and slipped her other fingers into a back pocket, pulling out three wrinkled dollars. "This all I got today." She held them out to me. "You want it? Go ahead."

It wasn't enough. Not nearly enough. Maybe she had to

take care of people, but I had to take care of people now too. I frowned at the bills. "You spent the rest on gin?"

She stared at me before she answered. I guess she was surprised. "Do I look like I'm drinking to you?" She slid the money back into her pocket.

I tried to think of what Shug might say. "Maybe not right this second."

Jywon made a whooshing sound with his mouth. Janelle looked more than surprised now. She looked as if I'd pulled a gun on her.

I kept on. "I guess you're just waiting until somebody takes this baby away."

She tried to slap me with her free hand, but I was too quick. She just swiped air. I backed up more into the open doorway, expecting for her to try again, but she didn't. Instead she huffed out some kind of sigh and lifted the newborn back to her shoulder. She huffed again. "I can't hardly believe you."

We were quiet for a minute. All of us. Sienna had her big eyes fixed on me. Jywon had his little ones.

"I'm not coming back again," I told Janelle. "DYFS will figure it out. And they'll investigate you and take everybody away." I believed myself for a minute and thought about how she would cry all night. "I'm sorry for that."

"Well, life is not no storybook," Janelle said. "I see you worked that out by now."

Sienna kept peeking out at me. I wanted to smile at her, or wink, but I didn't know how right then.

"If they investigate me," Janelle pointed out, "they going to investigate you. Jywon know where you at. He'll be right delighted to tell them." She wasn't saying it unkindly; just as a point to consider. But Jywon smirked and did something obscene with his hand at his crotch behind Janelle's back. Then he turned and walked away somewhere.

I looked after him while I spoke to Janelle. "You need to watch Jywon around the little girls."

Janelle shook her head. "Please," she said. "Jywon harmless."

"You need to watch," I repeated.

Janelle nodded. "All right then." She jiggled the baby a beat and then rested her other palm on the top of Sienna's head. "See you."

Part of me had known it wouldn't work. None of it. Celie would have known too. I guess I was foolish to have hoped otherwise.

At the library I kept my head down, hiding *How to Deliver a Baby in an Emergency* on the table but under my puffy coat. I read the chapters I needed half-shaded beneath the gray fur-lined hood. Every time anybody came close—the Puerto Rican male librarian named Daniel or the white female—I used the math textbook to knock-slide the baby book all the way under.

I didn't want to be reading about how to deliver babies at all. I didn't want to be staring at geometry, either. I wanted to be far away from babies and math and Daddy. I wanted to be riding an elephant or on a front porch fanning flies with Celie and Nettie. I wanted to be reading *The Color Purple* over and over until I was so far inside it, I wouldn't even remember myself.

I didn't know how to discuss it, though, and so even though a part of me hoped to see the librarian with the clacking necklace, another part of me was relieved she never showed up, covering for anybody.

I took notes and looked at pictures. Whenever there was a working computer, I put my name on the list to use it, so that I could search YouTube videos and websites. It wasn't that hard. If everything went fine, there wasn't that much to know. But all sorts of things could go wrong. The baby could come feet first or with the cord around its neck. Lollipop could bleed to death. I wasn't sure how a baby could get out of an eleven-year-old girl. It didn't make sense to begin with, even with a full-grown woman. And Lollipop was some-where around seven months now. I needed an A in this. I couldn't fail.

I never actually failed a class before last year. Now I was getting Fs in English and math, both. I thought I would get called out by a guidance counselor, but it hadn't happened yet. My English teacher did keep me one day, though. It made me nervous, because I was scheduled for a party. Daddy was picking me up in the Escalade, and he would be furious if I was late.

"You're struggling in my class," Mr. Davis told me. He was the color of a tree trunk at dusk—it made me think of down south—and his hair was shaved close to his head. "As you know, your tests have not gone well." His round eyes made him seem surprised all the time, but nothing else about him seemed that way. Mostly he was calm and solid. Trevor said he used to be in the military. "And you haven't turned in homework assignments for a while."

I glanced at the clock. Mr. Davis noticed. "Are you expected somewhere?"

"Yes."

"I'm available after school for help. I stay an hour later Tuesdays and Thursdays for students to drop by."

I nodded.

"I notice you're falling asleep in class frequently."

"I'm sorry."

His round eyes looked at me, seeing me, just a little bit the way I once thought Daddy used to see me. But I had been so stupid to think that. "You don't have to be sorry." His voice was kind, but Daddy's had been too. "I'm just wondering if there's any way you might get more sleep at home."

"Okay."

"I would be happy to speak with your parents or parent or guardian, if that could help."

I tried not to show panic. "I have to go. My boyfriend is waiting for me."

He frowned and looked past me, then at me, then past me again. But he couldn't figure it out. So he excused me instead.

Lollipop was getting big enough to really notice, so not many men wanted her anymore. On the other hand, the ones who did were apparently paying top dollar. *Frogs,* Celie might say. *They all frogs to me.* It made me want to laugh and cry both at the same time, what Celie thought of men.

Lollipop was tired, and she said her legs jumped around at night. But she was proud. "I'm making all of us rich," she boasted, patting her round belly.

We were in her hotel room, and I was trying to explain to her how she needed to breathe during contractions. She didn't want to listen.

"Daddy didn't want me to know, but that last date from Tuesday told me how much he paid."

She wanted me to ask, but I couldn't. I could hardly look at her myself, much less think about her with a date. It was too messed up.

"Three thousand!" Lollipop shouted. "Three thousand!"

I guess she learned her numbers. "Lollipop, I don't care how much anybody paid for you. I have to get that baby out of you safely, and I need you to pay attention to me."

"Stop worrying, Dime," she pouted. "It's not going to be a big thing. I'll just go away when it's time."

"You can't go away from a baby coming out of you!" I still didn't know if her ignorance was an act or not.

"You can go away from anything," Lollipop said. "I do it all the time so that when it hurts, nothing hurts."

"I don't know what you're talking about." But I did. She was talking about what I imagined when I tapped on the gray brick, hoping for an escape route. Except I think what Lollipop was telling me was that she really knew how to make it work. How to go far away so that she wasn't feeling or thinking anything when her body was right there.

"If it's a boy, I'm going to name it Ray, after Ray, since I'll never see him again," she said matter-of-factly. "And if it's a girl, I'm going to call her Rayelle after him too." She thought for a second. "You think Daddy will put the baby in here with me? Or do you think he'll keep the baby back at the apartment?"

"I don't know, Lolly," I told her. "I really don't know."

Fake snow and candy canes were up on the walls at school. In the front lobby, just past the metal detectors, they put up a plastic Christmas tree. Two days later it was knocked over and half-crushed. TV commercials were filled with red and green and silver and gold and "We Wish You a Merry Christmas" and "Jingle Bells" and "The Little Drummer Boy." The Puerto Rican man and the white woman pulled out books on Christmas and Hanukkah and Kwanzaa. I watched them set up the display the day I was studying breech births for the fourth time. My librarian showed up again, her fingernails freshly silver with green ribbons painted perfectly on each thumbnail. She had no idea I was on my third reading of *The Color Purple*. Or that I had even looked at it yet.

"I hope you'll discuss it with me the next time we cross paths," she said. "It really is challenging."

I nodded.

Daddy bought us Christmas-colored bras and panties, and Brandy got a new coat, red on the outside and black lining on the inside. Lollipop didn't get one because she wasn't allowed out. Three different dates gave me red-and-white-striped candy canes.

Then L.A. came back. Wearing a new sweater jacket that went to her knees. I'd forgotten about the gap in her mouth.

She decided to hang tinsel all over the apartment within an hour of walking in the door, dragging Lollipop's pink and white suitcases behind her. "It is slow down there." She poked her tongue through her gap. "I mean, slow."

"What are those Russian girls like?" Brandy asked.

I wanted to know why she was back. Was it just for Christmas? Did Daddy miss her?

"Slow." She pulled out another piece of tape and attached her green tinsel to the top of the TV. "We going to switch," she said. "After the baby come, you going down south and I'm staying up here."

"Yeah, but until the baby come, you working the street with me," Brandy said.

"I'm not working no track." L.A. twisted the tinsel so that it curled around the edges of the TV, all the way around. The locks turned, and Daddy walked in as L.A. kept talking. "I'm doing outcalls and parties. Daddy say Christmas season more profitable up here than down south. If I bring home a certain Christmas quota, I'm getting a new tooth."

"Who say you getting a new tooth?" Daddy asked. He hung up his new black-and-brown coat—Brandy said it was *shearling*—and then thumbed his phone without looking at us as he walked to the couch.

"You getting it for me," L.A. said. "Don't play like you ain't."

"How much does a new tooth cost?" Brandy asked.

"More than you make," L.A. said.

Daddy ignored them, tapping his phone fast. I wondered if he was texting Eagle. And I wondered what a new tooth cost. A hundred dollars? A thousand? Why didn't Daddy just get her a new tooth right away, because—except for the true freaks—wouldn't it likely turn off most dates?

"Dime, get me a beer," Daddy said.

I went to the kitchen to get a forty. When I came back and handed it to him, he pulled me down onto his lap. "You studying hard?" he asked.

"Yes."

"Good," he said. "We all counting on you."

The one they called Dime didn't see it coming. That's how Truth would begin this next part. *She thought she had grown up enough by now and knew enough by now not to be surprised by anything anymore. Not by Daddy cooking the household's Christmas Eve turkey himself. Not by Daddy ordering them all to work Christmas Day. Dime was sure nothing would ever surprise her again. But she was wrong.*

Daddy was home when I came back from the library. He was in the best mood I'd ever seen him in. If I didn't know better, I might even think he was drunk or high. Instead of telling me to hurry up and change, he took me into his room, tossed me onto his bed, and got himself naked in two seconds. His new scar bumped a short line on his chest. His muscles were tight and his shoulders bulged. He was standing up straight—every part of him—grinning.

"Just had me a conversation with Uncle Ray." He dragged me down the bed by my ankles. "You know what you doing birthing that baby, right?"

My bottom was at the bed's edge, so I lifted my hips. "Yes." Lollipop had never been to the clinic. What if she had high blood pressure? What if she had gestational diabetes? What if the baby was a boy, and Uncle Ray didn't want to buy a boy? I guess that was Daddy's problem. Or maybe Uncle Ray did want to buy a boy.

"Ain't nobody seen you reading about it?" He wiggled my jeans down and then tugged them off.

"Nobody knows," I said. I was more used to pretending now, plus I knew he knew I was scared about the baby, so it was okay if I didn't pretend as well as I usually tried.

He was in a hurry, and it was over fast. He dressed right away. "I'm out," he told me. "You stay. I'm a be back in a while. Take you a shower and wait for me clean."

"What about work?" I asked. "What about my quota?"

He flashed his *D*. "You getting a little vacation this afternoon." He smiled. "Business booming."

He hadn't taken me twice in the same day since before down south. I wished I hadn't been the only one home. If L.A. had been here, he probably would have taken her instead of me. I had to hope that when he came back, he would want it fast again so it would be over quickly. I listened to him leave, to the locks on the door clicking into place. Then I lay there, wondering how much time I had. It was strange not to have somewhere to go, something to do. I was just about to get out of the bed and get into the shower, when I heard the locks again. I thought it was Daddy, forgetting something, and I almost called out. But it wasn't Daddy. It was L.A. and Eagle.

"Whippet got the spot set," L.A. said. I heard her walk to the refrigerator and pull something out. "Philadelphia."

"I do not trust Whippet." I heard Eagle scrape a kitchen chair as he sat down.

"Well, he got the spot set." L.A. sucked her teeth. "Anyways, I don't trust you."

"I have buyer," Eagle said, in an impatient tone, as if he had said it lots of times.

"How do I know you ain't playing me?"

There was a silence. Then L.A. sucked her teeth again. "Lollipop's people going to pay forty grand for a baby?"

"Yes."

"So that what you and Daddy been planning? To sell the baby back down south? To her uncle Ray or whoever?"

Eagle must have nodded.

"But you and me and Whippet. We selling it to someone different?"

"Not so much money," Eagle said. "Not so much like from Raymond. But mine people disappear. Impossible to find after. Safe."

"How much I'm a get?"

"We divide. Whippet. You. Me. Seven. Eight thousand."

"Each?" L.A. asked. "Or we got to split that?"

"I tell you many time," Eagle said. "Each." He must have handed her his phone. "Call. Make plan."

"You sure Daddy not coming back here?"

"He bring date to little girl. We have hour."

"What is your people doing buying a baby anyways?"

I didn't hear Eagle answer.

"What people buy babies for?"

Eagle still didn't say anything.

"Eight thousand?" L.A. said.

"Seven. Eight." Then Eagle sounded impatient. "Make call."

I heard silence. And then I heard L.A. talking. "It's me. Yo. He right here. You still got the spot set? We got a buyer. Uh-huh. Yeah."

I didn't move inside the satin sheets. I tried not to breathe. I tried to stop my heart from pounding so loud.

Eagle and L.A. left.

What? What? What? What? What? What?

Daddy came back.

"Why you ain't showered?" he asked me.

I couldn't answer. I couldn't move.

"I told you get clean," Daddy said.

"I feel sick," I whispered.

He kicked his door shut and flashed his *D*. "You lucky I'm in a good mood." He dropped his pants. "Try this," he said. "This make you feel better."

Dime used to be foolish, Truth would write, *simple even. But she had learned a lot in a short space of time.* He would pause, thinking about how I had grown up and become wise. Then he would continue. *I'm guessing that by now you understand what I will be asking you to do with this note and package.* If Truth were real, he would be so worried. *I'm almost finished,* Truth would add. *If you could just read all the way to the end. It would mean so much.*

Chapter Thirty-Three

THAT SEEMS LIKE yesterday and also an entire lifetime. Nettie said it best in one of her letters to Celie: *Time moves slowly, but passes quickly.* Either way, the fact is that Lollipop could give birth any second. Brandy and I are supposedly prepared: I made Daddy buy sheets, extra-thick towels, straws, two fleece baby blankets. Soap and disinfectant wipes and gloves and formula and a box of diapers, and other things the books and websites said I'd need. It's all stored under the beds in the hotel.

Daddy's had the two end rooms opposite each other on the top floor of the hotel all this time. He's planned it, hoping it will be harder for "guests" in the other rooms to hear Lollipop scream if she's up high in a corner. Also the live feed is off. Lollipop only does scheduled time slots now. Brandy says Daddy is being more careful than usual since Lollipop is so pregnant. She says Daddy doesn't want too much word getting out what he's selling right now because a pregnant eleven-year-old is a squad magnet for sure. Daddy shrugs and says he's not worried, but it's just that people pay more money if they have to wait to watch.

He sent L.A. back down south right after Christmas. He sent her with Eagle straight from an overnight. She must have been pissed off. I don't know how she and Eagle and Whippet are planning it: What can L.A. do from all the way down south? Even the "spot," whatever that is, is in Philadelphia. Maybe Whippet's going to drive down south to pick up L.A. and bring her back to Philadelphia with him, and they're going to wait there for Eagle to call or come with the baby. Except if I was L.A., I wouldn't trust Eagle as far as I could throw him. Or Whippet. Why does she think they even need her? Maybe there's more than one spot and they're going to have to take the baby somewhere after Philadelphia and will need some-body who looks like a mother to get to wherever they're going.

Between preparing to deliver the baby and trying to hide what I know and trying to figure out L.A.'s plan, I can hardly think straight. I want to go right back to *what?* But I can't.

Lollipop is pregnant, and there's going to be a baby, and I have to save it.

All Daddy talks about with me is baby plans.

"When she starts up that labor, you tell Eagle immediate. He going to find Brandy. Then you and her getting that baby out."

I nod.

"After it finished, you scrub up good."

I nod again.

"Keep Lollipop in the bathtub for all the blood. Easier to clean."

"Did you ever see a baby born?" I am wondering how he knows there will be so much blood.

He laughs, flashing his gold *D*. "I got born, didn't I?"

I stay quiet after that. I'm afraid if I say much more, I'll somehow reveal what he still doesn't know about L.A. plotting with Whippet and Eagle. It doesn't feel real to believe that people actually buy babies. But maybe that's not so different from buying Lollipop for an hour. Or buying me. I'm wondering if L.A. and Eagle and Whippet will keep the promises they made to each other. Maybe one of them will play the others. Maybe all of them are hoping to play the others. It's hard to say.

I just hope I can keep it from Brandy. I don't want to involve her. I don't want her getting beaten again, or worse. I did look for her powder. I've looked for it three times, when

I had the chance. It's not anywhere. Not tucked inside the foot of my sleeping bag, not slipped in with the tampons or folded between socks or behind the padding of a bra or anywhere. And I can't ask her again, because it's just too dangerous for both of us if she knows I'm up to anything.

I still know I'll have to kill myself. I'll have to do it before anybody finds me, especially because they all will want to make sure I die hurting.

Between two thirty and seven thirty each morning I lay my head on the royal-blue pillow I got so long ago from Daddy. I breathe as evenly as I can, reading, or trying to decide how to write the note and also how to end my life when I'm finished doing what I'm going to do.

I still don't know which voice to use for the note, which one will be the most effective.

And I still don't know which method to use to kill myself. What will be the most painless, the least terrifying? Throwing myself in front of a car doesn't seem 100 percent certain. I could just lose a leg or become paralyzed. It would hurt. Grabbing Eagle's gun off the front seat is too risky. He's faster than I am, and stronger. Daddy always has his gun on him now. I think he sold the pearl-handled one. The same three times I looked for Brandy's card in the powder,

I looked for that gun, too. It wasn't anywhere. I don't have drugs or medicine to overdose. I thought I could get some from Stone's girls, but everybody would see me, and Stone himself might hand me over to Daddy. There's a bathtub in my hotel bathroom, but not enough time for me to bleed to death in there before they'll all find me.

It's going to have to be one of those bridges. There are a lot that cross the river.

Brandy surprises me. "What do you think Daddy going to do with that baby?" she asks one Sunday. We're cleaning up in the kitchen from early dinner before going to work. Daddy is out.

I shrug.

"You think if it's a boy, Daddy going to take him for his own?"

"What if it's a girl?" I ask back.

"Maybe raise her up too? Be nice to have a baby around."

Hearing her wish for that, as silly and stupid as something poor Lollipop might think up, gives me crazy thoughts. Thoughts that don't go together but all seem important. "How much do you remember your grandmother?" I ask.

"What?"

"Like what do you remember?"

"The way she did up my hair," Brandy says. "The way she sang. She sang from *Thriller* all the time and also Marian Anderson." She starts dancing around. *"Billy Jean is NOT myy looover. She's just a girl who says that III am the onnnne. But the KID is not my sonnnnn."*

"I remember a lady," I interrupt.

She stops singing and raises her eyebrows instead. "You talkative today."

"She used to read to me," I say. "On a rocking chair. She had a watch."

"Why you telling me this?" Brandy asks.

"In case a lady like that ever comes by," I say. "You can make sure she knows I remembered."

Brandy puts her hands on her hips. "You gone crazy, Dime? The hell you talking about?"

"There's a gray brick in the alley behind the third house by the track," I tell her. "Sometimes I think if I push it just the right way, I can find that lady."

Brandy bugs out her eyes. "I always knew you was psycho."

"I'm just saying," I say. "Maybe you could find your grand-mother too."

"Shut up."

"She used to read to you, too, didn't she?"

"Shut up, I said."

"*Goodnight Moon*, right?"

"You walking on thin ice."

"You should apologize to Lollipop for what you did to her."

"I did that already."

"You did?"

"Please," Brandy says. "Don't be so surprised."

"I'm not surprised," I say. "And just because *Goodnight Moon* bothers you, doesn't mean you have a right to beat little girls."

"I want to pretend I don't know what you talking about, bitch," Brandy tells me. "But I'm so taken back that you talking so much, I'll just let it lie."

Since I know what I'm going to do, and I know there isn't much time left, I don't bother to keep trying at school. Ds and Fs don't really matter anymore. Instead I think about what it will be like to jump off a bridge. I tell myself that maybe I will get to be on John Edward, after all. Just not from this side. Maybe it was a grandmother or an aunt or possibly even my own mother. Whoever it was with the scratching watch and the barbecue potato chip breath will be searching for me. And John Edward will say, *She wants you to know she is with the elephants, and they are taking care of her, and she is okay.*

I imagine that, but mostly I just concentrate on remembering the books I've always loved. Or on hiding my flashlight inside my sleeping bag while rereading *The Color Purple*, the only book I have left. I burrow inside the pages of my memory and of my thick paperback in the early morning between two thirty and seven thirty. The time when I'm so tired I can hardly keep my eyes open, but the characters are so alive I can't close them. Scout, Tom, Boo, Janie, Charlie, Alec, Carrie, Katniss, Cathy, Mandy, Charlotte, Corduroy, Max, James, Wendy, Celie, Nettie, Shug.

The stories and the characters begin to overlap, to blur together, but their hearts are all the same. And that helps.

Chapter Thirty-Four

IT HAPPENS EARLIER than I thought it would. I've just arrived after school, and I'm in Lollipop's hotel room doing her hair, getting her ready for a show at four. It's Friday afternoon.

"Dime?" Lollipop says. "I'm peeing on myself."

She's dripping a puddle on the carpet. *Thank you, Jesus,* I say to myself, even though I never talk to Jesus. "Get over the toilet." *Thank you for letting me be here when it begins. Thank you, thank you, thank you.*

She runs to the bathroom, leaving a liquid trail behind. I blot it up as best I can and follow her. When her stream slows to a trickle and then to a stop, I wipe her legs dry and bring her a fresh change of clothes.

"It doesn't hurt at all," Lollipop says. She looks down

at herself, pulling her waistband out. "I don't see a head or anything."

"Lollipop, I told you so many times it could be hours before you feel any pain. It could be a day or more before that baby comes out." *Please let it be tonight. Please, please, please.*

I lead her back to the computer. "Now do your show and then get in bed and rest," I tell her. "If you start getting pain, don't worry. It will stop in a minute and then it won't happen again for a couple of hours. Do not say during your show that your water broke. Do not say that. Daddy said so, okay?"

"Okay," she says. "Can I have the orange ribbons, though?"

I'm betting that since she is so young and since this is her first baby, nothing much will happen soon. I am praying that baby will wait until later, until after dark, until long after dark. Even though I don't pray, I am praying and praying and praying.

I have three dates all in a row. The first is one of those stupid ones.

"I like that color," he says, about my fingernails. They are the same blue as my pillowcase. He's sitting on the edge of the bed and hasn't even taken off his shoes. "Do you do them yourself?"

I shake my head. Brandy does them for me.

"How old are you?"

"Nineteen," I lie, and I start to undress him, since he doesn't seem in any hurry.

"Wow. You look younger." He's wearing boxers, and he has a gold chain around his ankle. "What do you use this money for?" He slips off his own shirt, and I work on his pants.

"I pay for classes at Rutgers," I say. "I want to be a teacher."

"That's a great goal," he says. "I bet you make money fast doing this."

I nod again.

"You have any brothers or sisters?"

"One brother and four sisters," I say. *Jywon, Vonna, Sienna, Lollipop, Brandy*.

"It's nice to have a big family," he tells me.

I start to touch him, just to keep things going. He's white, but his skin has that red tint some white men have.

He stops me. "Don't be scared, okay?" he says, which scares me. "I'm going to take care of myself," he says. "You just stand there and hit me."

"Hit you?"

"Yeah." His red face turns pink. "It really turns me on," he says. "Just slap me around a little." He picks up my hand and makes me hit his cheek the way Daddy slaps me.

"Oh," I say. "Okay."

*   *   *

The second john folds me over the edge of the bed so that he can stand behind me. He takes forever to finish.

The next one has a limp and asks me to sit on his lap facing him. It takes him forever too, and the whole time all I can see are the shades of pink inside his huge nostrils.

Finally I have a break and I can check on Lollipop. She's fast asleep in her bed. It's almost six. I have fifteen minutes before my next date. I spend it frantically trying to write my note. I've been using the empty pages left in the back of my old English notebook. It has to be perfect. I've been working on it for so many weeks. But I still don't know how to do it. Who to be. What to write. I start and stop five times, then six. I hear footsteps approaching my door. My date. I slide my English notebook and pen under the bed.

I'm back in Lollipop's room at seven, carrying a bag of cheeseburgers and fries. Eagle is following me because I couldn't figure out how to stop him. I hope Lollipop's still asleep. She's not. She's sitting up in bed, watching Nickelodeon.

"How you feel?" Eagle asks.

I hold my breath, silently begging her not to tell him

her water broke. Not to get a contraction. She ignores him, spaced out on the television screen. I scrabble a french fry and try to eat it, faking calm.

"I ask how you feel!" Eagle says more loudly.

Lollipop glances at him. "Sorry," she says. "Fine, thanks."

Eagle looks at her for a minute and then strides over to the bed. He pulls the covers down and looks at her belly for a long second.

"What?" Lollipop asks. She looks at me. My cold nerves are leaping all over the place. "What?"

"You have date tomorrow. Eleven. Two hour." Eagle doesn't bother to replace the covers. He just marches out of the room.

Lollipop glazes over at Nickelodeon again. I turn the TV off and wait a minute for her to snap out of it.

"I have to go back to my room," I tell her. "I'm working again in ten minutes. Did you have another contraction yet?"

She nods. "Yeah," she says. "It hurt bad but it's over now."

"How long ago?"

"*SpongeBob SquarePants* twice, *Victorious*, and then most of *Drake and Josh*."

About two hours.

"I'm going to come check on you as much as I can," I tell her. "You keep track of the pains. That means you have to remember how long between each one. Okay?"

"Is the baby coming tonight?"

I think of the man arriving at eleven tomorrow. I feel icicles over my body. "I hope so."

The one they call Dime usually has a steady stream of dates during the late afternoon and into the night. Eagle, working for Daddy, brings the johns in, mostly from the Newark airport, when he isn't driving Brandy to a party or to a private indoor event. This means that Dime has to turn tricks and check on Lollipop without letting her dates, Eagle, or Lollipop know what she's up to. Truth would put his pen down to shake out his hands. *I haven't meant to write so much,* he might add, after a minute. *It's just that I know I'm complicated and hard to understand. I'm sorry,* he would write. *All I'm trying to do is ask for help.*

Lollipop's labor goes just like the books and the videos said they would, except faster for a first birth. It's good that it's going faster, because if it lasts until daytime tomorrow, it will be much harder for me to do what I need to do. I pray and pray and pray.

After every trick, I make myself walk and not run across the hall into Lollipop's room. I manage to scrub the bathtub with Clorox and spread clean towels on every surface. Once or twice when I walk back, the men are waiting by my door already, and I act like them waiting for me to show up is normal.

Twice I see Eagle walking toward our rooms. Each time, I am calm in the hallway. "Nothing yet," I say to Eagle. "I just checked."

He believes me and turns back around.

By midnight I have Lollipop right outside her bathroom, propped up on pillows, praying Eagle won't come in. If he does, I'm planning to shout, "Hurry! It's happening so fast! Get Daddy and Brandy!" As if I never had time to tell him it had started. If that happens, I guess I'll have to try to take Lollipop with me as soon as he leaves, but I don't know how on earth I can drag her, in labor, out of the hotel.

The good surprise is that Lollipop really can go away: She goes wall when the pains get bad, and she's been staying wall for longer and longer in the past hour and a half. The bad surprise is that makes it harder to time how far apart the contractions are and harder to help her move around. The books said to try kneeling or to rest on all fours, squatting or leaning forward on your knees with arms on a table or something. But it's hard for me to get Lollipop up and moving. She just wants to be left alone to lie in one spot.

"Sorry," I keep saying. "I'm not trying to hurt you." Her wall scares me. It's as if she's dead.

I have to remember to rearrange my face when I rush back into my room for the next john. I have to remember to act the way they expect me to act so I can get them out of there fast and go check again.

"Take a shower," one date tells me. I don't want to. I don't want to take the extra time. I end up taking the shower but ignoring what he asks me to do next. Instead I wrap my mouth around him, pretending that I love to do that so much I just can't help myself. I figure that will finish him off fast, and it does.

At about one thirty in the morning, the contractions get closer together. They are about ten minutes apart. The books say when they get to two minutes apart I have to be ready to catch the baby. *Thank you,* I tell Jesus, my new best friend, who I doubt I even believe in. *Thank you for having this happen on a Friday night.* On weekend nights Daddy makes me work straight through until six or seven. If this was a school night, Eagle would be looking to take me home in half an hour. *Thank you, thank you, thank you.*

I think it's time to get Lollipop into the bathtub, but it's hard to coax her to come out from behind her wall.

"Come on," I keep saying. "Lolly, come on. We have to get you into the bathtub now. Lollipop? Lollipop!"

Finally she comes back with a rush of breath. She wails. "It hurts!"

"I know," I tell her as kindly as I can. "It's going to hurt a lot more, too. Bite on this." I hand her a wet, rolled-up towel, wait until the contraction seems to end, and then haul her to her feet. "You have to try not to make any noise, okay?"

"Where's Brandy?" She's moaning and crying.

"It's not time for her to come yet," I say. "I'm going to get her soon. It's going to be okay. You're doing a great job. It's going to be okay." I half carry her the few steps into the bathroom and then help her step up and over into the tub.

"Don't be nice to me," Lollipop sobs while I try to get her on all fours. "If you're nice to me, it's harder to go away."

"Well, Lolly, I can't be mean."

She starts crying and moaning louder. I'm so afraid Eagle will hear. "I just want to go away," Lollipop cries. She drops her head into her hands, belly hanging down and butt in the air. "It really hurts, Dime. It really hurts a lot."

Somehow nobody hears. Between tricks I walk across the hall to help Lollipop in all those different positions. I try to help her breathe. Most of the time she is wall and not present. Some of the time she comes back to me and either screams, *Where is Brandy, where is Daddy? Where is Uncle Ray?* or just screams without words.

The contractions are five minutes apart now, and I'm pretty sure she's done about four of them without me in the bathroom with her. "Am I really not ever going to see him again?" she asks, holding her breath.

"I don't know," I say to her. "Breathe."

I am hot and sweaty and dirty. My next date is in fifteen minutes at three thirty. Lollipop is shaking and wailing. I look between her legs. Everything looks the same, but different. I don't know if the baby is ready, and I don't know what to do. So I just make a choice and wash my hands again, then walk down the hallway to the elevator. It's hard not to run, but that would be stupid, so I walk as normally as I can manage out to the street and wait for the town car to appear. In a few minutes, Eagle cruises to the curb, puts on his flashers, and rolls down his window.

"It's time," I tell him. "She's just starting. You should probably go get Brandy." I try to act like there's no hurry, like I'm not in a hurry, so I lean in.

"The baby?" he asks, as if to make sure.

"Yes," I say. "Her water just broke, so there's plenty of time." I pause, wondering if he even knows what water breaking means. "But you should probably tell Daddy and see if he wants Brandy to come now. Or what he wants to do with her eleven tomorrow."

Eagle nods, I straighten, and he rolls up the window. He will send my date away and then go get Whippet. I'm counting on that. I walk as slowly as I can back toward the hotel door. Eagle and Whippet and L.A., wherever she is, will believe they have hours to find their people, to arrange their meeting, to take the baby.

I have time now, I tell myself, forcing myself to walk to the elevator, to walk until I'm back in Lollipop's room.

The baby's head is crowning, and Lollipop is screaming as I reach her. I know I need to wash my hands all over again or at least put on sterile gloves, but there's no time.

"Breathe," I tell her. All of a sudden she smiles a grimacy smile, and the baby's head pops out. And stays there, stuck. Lollipop is flat limp on her back in the tub, with that baby's head almost resting on the messy, slippery bottom. I haul her up to the tub's edge and perch her bottom on a pillow there so that the baby is pointing downward. "Hold yourself steady," I order her, because I can't do what I have to do and keep her from slipping back down at the same time. She braces her palms on either side of her and does her best, crying and moaning. I wipe guck off the baby's face with a clean washcloth from my stack. The baby's face is blue. I'm trying to ignore the way it's just poking out of Lollipop. I'm trying not to panic, and then the baby's head turns to the side, and a shoulder slides out. Then the whole baby is sliding out, and I grab a clean towel just in time to catch it. But it's still blue. I wipe its face again and rub it all over while Lollipop slides down back inside the tub. I keep rubbing, but the baby doesn't cry. Then I remember the straws, and I'm not sure if I should wipe alcohol over one first. I'm too scared, too much in a hurry, so I don't. I just poke the straw at the baby's tiny nostril and I suck on it, pulling out the guck. I suck more out and then switch to the other tiny nostril. I keep going back and forth until there's no more guck. Then I stick my pinky inside the baby's mouth to wipe out anything left. The baby begins to pink up and cry. The crying sounds like a little toy, squeaking, like it's not even human. It is so cute, I can hardly stand it. I settle the baby on top of Lollipop. She pulls it up to where she can properly look. "Rayelle."

"Hold her carefully," I say. "And be still. We have to get the placenta out."

"The wha?" Lollipop says, and then she gasps and the placenta oozes out. She look down at it and yells, "Eeeew-wwwww, gross!" And then she looks back at the baby and laughs and laughs, lying in the bathtub full of guck and blood. The baby keeps squawking those toyish squawks. I grab the dental floss from a plastic Baggie off the sink and the new CVS scissors and wipe them with an alcohol wipe. Then I pause. Some of the books said to wait twenty minutes. Others said to watch until the cord seems to stop pulsing. I'm not sure what to do. I don't want to hurt the baby or Lollipop. But if I take too long . . .

"Hold Rayelle toward me," I tell Lollipop. "Don't you dare drop her." She does as she's told, and I use dental floss to tie the cord a few inches from Rayelle's belly. Then I cut the cord. It's difficult. It's like cutting old meat, and it takes a long time. The scissors are not sharp enough.

But I do it, and when I'm finished, I put the baby back on Lollipop's belly. I turn on the bathwater again and try to clean a little. The placenta is huge, though, and goo and blood fill the tub.

"Where's Brandy?" Lollipop says, cradling Rayelle in the towel. "Where's Daddy and Eagle and L.A.?"

"I'm going to get them now," I lie. "They're just outside waiting." I take Rayelle from her. "I'm going to bundle her better," I explain. "And bring her out to them, and then we're all going to get you cleaned up and out of this tub."

I move as fast as I can, wrapping Rayelle now first in one of the two fleece blankets and then in a towel. I twist off the cap of the formula bottle and slip it in the baby's mouth. She sucks right away.

I look at Lollipop, a bloody, happy mess in the filthy bathtub. "Press on your belly, here," I show her, placing her hands beneath her belly button. The books say she could bleed to death if I don't make sure. There's more I wish I could express to her, but there's no time, and I don't have the right words. "I'll be right back," I lie again, my dead soul half breaking and half singing. "I promise."

My paperback sits at the bottom of the knapsack beneath two fresh towels and the second fleece blanket, all folded into rounded rectangles. I lay the wrapped baby on top of the stack and zip up around her until only her face shows. Then I prop the bottle in her mouth, knowing it will fall out and worrying she will fall out too, or suffocate. I grab the piece of paper and the flashlight pen I told Daddy to buy at CVS so that I could see all the parts of Lollipop I thought I'd need to see, shrug into my black puffy coat, slip the heavy knapsack on, and try not to run.

I can't leave her at the hospital, because it's too close and Daddy or L.A. could have time to find both of us there and also somebody might see me and call the police. I can't leave her with the police, because they will arrest me and give the baby to L.A. or to foster care, and also Daddy or the others might find me before I even get to the station. But even though it's far away—really far away—there is one place I can go. I know how to get there, because I've spent a lot of time looking out car windows, noticing.

It's dark and cold enough that there are hardly any people out. I just duck my head and try to be invisible. I check on the baby with my palm reached up high and back. The bottle has fallen out and she's not making any sounds, but I can feel her exposed face, so if she's dead, it's not from suffocation. I walk and walk, trying to think of what to write down on my note.

It's a beautiful thing when it's two young people in love, I could write. *So give this fresh baby a chance to know what that's like someday. . . .*

She squawks, still alive. I'm nervous about the temperature. They say newborns get cold so fast, and somehow Daddy and L.A. didn't get a hat for her, even though I told them they had to. Babies lose most of their heat from their head, and it must be about five degrees out. I can't feel my own face. I'm worried.

You take this newborn bitch, the note could say, *and you consider it a gift. You sell it to the highest bidder, and you will have more of me than you ever dreamed was possible.*

I reach up behind my neck again to her face and feel a tiny warm mouth find my pinky. I keep my hand there to let her suck, and I twist it a little as I walk, trying to make my palm be a cap for her.

What lies here before you, I could try, *is both amazing and upsetting. Please tend to her as I wish all people would tend to me.*

I arrive. It must be about five o'clock. Quiet. I'm shivering and sweating at the same time.

I climb the four steps, carefully ease the knapsack onto the ground, unzip it, and pick up Rayelle. I hold the bundle of her under one arm like a football while I pull out the towels and fleece, unrolling and draping them over my shoulder. I reach to the bottom of the knapsack with my free hand and find the book. *The Color Purple.* I place it on the ground just in front of the door, title facing up and edges squared. I tug the linens off my shoulder, using the towels to line the knapsack and the fleece for a final warm layer. I pull the fleece longwise so that it covers the top of the baby's head and the tips of her toes. She squawks while I arrange her like a princess on top of the padding and near the knapsack's opening so that she can breathe. I sit on the frigid cement and cradle the knapsack in my lap to keep it as warm as I can.

I pull out my pen flashlight and crumpled, bloody paper. There's not enough time to write it the way I had hoped I would. There's too much, and it's too complicated, and there are too many voices. So I give up all my fancy ideas and just try to make it legible.

Please make sure this baby gets a good story.

I slide the note beneath the fleece folds. I stay hunched over for as long as I can before I imagine that people will come along and see us. A glow of light begins to seep into the air. There is nobody around anywhere. The glow lightens and lightens until it is sun bright and the outlines of buildings and cars and trees and hydrants and mailboxes are crisp, glinting. It's hard to put Rayelle down, but I might already have waited too long, and I need to get to a bridge. So I rest her gently next to the book, in front of the library door, beneath the green statues guarding the archway. I tuck her in as best I can and kiss her cheek.

And then I go.

Dime

I HAVE NO idea what made me take off the puffy black coat with the gray fur-lined hood all those years ago. Maybe I thought I would fall faster and harder. Maybe I thought that being coatless would numb my body in the cold, so that somehow I would feel less pain both hitting the water and drowning. Whatever the reason, when I dropped Daddy's gift on the icy ground, an inside zipper gaped open. I had never known that zipper, or the pocket it sheltered, existed.

The corner of something slight and cream colored slipped out. It was a business card. It smelled of face powder.

Pamela Terrence, it read. *The North Star.*

Sources

The following nonfiction books contributed to my attempts at understanding human trafficking:

Bales, Kevin. *Disposable People: New Slavery in the Global Economy*. Berkeley, CA: University of California Press, 2004.

Bales, Kevin, and Ron Soodalter. *The Slave Next Door: Human Trafficking and Slavery in America*. Berkeley, CA: University of California Press, 2009.

Gobodo-Madikizela, Pumla. *A Human Being Died That Night: A South African Story of Forgiveness*. Boston, MA: Houghton Mifflin, 2003.

Hayes, Sophie. *Trafficked: The Terrifying True Story of a British Girl Forced Into the Sex Trade*, Naperville, IL: Sourcebooks, Inc., 2013.

Kara, Siddharth. *Sex Trafficking: Inside the Business of Modern Slavery*, New York, NY: Columbia University Press, 2009.

Lloyd, Rachel. *Girls Like Us: Fighting for a World Where Girls Are Not for Sale, an Activist Finds Her Calling and Heals Herself.* New York, NY: HarperCollins Publishers, 2011.

Malarek, Victor. *The Natashas: Inside the New Global Sex Trade.* New York, NY: Arcade, 2004.

Mam, Somaly. *The Road of Lost Innocence.* New York, NY: Spiegel & Grau, 2008.

Phelps, Carissa. *Runaway Girl: Escaping Life on the Streets, One Helping Hand at a Time.* New York, NY: Viking, 2012.

Skinner, E. Benjamin. *A Crime So Monstrous: A Shocking Exposé of Modern-Day Sex Slavery, Human Trafficking and Urban Child Markets.* Edinburgh: Mainstream, 2008.

Slim, Iceberg. *Pimp: The Story of My Life.* Cash Money Content, 2011.

Smith, Linda, and Cindy Coloma. *Renting Lacy: A Story of America's Prostituted Children.* Shared Hope International, 2009.

Another nonfiction book, written by a survivor and published after *Dime* was completed, is an excellent resource:

Smith, Holly Austin. *Walking Prey: How America's Youth Are Vulnerable to Sex Slavery*. New York: Palgrave Macmillan, 2014.

The following documentary films contributed to my attempts at understanding human trafficking:

Not My Life

Very Young Girls

Another documentary film, released after *Dime* was completed, is an excellent resource:

3AM Girls

At the time of the publication of this novel, there are many organizations that provide direct services to survivors of domestic human trafficking. These shelters are listed by state at sharedhope.org.

Another helpful resource for victims, survivors, and anyone interested in more information is the National Human Trafficking Resource Center: (888) 373-7888.

Text INFO or HELP to BeFree (233733) or visit befreedayton.org to receive help, report a tip, or request information or training.

A Reading Group Guide to
Dime
by E. R. Frank

Discussion Questions

1. Describe the settings of the novel, including the road trip. How important is setting to the story? What would the impact be if the story were set in a different large urban area?

2. Give specific details about the apartment and discuss how Daddy uses the spaces in it to reward and punish the girls. What does Dime value in the apartment?

3. Dime, who loves to read, makes many references to books. What role do children's books play in the narrative? Which novels are important to her and why? If you're familiar with one of the novels she mentions, talk about its significance in the story. Discuss why reading and the library are so important to Dime.

4. Describe Dime, how she changes in the story, and what causes those changes. What are her memories of being young and why do they matter? What role does school play in her life? What losses does she suffer in the story?

5. Discuss Dime's foster situation with Janelle and what prompted Dime to leave. How did Janelle's treatment of Dime change over the years? In what ways was it not safe for Dime at Janelle's?

6. Daddy manipulates Dime and the rest of the girls. What words and actions does he use with Dime at first to get her to stay? How does his approach change when he wants her to work as a prostitute? Discuss why she finally sees through him.

7. Compare Daddy's treatment of Dime to how he treats the other girls. Discuss the role of sex, jealousy, and violence in how he controls the girls.

8. Dime blames herself for "choosing" Daddy and a life of prostitution. She says, "I didn't want to have to be a ho anymore. But I chose it, so now that's all there was for me." Using examples from the narrative, explain why she believes it was her choice. In your opinion, is that all that's left for her? Discuss what her other options, if any, might be.

9. What is L.A.'s relationship with Dime, Brandy, and Lollipop? Cite evidence from the text that provides clues to her background and analyze how that affects her actions. Describe how she changes over the course of the novel.

10. Describe Brandy, her background, and why she is grateful to Daddy. What do Brandy and Dime have in common?

How are they different? Point to scenes that show how they feel about each other.

11. Daddy and the girls, who are called wifeys, form a distortion of a real family. Analyze the theme of family and belonging in this novel. What does Daddy's household, harmful as it is, offer that resembles a family? What are the girls' experiences with families in the past?

12. How does the introduction of Lollipop into the group propel the plot forward? Describe her background and how she ends up with them. How does her presence motivate Dime to take action?

13. Discuss why Dime is so determined to save the baby. What do you think the rescue symbolizes to her? What are Dime's plans, how does she prepare for them, and how well does she execute them to save the baby? Talk about what the consequences of the baby disappearing might have been on Lollipop and Brandy.

14. This novel explores power and its abuse on various levels including the rules on the street about how prostitutes interact with pimps. Describe "reckless eyeballing," explain why Whippet slaps Dime, and discuss what purpose rules like this one serve for the pimps.

15. The issues of child sexual abuse and prostitution are interwoven in the lives of the girls in this novel. Describe the role sexual abuse played in the earlier life of each

girl. In what ways did the sexual abuse make it easier for Daddy to turn the girls into prostitutes?

16. Dime quotes from *To Kill a Mockingbird* about courage. Discuss the theme of courage in *Dime*. How does the quote apply to Dime's life and actions?

17. The prologue and various chapters throughout the book focus on the note that Dime is trying to write. Why does the author structure the story like this rather than in straight chronological order? Why does she repeat most of Chapter One in Chapter Twenty-Eight? Discuss the effect of the novel's structure in terms of suspense and emotional impact.

18. The prologue and opening chapters also foreshadow much of the later action and give hints about the characters. Find specific examples of this, including Dime's reference to suicide, and relate them to what happens later in the book.

19. Dime plays with the idea of who should be writing the note, based in part on the narrator in *The Book Thief*. Compare the voices that she tries out and how effective they are. Discuss the one-line note that she ends up writing and how it ties into the rest of the book.

20. A continuing metaphor throughout the book has to do with heat and cold that Dime feels inside. Find examples of this, such as the reference to a volcano, and trace how

the metaphor changes in the course of the story. Analyze how effective the images are in conveying Dime's emotions.

21. After her first time as a prostitute, Dime says that "There hadn't been any tunnel or light or angels singing, but I know that I had died." Discuss what she means and why the author chose that metaphor and the details she uses. What is the relationship of that passage comment to the final paragraph of the book, just labeled "Dime"?

22. Discuss what happens to Dime on the bridge at the end of the book. Based on her previous actions and her strength of character, speculate about what might have happened to her after she found the business card in her coat.

23. Find places in the text where Dime deceives herself about Daddy's intentions yet reveals enough in her narrative that the reader knows she's wrong. How does the author convey both Dime's self-deception and the real situation? After reality sets in, Dime says, "I was fuzzy on a lot of things." How is this fuzziness reflected in her narration?

Guide written by Kathleen Odean, a former school librarian and Chair of the 2002 Newbery Award Committee.

This guide has been provided by Simon & Schuster for classroom, library, and reading group use. It may be reproduced in its entirety or excerpted for these purposes.

Discover the gritty world of acclaimed author
E. R. FRANK.

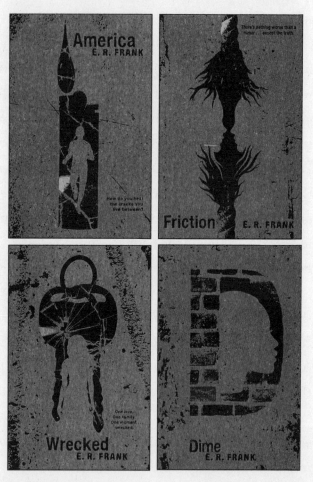